A REAL KISS

Philip's lip curled. "You're in quite a hurry, Olivia. Don't worry. Thornton won't slip out the back door."

"Thank you for the buggy ride. I'll see you on Sunday." I rubbed two fingers against my temple to ward off the pain.

His jaw tightened. "Don't let me keep you from your lord and master."

Headache forgotten, my own anger flared. "No man is my lord and master," I said, and turning my back on him, I reached for the door handle. Strong hands spun me around and his mouth came down hard on mine.

There was anger and possession in the kiss and when he let me go, he said, "Now you can go inside. And when that fop kisses your hand, you'll remember how a real kiss felt."

ANNE KNOLL

THE HOUSE IN THORNTON WOOD

LOVE SPELL BOOKS ⬧ NEW YORK CITY

For Charlie,
who turned my gray skies into blue again.

A LOVE SPELL BOOK®

April 2002

Published by

Dorchester Publishing Co., Inc.
276 Fifth Avenue
New York, NY 10001

ISBN 0-505-52477-5

THE HOUSE IN
THORNTON
WOOD

A word is dead
When it is said,
Some say.

I say it just
Begins to live
That day.

—*EMILY DICKINSON*
COMPLETE POEMS

Chapter One

Mr. Tattersall, the late Lord Wynfield's solicitor, walked back to the house with me after my mother's funeral. I supposed he had been sent to represent the family, for neither Lady Wynfield nor Caroline had attended.

My mother had been Caroline's governess, and when I was a child, we had lived at Wynfield Towers. Mama and I had been treated with the greatest respect and indeed with affection by the whole family, but things had changed after Lord Wynfield's death.

Caroline had been about fifteen at the time, and, as my practical mother had pointed out to me, at Caroline's age, she was hardly in need of a governess.

Mama had been prepared to accept a position as housekeeper to the local vicar, as it would have been hard to find another family that would allow a governess to bring along her own child.

1

At the age of eleven, I found this hard to understand. Wynfield Towers had been my home since infancy and I didn't see why we had to leave just because Caroline had grown up and no longer needed a governess.

Mama had very patiently explained that we were not family; we were employees, which of course, I knew, but preferred to forget. I was rather spoiled, I'm afraid, having been treated like a little pet by everyone, family and servants alike.

I have since learned to understand and accept class distinctions, which are rather rigid in England as well as every place else, I suppose, with the exception of America.

Lord Wynfield solved the problem of another post from beyond the grave though, for when the will was read, my mother had been left a monthly pension and this cottage to live in for the rest of her life.

It was a cozy little cottage, small, but big enough for Mama and me. I would miss it, but in a way I was relieved to no longer be under obligation to the Wynfields.

Unlocking the door, I invited Mr. Tattersall inside.

"Can I offer you a cup of tea?" I asked.

He smiled and handed me his hat. "I was hoping you'd suggest it."

He looked nervous, poor man. Surely he didn't think I was expecting to stay on here.

Lord Wynfield had certainly been our benefactor, but after his death, Lady Wynfield and Caroline, too, had seemingly dismissed us without a backward glance.

I fixed the tea tray and carried it into the parlour.

"Ah, that looks inviting," he said, taking the tray from me and placing it on a low table.

Looking ill-at-ease again, he accepted the cup I offered him. "Your mother's illness kept you confined, didn't it my dear?"

Taking advantage of the opening, I said, "Mama was bed-ridden for a long time, but we were happy together, Mr. Tattersall. However, now I must look to the future. I'll be vacating the house, as I shall be moving to London and taking a position as a governess."

He looked greatly relieved. "I see. I'll advise Lady Wynfield of your decision. Of course there's no rush. Take your time, my dear."

"I shall be leaving in the morning," I said. "So, if you wish to catalogue the furnishings, please feel free to do so now, Sir."

A rosy-cheeked, round-faced little man, Tattersall waved a pudgy hand in the air. "Nonsense, wouldn't think of it, my dear. Lady Wynfield and Lady Caroline were truly sorry they couldn't be here themselves."

"I'm sure they were," I said.

It was foolish, but I couldn't help feeling just a little resentful. They had never once visited or even written to Mama and although she never reproached them for it, their careless dismissal of a once-close association must have been hurtful.

"Have you sufficient funds to tide you over until . . ."

"Thank you," I said. "You've been most kind, but I shall do just fine on my own."

After he left, I reproached myself for acting like a fool. I didn't have to accept the money, but why had I said I would be leaving in the morning? A week or even a month's grace period would most certainly have been agreeable to the old solicitor.

Why had I let my pride goad me into asserting an independence I had yet to earn?

I had no post and very little money. How would I manage until I found a position?

Like a country bumpkin catching her first glimpse of big-city life, I stood outside Waterloo Station staring in confusion at London's bustling activity.

Carriages and hacks clattered over the cobblestones, miraculously missing each other as they fought for space on the narrow street to discharge their passengers.

Dark-suited businessmen and top-hatted aristocrats accompanied by elegantly dressed ladies poured out of cabs and carriages and hurried into the station, trailing a string of luggage and lackeys behind them.

After several futile attempts, I managed to engage a cab. "Can you suggest an inn, one that is respectable, but not expensive?" I asked the driver.

His face, peering down at me from the opening, looked dark and sinister. Without giving me an answer, he flicked the reins, causing the carriage to lurch forward as we joined the melee in the street.

I gasped as wagons and drays flew past my window so perilously close that I shall never know how we missed crashing into them. Fool, fool, I chided myself. This man could be taking you anywhere.

All the harrowing tales I'd ever heard about London came back to haunt me. I should have asked the station master to recommend an inn, not some wild young cab driver. Why, the man could be a procurer on the lookout for country girls arriving in town with no connections.

When he slowed down, I thought to open the door and escape, but before I could gather my wits, we had stopped and the door was suddenly opened for me.

" 'Ere ye be, Miss."

I stared up at a pink-faced jovial-looking man with white, muttonchop whiskers.

This was a different driver. The other one had been young and dark-complected, I recalled.

Stepping out, I glanced quickly around the deserted street. "Where's the other driver?" I asked.

He looked perplexed. "I be the only driver, Miss."

"Where's the inn?"

He pointed to a small neat-looking house. "This be Cousin Carrie's, Miss. You'll like it fine 'ere."

Either he's crazy or I am, I thought, but he had my luggage and was already walking up the steps with it.

Cousin Carrie proved to be a pleasant, motherly sort of woman. The house looked clean and the rent was reasonable, so I paid the driver and convinced myself that I had been mistaken. After all, the carriage had been dark. I had only caught a quick glimpse of the driver, and at an odd angle to say the least.

My room on the third floor was small but adequate, and after all, I didn't expect to stay very long. A prosperous, overcrowded city like London should offer a young woman with my education more than a few opportunities to work as a governess.

I was inexperienced, it was true, but I had been taught by an expert and I had letters of recommendation from the parish priest, my mother's doctor, and if necessary I knew I could count on Mr. Tattersall to solicit a letter from Lady Wynfield.

My landlady who insisted right away that I, too, call her *Cousin Carrie* made me feel wonderfully at home from the very beginning.

There were five other boarders, all of them genteel ladies as warm and friendly to a stranger as their hostess.

Two were elderly sisters who obviously had seen much better days. They were spinsters, and Cousin Carrie confided to me later that they had depleted their inheritence and been forced to sell the home their parents had left them.

The other three ladies were middle-aged women who worked for a living. One, a seamstress, owned a little dressmaking establishment around the corner, and the other two worked for her.

I, of course, was the youngest and they all assumed a protective attitude toward me that was reminiscent of my days at Wynfield Towers.

I felt I had come home, and although it was only a temporary haven, I was to look back on it with nostalgia in the terrifying days that lay ahead.

The sisters, Miss Mary and Miss Sara Mead, had a nodding acquaintence with some of the older members of London society and I gathered that when their father, a respected doctor, had been alive they had moved on the fringes of the aristocracy.

They graciously provided me with the name and address of a woman they knew who specialized in screening applicants for positions in wealthy homes, and, armed with my letters of recommendation, I set out the following day to file an application.

The House in Thornton Wood

I was used to walking—everyone in the country is—but walking through the streets of London was an experience I found appalling.

I hadn't taken a hack because I wanted to save the money, but after ducking the contents of a chamberpot being tossed out a window, I hailed a passing cab and was happy to pay the fare.

Mrs. Truesdale lived in an old but respectable part of town. The three-story house faced a small park, and as I alighted from the cab, I caught a glimpse of a young man standing at its entrance. A shiver ran down my spine, for he looked like the man I had seen through the roof of the cab.

My attention was diverted by the driver demanding his fare and after rummaging through my purse, I scooped up a handful of coins and most likely overpaid him.

Glancing quickly back to the park, I saw no one. The man had completely disappeared, and without thinking, I crossed over and looked up and down the deserted street. Determined to convince myself that I had, indeed, seen such a person, I opened the gate and entered the public garden.

Lush shrubbery grew on both sides of a long, winding path. I walked slowly down it for several feet and not a living soul did I see, but my ears picked up a faint rustle in the undergrowth.

I was a country girl and as a child I had spent many hours roaming through the woods behind our little cottage. Something, either animal or human, was hiding in those bushes. Picking up my skirts, I broke into a run.

"Halt or I'll shoot," a high-pitched voice called out,

and looking back, I was embarrassed to see a small boy emerge from the shrubbery and point a toy rifle in my direction.

Swaggering up to me, he said, "It's a good thing you halted. I shouldn't want to shoot a lady."

"You must forgive me for trespassing," I said. "I didn't know this was a battlefield."

"That's all right. Ladies don't understand about war."

"True," I said. "Am I free to go now?"

"Oh, quite."

"Then perhaps I could ask you a question. Did you see a man enter the park a few moments ago? He was dark and rather foreign-looking."

He shook his head vigorously. "I would have captured him, for sure. No, Miss. Nobody came in but you."

Strange, I thought, but then the man could have stepped into a passing carriage, I supposed.

I crossed the street and in a matter of minutes was seated in Mrs. Truesdale's well-appointed front parlour.

Glancing around the room, I could almost imagine myself back in Wynfield Towers. Delicate golds and vibrant blues dominated the colour scheme and I could have sworn the Aubusson carpet was one I fondly recalled from the days of my early childhood.

A pretty woman in her mid-forties, Mrs. Truesdale was not unlike Lady Wynfield with her well-modulated voice and graceful mannerisms, and I wondered if the Mead sisters had been mistaken. Surely this obviously well-to-do woman would not be engaging in business transactions for her friends.

Astutely reading my mind, she said, "I'm only

slightly more fortunate than Mary and Sara Mead. Although I was unable to keep my home after my husband's death, I was able to keep most of the furnishings." Then she smiled and added, "You have indeed come to the right place, my dear. What might I do for you?"

Her candor gave me courage. "I must find a position. Miss Mead said you could help me."

"What kind of position? Companion, social secretary?" She was eyeing me shrewdly. "The Duchess of Hargraves is in need of a social secretary."

"I'm sorry. I'm looking for a post as governess."

She seemed surprised. "You don't look like a governess, but how ironic! I haven't had a request for a governess for sometime now. They're almost out of fashion, you might say, what with all these boarding schools for young ladies coming into vogue."

I stood up and held out my hand. "Thank you for seeing me, Mrs. Truesdale. If you do hear of anything . . ."

"Please, sit down," she said. "What I meant was, it is ironic that you came today because right before you walked in that door, a messenger brought me just such a request."

She opened the envelope I had given her, and putting on her spectacles, she began to look over my statement of qualifications and the letters that had been written on my behalf.

I held my breath in anticipation and silently prayed, "Please God, let her give me a chance."

Removing the spectacles, she gave me a wistful little smile. "Your qualifications are excellent, my dear, but you're so young and this position is in a rather remote area of Northumberland."

"Oh, I don't mind. I've lived in the country all my life."

She gave me a resigned look and continued. "I know something of the family. Sir Evan Thornton is a widower. His third wife just recently died, but the daughter is by his second wife. There is only the one child, and she would be about fourteen."

"I would be interested in the position," I said eagerly, but she ignored me, seemingly lost in her own thoughts.

"I met Sir Evan once. It was many, many years ago. I was sixteen or seventeen and he couldn't have been too much older, himself. He was a handsome devil, but quite the rake. I seem to recall he married rather young. It was an arranged marriage. The families were neighbours and the children had been promised to each other since birth. Barbaric custom!" she said, shaking her head. "The little child bride died about a year later, I recall. There was some tragedy connected with her death, but I can't remember just what it was."

"I would be interested in the position," I said again, and this time she answered me.

"I can only recommend you to Sir Evan, and I will certainly do that, but I do wish you'd consider working for the duchess."

"I know nothing about being a social secretary," I said.

"My dear, I will train you myself. You're a very intelligent young woman. You'll have no problem, I assure you. The duchess is in London for the season and then she takes her whole retinue to Foxleigh Manor for the summer. It's a brilliant post. Think of the connections you could make. With your looks, you'd be certain to make an advantageous marriage, too. How old are you, my dear?"

"Twenty-two."

"Why bury yourself in the country at your age?"

"I love the country."

She shrugged. "Well, at least I tried. I'll write to Sir Evan and give you a glowing recommendation. Unless he has already hired someone, you can be assured the post will be yours, my dear."

I took her outstretched hand and thanked her.

"Don't thank me yet. I'll be in touch as soon as I hear from Sir Evan, and in the meantime, if you change your mind, remember, London and Foxleigh Manor can be yours."

I was in a state of exhilaration. What luck! For once, I was at the right place at the right time. It never occurred to me to question the strange twist of fate that was drawing me like a magnet to Thornton Wood. Or moreover, why Mrs. Truesdale seemed reluctant to send me there.

I didn't hear from Mrs. Truesdale for four long weeks, and just when I had convinced myself that I would not be going to Northumberland, I received a letter from her.

She said that she had heard from Sir Evan, and if I still wanted the post, I should see her on Friday afternoon at four o'clock.

I was elated. My funds were almost depleted and the ad I had placed in the *London Times* had produced no leads at all. So, on Friday afternoon I set out for

Mrs. Truesdale's prepared to accept whatever offer Sir Evan might have made.

I was not without reservations. Sir Evan's daughter was already fourteen. I would have felt on safer ground with a younger child, even a boy, I mused, recalling my instinctive rapport with the little soldier in the park. But, in my innocence, I assumed I would overcome whatever awaited me at Thornton Manor.

Mrs. Truesdale greeted me warmly, and ushering me into her charming parlour, she said, "I'll let you read Sir Evan's letter. It's a little mysterious, but he has made you an offer and I daresay you'll be accepting it."

The monogrammed stationery was black-bordered, indicating that Sir Evan's third wife had only recently died.

Dear Mrs. Truesdale,

Your kind letter together with your client's application arrived today. I sent no messenger, but after giving the matter consideration, I have decided that my daughter, Vanessa, would benefit immensely from the services of a governess. I would therefore like to engage Miss Olivia St. Claire for such a position at a salary of 30 pounds a year.

My solicitor, Mr. Henry Collington of 156 Regency Street, London, has been authorized to provide your fee and to make arrangements for Miss St. Claire to travel to Thornton Wood.

With deep appreciation for your assistance in this matter, I remain,

Sincerely yours,
Sir Evan Lawrence Thornton

I was puzzled. "But, if the messenger didn't come from Sir Evan, who . . . ?"

Mrs. Truesdale shrugged. "A mutual friend, probably, or perhaps it was fate. What does it matter anyway? All three of us stand to benefit from the arrangement."

There could be no argument with her logic, so I smiled and said, "You're absolutely right and I for one couldn't be more grateful."

"Fine. I hope you'll be happy at Thornton Wood, Miss St. Claire, but if not, come back to London. I'm sure I can find you something else."

I shook my head. "I always finish what I start."

"A noble goal, but not always a prudent one, my dear." Then suddenly clasping my hand, she added, "Please write. I want to know how things are at Thornton Wood."

I gave her an absentminded, "Of course," and she went on to say that I should be hearing from Sir Evan's solicitor within a few days.

She seemed withdrawn and I wondered if she was having second thoughts about recommending me. Perhaps she thought I was too young to cope with a fourteen-year-old.

I smiled and held out my hand. "Good-bye, Mrs. Truesdale and thank you. I shall never forget your kindness."

"Just don't forget to write."

When I didn't immediately respond, she added, "The town of Thornton Wood took its name from the vast forest that surrounds Thornton Manor. I don't know how things are today, but years ago, the area was plagued by bands of roving Gypsies. You'll have to travel by coach, so if you meet up with a caravan, I would advise you to hide your valuables."

After London with its tossed chamberpots, wild carriage rides, and mysteriously vanishing cab drivers, I found Mrs. Truesdale's concerns a little ludicrous. Nevertheless, I assured her that I would be careful and I promised faithfully to write and let her know how I was getting along at Thornton Manor.

As I walked down the steps, I could have sworn the same dark man who seemed so often to appear on the periphery of my activities peered out at me from the window of a passing cab. It was dusk, and of course I couldn't be positive, but the disturbing incident made me grateful to be leaving London.

Either the stress of city living was causing me to become unhinged, or someone was spying on me.

Chapter Two

Your fare has been paid, so don't let the coachman tell you otherwise, Sir Evan's solicitor had cautioned me. Then chuckling to himself, he'd added, *I don't think you'll have to worry, though, Sir Evan Thornton's name will be enough to guarantee your safety.*

Now, seated on a train bound for York, I wondered what he had meant. Was this Sir Evan some kind of ogre?

Well, he shan't intimidate me, I decided, and still chafing over the Wynfields' snub, I told myself that I would never become beholden to an employer the way my mother had been.

Poor Mama, I mused. Did she really have a choice? Lord and Lady Wynfield had been good about letting her bring me to Wynfield Towers. Of course she would be grateful. My welfare had always been foremost in

15

her mind, but the ghost of a suspicion too ugly to voice sometimes plagued me with disloyal thoughts.

Once Lord Wynfield's will had been read, his wife and daughter had turned away from us. No visits, no letters, and this after twelve years of our being treated like family. Had Lord Wynfield's beneficence to my mother caused them to view our relationship in a different light?

My mother rarely spoke of my father, only to say that his name was John St. Claire. He had been a fine, upstanding man who had died young, and that was the extent of my knowledge. My mother didn't even have a picture of him.

Such thoughts made me feel disloyal, and more so now that my dear mother was gone. Gentle, kind, and with a rigid sense of morals, Jenny St. Claire had been almost spinsterish. How could I, who had loved her so dearly, even think such dreadful thoughts!

Would that I could be more like her, I thought, for I saw none of her sterling qualities in myself. Maturity and my mother's gentle guidance had tempered some of the wild impulses of my youth, but even now there were times when I craved adventure and something more, though I had no earthly idea what it could be.

Glancing down at my left hand, I studied the ugly birthmark that covered it. Whenever possible, I wore gloves, for the raised red mark caused people to stare, and as a child I had been taunted and told it was the mark of a witch.

In fact such cruel teasing had decided the course of my early schooling. Shortly after we had moved from Wynfield Towers my mother, probably thinking I needed playmates, enrolled me in the village school.

My fancy, hand-me-down clothes made me stand out among the peasant children like a peacock in a chicken pen and my disposition didn't help matters either, for I had grown spoiled at Wynfield Towers. At any rate, the birthmark gave them an excuse to torment me.

Witch, witch, the devil's marked her for a witch.

After a few days, I lashed out in anger and, mumbling some mumbo-jumbo, I laid a curse on one of my worst tormentors, a big-boned farm boy who towered over the teacher, but couldn't seem to get out of the third grade.

The boy became sick that very night. My mother figured he'd been smoking corn stalks behind his father's barn, but all of the children and not a few parents put the blame on me.

It was the only time I ever saw my mother angry. She removed me from the school and I was secretly satisfied to hear her give the teacher quite a dressing-down for allowing such ignorance to go unchallenged.

After that, I was tutored at home and I spent my free time playing near the woods behind our little house with all kinds of fascinating imaginary companions.

Turning my attention to the window and the passing scenery, I felt a little nostalgic for Sussex. In spite of everything, my mother and I had been happy there and it was certainly beautiful country. Yorkshire was a little bleak in comparison.

It was late afternoon when we arrived in York. I had never been in the city before, but I was familiar with its history. My mother had been a wonderful teacher, and although we never left Sussex, we traveled through the pages of history to other lands and other times.

The coach would not be leaving until morning, the Scottish station master informed me, and I was pleased to have some time to spend in York.

There was much I wanted to see; the funny, narrow little streets, the great cathedral with its impressive stained glass, and the 13th-century wall that still encircled the city. There were four gates, and one of them, Micklegate, had given me nightmares as a child. It was here, according to history, that the bloody heads of traitors had been displayed, a warning, no doubt, to travelers arriving from the south.

Sir Evan's efficient solicitor had recommended an inn, should I be required to spend the night.

"Where might I find Heversham Lodge?" I asked the obliging station master.

"Across the road and next door to the livery stable," he answered in his soft brogue. "Dinna have a care aboot your luggage, Miss," he added, and snapping his fingers, addressed a gangly youth who was sweeping the floor. "Carry the lassie's belongins over to the inn."

I was shown to a small, pleasant room and after washing my face and hands and brushing the soot from my clothes, I took a walk through the town.

York had at one time been a Viking stronghold and vestiges of that era could still be found in the street names, Ousgate, Skeldergate, Nessgate, and Goodramgate. I found the use of the Scandanavian "gate," for "street," odd, but quaintly charming.

I had a wonderful time sightseeing on my own, and although I truly missed my mother, there was something exhilarating about the freedom I now possessed.

Wandering through the ancient, winding streets, I projected myself back to the days of the Vikings when York had been known as Jorvik. I pictured the horn-helmeted barbarians who had conquered the city, and for a split second, they were as real to me as the imaginary playmates of my youth. Giants with flowing blond beards and icy blue eyes. Did their souls still roam the quiet streets?

The thought returned me abruptly to the present. There were no other people walking about now, and as dusk began to fall, I hurried along, my mother's disapproving voice ringing in my ears.

The silence was suddenly shattered when a door opened and a group of working men spilled out of a pub. Their raucous laughter and heavy footsteps followed me down Goodramgate. Glancing back, I quickened my pace, but their longer strides were easily closing the distance between us.

They were obviously drunk and one of them shouted, "Say, Doxy!"

My heart began to pound and I chided myself for getting into such a predicament. I should have been alert and not daydreaming about Vikings. I began to pray and just then the tall figure of a man suddenly materialized from the shadows and walked past me.

It was dusk and the street lamps had not yet been lit, so I couldn't see his face, but after he had passed, I heard one of the men behind me shout, "What the bloody 'ell! Did you see thot?"

Glancing quickly over my shoulder. I saw that my pursuers had stopped and were standing in the middle of the sidewalk. Something else had obviously caught their attention, and taking advantage of the opportunity, I broke into a run.

Fear added wings to my feet and despite a long skirt and tight corset, I ran without stopping until I reached the inn. I didn't stop trembling, though, until I was in my room with the door safely locked.

Early the next morning, I was in a coach bound for Northumberland, England's farthermost county on the Scottish border. Two other passengers, Mr. and Mrs. Brighton, shared the coach with me, but they were only going as far as Thirsk.

When I told them where I was going, Mr. Brighton looked askance at the old coach and remarked that he wouldn't want to be traveling a great distance in it.

His words confirmed my own doubts. The ancient coach rattled and shook over the streets of York. How would it fare on the long stretch of unpaved country roads that lay ahead?

The Brightons were a pleasant, elderly couple, but Mrs. Brighton was an incessant talker and I was grateful for the solitude I enjoyed after their departure in Thirsk.

I spent time preparing for the classes I would teach at Thornton Manor and wondering about my pupil. Vanessa Thornton was fourteen and probably a little giddy. I would have to be firm, but it wasn't in my nature to be stern and I found myself looking forward to developing a warm and companionable relationship with the girl.

Thornton Manor was surrounded by a vast woodland, I had been told, and I thought about the wonderful opportunities that afforded for nature walks and picnics. In another month, it would be summer, and we could be taking our studies outdoors.

My thoughts turned then to the master of Thornton Manor. How unfortunate to have lost three wives. From Mrs. Truesdale's comments, I gathered Sir Evan was close to her own age, which I judged to be about forty-five; not young, but certainly not old, either, for a man.

We stopped at a roadside inn and the driver seemed concerned about one of the coach's wheels. I overheard him ask the innkeeper if he could give him a hand to tighten it, but the man replied that he was an innkeeper and knew nothing of carriages.

My lunch consisted of mince and dumplings with a pot of tea. It was satisfying, hearty fare and after refreshing myself, I joined Mr. Glace, the coachman, for the last leg of our journey.

The country was wild and beautiful, but by late afternoon I was growing restless. We should be arriving at Thornton Wood before nightfall and from there it would be only a short distance to Thornton Manor. Thank God, I thought.

I had nodded off, and a sudden jolt threw me to the floor. Confused and panic-stricken, I was almost afraid to raise myself up to look out the window. I had been dreaming that we were traveling down the side of a cliff and the way the coach was leaning, I was sure we were hanging over the edge.

Mr. Glace suddenly appeared in my window and said, "The wheel's come loose, Miss. Take care getting out."

I made a cautious exit and once outside, my hopes fell. The wheel was not only loose, it was completely off and the coach lay in the road like a fat old drunk.

I looked around. Not a house was in sight. "What shall we do?" I asked.

He shrugged. "Wait for 'elp."

Wonderful, I thought. We hadn't passed so much as a farm wagon since we'd left Thirsk.

Scanning the open field to the right of us, I saw something bright moving in the distance. It was a wagon of some kind, and pointing, I said to the coachman, "Look over there."

He shielded his eyes with his hand and watched it approach. "Bloomin' Gypsy caravan," he muttered under his breath. Then he turned to me and said, " 'Ide yere money, Miss. They're a light-fingered lot. Crafty, too," he added, "but maybe the bloody 'eathens can get the wheel back on."

I didn't put too much stock in the coachman's gloomy views. Although I had never met any Gypsies, I had read about them. Their unconventional lifestyles and strange customs had seemed rather adventurous to me.

As the wagon approached, I could see that although brightly painted, the caravan was a little shabby-looking. I was disappointed, too, that there were only three men in it. I had hoped to see colorful women decked out in spangles and beads.

The Gypsy men shook their heads at the disabled coach and gave each other knowing looks. "We're headed for our campsite," the spokesman said. "You can be our guests, and we'll fix the carriage in the morning."

The coachman looked outraged. "I don't want to go to your camp. I'll pay you to fix the wheel now."

The Gypsy smiled and shrugged. "We see you in the morning, then."

The sun was going down. No other wagons were going to come along now, I reasoned, and the Gypsies seemed friendly enough. "I think we should go with them," I told Mr. Glace.

Ignoring me, he stared them down, but when they called his bluff and walked back to their wagon, the taciturn old coachman called out, "Wait. We'll go with you."

Giving his companions a triumphant look, the spokesman nodded and the other two hurried back and eagerly began to unhitch the horses.

They led the animals across the field and Mr. Glace and I followed. The dour old man looked at me and muttered, "Now they 'ave the 'orses."

"They could have taken them anyhow," I countered.

I'd had no dealings with Gypsies, but I was aware of their reputation, and at the first opportunity, I told them that I was traveling to Thornton Manor. "No doubt you've heard of Sir Evan Thornton," I said.

They seemed to find this of interest and I felt a little better about our situation.

The campsite was located in a clearing about half a mile from the road, and as we approached it, several women and children emerged from a second wagon and gave us curious stares.

The children's feet were bare and one of them, a toddler who looked to be about two, was naked. He clung to his mother and stared up at us with soulful black eyes.

The women looked exotic and I was not disappointed. Long, dangling earrings, bracelets, and beads flashed in the setting sun. They could have stepped out of the pages of my old history book. I was fascinated and a little surprised. They really are a handsome people, I thought.

One of the younger women smiled seductively at the leader, who had told us his name was Rashev.

The other two men tethered the horses and Rashev spoke gruffly to the Gypsy girl who had smiled at him. "See to the food, woman." He turned then to the coachman. "My woman will have the meal ready soon and we will eat."

I was afraid Mr. Glace might refuse, so I answered quickly. "Thank you for your hospitality, Rashev."

He smiled, showing a row of perfect white teeth, and the mental image of a jackal flashed suddenly before my mind. I shivered, though it was an unusually warm night.

There were four women, three of them young and an older woman that I took to be the grandmother. She sat on the sidelines holding the baby, while the younger women tended the fire and stirred something in a large cauldron over it. The men sat on the ground and smoked their pipes. The coachman had remained standing, but I seated myself on a large boulder facing the campfire.

Balancing the child on her hip, the older Gypsy woman peered into the pot and nodded to the other women who then began to ladle out something that looked like stew.

Rashev's woman picked up two steaming plates. Without saying a word, she presented the first one to Rashev and then stepping gracefully around the other two men, she carried the second plate over to the coachman.

"How much?" he asked sullenly, ignoring the woman and directing his question to Rashev.

The Gypsy laughed. "Eat, friend. We settle everything in the morning."

We had very little choice and I suppose the coachman reached that same conclusion because he accepted the plate and began to eat. I was served after the two men, but before the women and children.

The grandmother handed the baby over to his mother and joined us, while the other women fed the children.

"I am Sonia," she said, sitting down on the ground next to me. "Rashev is my son."

"It was kind of him to bring us to your campsite," I said. "Our coach broke down on the road."

"I know."

I wondered how she knew, since Rashev hadn't spoken to her yet.

I had removed my gloves to eat and could feel her eyes on my hand. Few people could resist staring at the ugly birthmark, but I had grown accustomed to stares.

"I would like to read your palm," she said.

Years of conditioning by my straitlaced mother made me hesitate, but then I told myself it was only foolishness. What harm could come of it?

"I've never had my fortune told," I said, and then remembering the coachman's warning, I added, "My fare's been paid in advance, so I don't have much money with me."

Her eyes traveled quickly over me from head to toe

and I began to feel uneasy. The only jewelry I possessed was my mother's cameo pin and I had forgotten to take it off after the coachman's warning.

"We'll trade," she said. "I'll tell your fortune and you can give me your pin."

There it is, I thought with a sinking feeling, but she was staring at my hat and reaching up, she removed my worthless hat pin. "Fair enough?"

I breathed a sigh of relief. "Fair enough," I said.

What she could possibly want with an old hat pin, I couldn't imagine, but I wasn't about to ask.

We ate then and I must say that I found the stew delicious. Mr. Glace must have thought so, too, for he had cleaned his plate. Taking notice of it, Rashev laughingly called out to his wife. "More food for our guest."

"I was supposed to arrive at Thornton Manor tonight," I told Sonia by way of conversation and also to ensure that the Gypsies knew I was expected there.

She nodded as if she already knew, but of course she couldn't have.

"I'm to be governess for Sir Evan's daughter," I explained.

She said nothing, and feeling a little uncomfortable, I asked, "Is the baby your grandson?"

I must have asked the right question for she smiled and her eyes grew dreamy. "Aye, and he has been given a legacy. He is destined to carry the torch that another laid down."

She didn't seem to expect a comment, which was just as well, as I had no idea how to reply.

Glancing at my empty plate, she asked, "Would you like more?"

"No thank you, but as you can see, I really enjoyed it. I don't think I have ever tasted the spices that were used, though. What were they?" I asked.

She gave me a mysterious smile and shrugged. "Our people use many spices from plants that grow wild in the woods. I don't know their names." She took my empty plate then and said, "I know how you English like tea. Before I read your palm, I'll brew some."

She stood up and collected the other plates and took them back to the younger women to wash.

Rashev went to his wagon, and when he returned, he was carrying a violin. "I will play for you now," he said.

Raising the bow, he began to play a hauntingly beautiful melody. A sad little tune, it was vaguely familiar. I thought I might have heard it before, but I knew that was impossible. The only music with which I was familiar was church music and the tunes played at the band concerts that Mama and I had occasionally attended in the village square.

The music, ending on a note that was achingly sweet, affected me deeply and when it was over, I felt like I had lost something.

Rashev's next selection was much faster in tempo. It had a primitive, wildly sensual quality about it. His wife, or whatever she was, began to dance and if I hadn't been so fascinated, I suppose I would have been embarrassed.

She moved with the music, all the while never taking her eyes off her man. The short, spangled skirt and low-necked blouse she wore offered glimpses of a voluptuous, honey-colored body.

The dance disturbed me, for I found it exciting and

wicked all at the same time. The music built to a frenzied crescendo and when it ended, the dancing girl threw herself on the ground at her lover's feet.

I caught a glimpse of the coachman's disapproving expression and blushed.

For a split second I had envied that wild and free Gypsy girl, but the English schoolmistress within me was horrified by my reaction.

Sonia came back with two cups. Handing one of them to the coachman, she said simply, "Tea." Then handing the other one to me, she whispered, "Drink and then come to the fire. I read the leaves and your palm."

When she was out of earshot, the coachman mumbled, "Pagan devils, wouldn't let 'er do it if I were you, Miss."

I drank the tea, which had a strong, minty flavor. "There's no harm in it, Mr. Glace. And, besides," I added, "we shouldn't insult them. They've been very kind."

He gave me an incredulous look. "We be lucky if they don't slit our throats for the horses, Mum."

His words unnerved me and a chill ran down my spine when I gazed at the faces of the three Gypsy men. In the flickering firelight their features looked hard and sinister.

My hand was still trembling when I held it out for Sonia to read my palm.

She studied it a moment, her face an unreadable mask. Then, turning my hand over, she touched the raised birthmark and said, "You are marked. That means you have the sight. Heed your visions and beware."

Releasing my hand, she turned her attention to the tea leaves in the bottom of my cup.

Her face took on a fanatical glow and she stared beyond me into the dark, farthermost reaches of the woods. Her eyes looked like the eyes of the dead and she began to chant in a voice that was strangely unlike her own. "Tongues of fire, light the pyre. The tide shall turn and the devil will burn."

Turning my head, I followed her gaze, but all my straining eyes could see was what looked like a huge vat standing upright on the ground. The illusion clarified itself when I blinked and saw that it was only the trunk of a felled tree.

My blood turned to ice then as the cup shattered, and the sound, like a tiny explosion, immediately brought the Gypsy woman out of her trance.

"What did you see?" I demanded.

She stared back at me with empty eyes. "You have a rendezvous with the Prince of Darkness in Thornton Wood," she answered.

Chapter Three

Rashev's wife handed the baby to one of the other women and hurried to Sonia's side. Flashing dark, accusing eyes in my direction, she said, "Stop questioning her. Haven't you done enough? Can't you see she's in terrible pain?"

The older woman's face was chalky white and her eyes were glassy. Recognizing the signs, I knew the Gypsy woman was suffering from an excruciating headache. "Is it because of what she saw?" I asked.

The Gypsy girl gave me a contemptuous look. "You people don't understand. 'Tell my fortune,' you say. You think it is a game. Come," she said to Sonia. "I'll help you to bed."

Leaning heavily on the younger woman, Sonia allowed herself to be led away, but as she was being helped into the caravan, I heard her say, "Tell Rashev

I must see him. I saw our vengeance in the girl's palm."

The coachman had taken in the whole bizarre performance and after the Gypsies had entered the caravan, he approached me. "Don't let them talk you into sleeping in their wagon, Miss. Mark my words. They're up to something. Blackguards," he muttered under his breath. "I'll not be closing me eyes this night."

But close them he did, for both of us grew drowsy almost immediately after declining Rashev's offer to sleep in the wagons. The last thing I remembered was the Gypsy's sly smile as he handed us blankets and slipped quietly away.

We've been drugged, I thought, for the coachman was already stretched out on the ground and snoring loudly. I wanted to run and hide in the woods, but I collapsed on the grass instead. It must have been the tea, I told myself before sliding into a deep, dark well of oblivion.

Several hours later I woke up trembling. I had dreamed about a large copper vat. It wasn't a nightmare, because nothing at all happened, ominous or otherwise, and yet I felt frightened and afraid to sleep lest I return to it.

Huddling inside the thin blanket. I thought to wake the coachman, but then decided against it. I didn't really think the Gypsies meant to murder us. Steal from us, to be sure, but why risk a confrontation over horses? The coachman was a blunderbuss and if conscious, he would only make matters worse.

I must have drifted back to sleep after all, for the next time I opened my eyes, dawn was creeping across the sky and birds were chirping in the woods.

I sat up suddenly and looked around. The wagons

were gone and the coachman and I were alone in the clearing.

"Mr. Glace, wake up," I said.

He awoke immediately, staring first at me and then with dawning recognition at the campsite. "Bloody thieves 'er gone and took the 'orses with them."

"At least we're safe, and not murdered in our sleep," I reminded him.

"Aye, but 'ad we woke up, they'd a done us in, Missy."

Pulling his blanket off, he threw it on the ashes of the dead fire. "Bloody 'eathens, ought to be 'ung, the lot of them." He stood up then and brushed off his clothes. "Come along, Miss. It's back to the road and seein if we can 'itch a ride with some farmer."

We tramped back the way we had come and I mentally took stock of our situation. It would be too much to hope that the Gypsies had left me my trunk. Looking down at my dusty traveling suit, I sighed. What a grand first impression I should make at Thornton Manor.

As we approached the road, I could just about see the top of the coach. Lo and behold, I thought. That looks like the trunk. But, of course it will be empty!

Mr. Glace ran ahead and a second later, he was shouting in an excited voice, his thick dialect disguising the words so that I didn't understand until I saw the coach for myself.

"The bloody 'eathens 'ave 'itched up me 'orses!" he repeated.

The wheel was back on and my untouched trunk was still strapped to the top of the carriage.

* * *

The House in Thornton Wood

Mr. Glace had informed me there was only one inn on the way to Thornton Wood and that we would stop for food and pick up any additional passengers. We would then drive straight through and reach our destination before nightfall.

I was ravenously hungry and the coachman must have shared my discomfort for the longer we rode, the more the coach picked up speed. It was with considerable relief, then, that I saw in the distance what looked like a roadside inn.

As we approached it, I was a little startled to see that the sign swinging in the breeze read, *The St. Claire Arms*.

They could be long-lost relatives, I mused, for indeed all of my father's family had long been lost to me.

It was an old inn and rather run-down, but the coachman said the food was good and the innkeeper seemed friendly. He was not a St. Claire, though.

"The name goes back a long way, Miss," he informed me when I asked. "None what 'ad the inn before me bothered to change the sign, so I leaves it up there, too," he explained.

I was the only guest in the small dining room. The coachman, who seemed to be on familiar terms with the innkeeper and his wife, was taking his meal in the kitchen. I was sure he would give his audience a harrowing account of our ordeal at the hands of the "Gypsy 'eathens," and I didn't doubt for a minute that he would credit himself with more foresight than he had shown.

I took a table facing the window, but in a dark corner of the room. I had no wish to be ogled should any gentlemen come in for a spot of ale.

Presently, a young barmaid brought me a steaming bowl of barley soup and a small loaf of crusty bread. She gave me scant attention, though, for her eye was on the window, and following her gaze, I saw that a man was hoisting a trunk onto the top of our coach.

Tall and good-looking, with dark brown hair that turned to copper in the sun, he was somewhere in his late twenties or early thirties. The slim but powerfully built young man cut a swashbuckling figure in his cape and boots, and the cheeky barmaid practically devoured him with her eyes.

Positioning his leg on the wheel of the coach, he reached up and strapped the trunk securely to the roof. Then jumping to the ground, he moved past the window.

A few seconds later the inn's creaky door opened and then shut with a bang. The sound galvanized the barmaid into action. Slinging my silverware down on the table, she arranged her face in a seductive smile and swaying her hips in a slow, suggestive manner, she sidled up to the man who stood in the doorway.

" 'Ave one more tankard," she said, standing as close as possible to him and smiling up into his face.

To my surprise and horror, he laughed and smacked her smartly on the bottom. "No more for me, Gracie. Now run along and tell that lazy coachman Dr. Mc-Allister's getting impatient."

He turned and left without spotting me and I was grateful for that much. The barmaid, brazen wench that she was, gave me a triumphant look as she headed for the kitchen. Good heavens, I thought, she thinks the prim little spinster is envious!

I was glad to hear a doctor would be traveling with us. No doubt, his presence would discourage that disgusting rake from getting out of line.

I had just paid my bill when Mr. Glace entered the room, and, walking over to my table, he said, "If you're ready, we'll be moving along now, Miss. Another passenger'll be joining us. Name's Dr. Philip McAllister. He's Thornton Wood's local doctor," he added importantly.

Thank God! The other one's not even going. That must have been the doctor's luggage that disgusting rake was tossing around, I decided, and picking up my purse and gloves, I followed the coachman out of the inn.

Before climbing up front, Mr. Glace opened the door for me and said, "Miss St. Claire, Dr. McAllister."

I entered the coach and was appalled to find myself staring into the smiling face of the rake from the inn.

Taking a seat on the opposite side of the coach, I acknowledged the introduction with a curt nod, but he was not to be put off. "I'm pleased to meet you, Miss St. Claire. It's not often we have visitors in Thornton Wood. Have you relatives living in the village?" he asked.

"No, I do not," I said stiffly.

"I see." He paused, but only for a moment. "Thornton Wood doesn't have much in the way of tourist attractions, but there's a fair coming up next month. Perhaps you can attend. If you plan on staying, that is."

"Perhaps I shall take my charge," I said, suddenly

35

deciding that it was useless to ignore him. After all, his conduct with the barmaid was none of my business and he was unaware that I had witnessed it. "I'm the new governess at Thornton Manor," I explained. Do you perhaps know my charge, Miss Vanessa Thornton?"

"Thornton Wood is a very small village, Miss . . ."

He paused, groping for my name and I supplied it, "St. Claire."

"Of course, like the *St. Claire Arms*. Are the names a coincidence or does your family have some connection with the original owners?"

"None that I know of," I answered.

His eyes twinkled with amusement. "I didn't think so. It was a rather notorious inn, or so I've heard, but that was long before our time."

With patrons like yourself, I thought, it will soon revert to type. I was glad I had caught a glimpse of his true character, for had I not seen him with Gracie, I might have been fooled into thinking him a gentleman.

Suddenly returning to the original subject, he asked, "Have you met Vanessa Thornton?"

"No, neither have I met Sir Evan Thornton. I was hired through an employment broker in London."

"I see."

His sudden silence annoyed me. Did he expect me to solicit information from him about the Thorntons? After what I had seen of his character, I certainly wouldn't put much stock in Dr. McAllister's opinion.

"And what of you, sir?" I asked. "Have you always lived in Thornton Wood?"

"As a matter of fact, I have. My father was a tenant

farmer. We worked Thornton land," he explained wryly.

I wondered how he had acquired a medical education, but his background and the candor with which he had revealed it served to justify him, to a degree, in my eyes.

Dr. McAllister's more rugged side and the veneer of gentility that masked it did not seem quite so reprehensible now that I knew a little of his history. I was baffled and a little embarrassed to find out that this dual aspect of his personality excited me.

I had been strictly raised, and although not allowed to associate with the village children, I used to hide, and like a caged canary, I would spy on them, the boys in particular, whenever I got the chance.

When they weren't in school or working on their parents' farms, they spent their time roaming all over the forest, a pastime that I, with my strict little boundaries, particularly envied.

How I longed to explore that fascinating place. Maybe I would discover a secret glen and catch a glimpse of the fairy folk who, according to my books, inhabited all forests.

Perhaps that was what had appealed to me about Thornton Manor. "It lies on the edge of a vast woodland," Mrs. Truesdale had said.

"Are you familiar with Thornton Manor then?" I asked.

He smiled, but it was a bitter smile and his intense blue eyes darkened with suppressed emotion. "It dominates the landscape like a great grey dragon guarding the woods." Then he recovered himself and said in a matter-of-fact tone, "I didn't see it from the inside, though, until I became a doctor and was treating Sir Evan's wife."

I wondered how the master of Thornton Manor felt about the tenant's son, who had risen above his station. Did Sir Evan resent dealing with the young doctor on an equal basis? Remembering the Wynfields, I rather thought that he might.

He broke the silence with a backhanded apology. "Forgive me, but I can't show much appreciation for manor houses. To my way of thinking, they are symbols of a feudal system that should have been discarded years ago."

His words implied a criticism of my employer and although I did not know Sir Evan, he had accepted me sight unseen, paid my traveling expenses, and offered me a generous stipend. I found it a little rude, then, for Dr. McAllister to make such a remark in my presence.

Feeling his eyes on me I glanced up, and was surprised when he chuckled.

"Now, I've shocked you, haven't I? You probably believe class distinctions are sacrosanct. Everything stays nice and orderly when one's place in the hierarchy is determined at birth. Right?"

He really is a rude man, I thought. "There's certainly room in the system for advancement," I said. "What about yourself?"

"Come on now, Miss St. Claire. You can't use me as an example—I'm a rebel. Not many people are, you know. But what about you? What made you decide to become a governess?"

"My mother . . ." I stopped. Blast the man. I'll not prove him right. "It's what I wanted to be," I said. "And now, if you'll excuse me, Dr. McAllister, I need to catch up on my reading."

I took the textbook, *England in the Sixteenth Century*, out of my bag and without thinking, removed my gloves.

I had only just turned the first page when he said, "That's a most unusual birthmark. I don't think I've ever seen one quite like it."

I put the book down and glared at him. He really was the rudest man! "I beg your pardon," I said icily.

"I'm a doctor, Miss St. Claire. I meant no offense and I apologize for my bluntness. I've been doing some experiments with herbs and plants. I'm not saying I could remove the mark, but I might be able to fade it."

"I came into the world with it. I'm satisfied to go out the same way," I said.

It was a lie. How many quarts of buttermilk had I soaked my hand in, hoping to fade this mark?

Unruffled by the rebuke, he calmly reached into his satchel. "Have an apple," he said, holding up a shiny red one for my inspection.

I politely declined and he proceeded to eat it himself. Returning to my reading, I found it hard to concentrate, for he was crunching on his apple, and with a sigh of resignation, I closed the book and looked out the window.

He took the gesture as an invitation to resume the conversation. "There's an apple tree at Thornton Manor. Has the biggest, most luscious fruit you can imagine," he said. "Old Sir Evan Thornton, the present owner's father," he explained, "set quite a store by that tree. Used to inspect it every day and wouldn't allow an apple to be picked until it was at its very peak of ripeness.

"One night a bunch of us rowdy little lads raided that tree and picked it clean. We divided the spoils and my ma made apple pies like I'd never tasted before. Course she didn't know where they'd come from," he added.

"Did she ever find out?" I asked before I could stop myself.

He nodded. "Old Sir Evan sent his overseer around the next day. The master of the manor was furious. Made my pa pay for the apples and I got a whaling, but they were still the best pies I ever tasted."

"Does your family still live in Thornton Wood?" I asked.

His lighthearted mood quickly evaporated and he said, "No. They moved back to Scotland after my father died."

The coach was rocking from side to side and I remember thinking that we were traveling at a dangerous rate of speed, when the next thing I knew I was pitched out of my seat, hurled across the coach, and plunked down in Dr. McAllister's lap!

Strong arms held me close as the coach rumbled and rocked and finally came to a halt.

"Are you all right?" he asked.

"I think so."

Sliding none too gracefully off the man's lap, I pulled my skirt down over my knees and blushed to the roots of my hair.

Reaching for the door and forcing it open, Dr. McAllister shouted, "Mr. Glace, are you all right?" Before jumping down, he cautioned me to stay inside. "I'll see to the driver," he said.

I poked my head out the window. The coachman must surely be hurt this time, I thought, but in the next second, I heard a familiar voice. "Bloody 'eathens didn't put the wheel on right."

"We didn't land in a ditch because the wheel came off, the wheel came off because we landed in a ditch," Dr. McAllister told Mr. Glace.

They had been arguing back and forth ever since the accident. I knew Dr. McAllister was right because what had come off the first time was the left wheel. That one was still on and it was the right wheel that now lay in the ditch.

"This coach is a relic and you have no business driving it at such high speeds." Dr. McAllister pulled out his pocket watch and checked the time. "It'll be pitch dark in another two hours. We can make it to Thornton Manor on foot before nightfall, and I say we stop arguing and start walking."

The coachman looked up at the younger man and shook his head. "I'll not be leaving me coach and horses for thieves to steal."

"Stay then. I'll send help from Thornton Manor."

The coachman turned to me. "You'd best be getting back in the coach, Miss. You'll be more comfortable inside."

"I'm taking Miss St. Claire with me," Dr. McAllister said.

The coachman looked dubious. "Tis a rough walk through Thornton Wood."

I recalled the Gypsy's words: *You have a rendezvous*

with the Prince of Darkness in Thornton Wood.

What did I know of Dr. McAllister? He might be a doctor, I thought, but his background had hardly prepared him to be a gentleman.

My unease increased as I stared at the man before me. In attempting to fix the wheel, his face and hands had become smudged with axle grease, giving him the appearance of a burly blacksmith. He had removed his coat and rolled up his shirt sleeves exposing hard, muscular arms that I would certainly have no defense against.

"I've decided to stay," I said. "After all, everything I own is in my trunk, and I certainly don't want to have it stolen."

He gave me an exasperated look. "Would you rather lose the trunk or your virtue?" he asked bluntly.

His crude remark left me speechless. Surely, the man was exaggerating. Or was he? Mrs. Truesdale certainly had tried to talk me out of coming up here. She had called it an *isolated* area, but had she meant Thornton Wood was a *dangerous* area, too?

"I shall accompany you, of course, Dr. McAllister, but mightn't we be accosted on foot as well?" It sounded prim and schoolmarmish and I could have bitten my tongue when he smiled.

"Don't worry about it, Miss St. Claire. I'll protect you. I'm no stranger to brawling and I always come out on the winning side."

I didn't doubt it for a minute, but who was to protect me from Dr. McAllister?

Chapter Four

We had been walking for over an hour, and the Cheviot Hills looked no closer than before. Hampered by my long skirt and shoes that were beginning to pinch, I had forced my traveling companion to match his long strides to my mincing ones and hence we had covered very little ground.

"I'm sorry. I'm not dressed for a hike," I offered by way of apology.

"You're doing fine. Remarkable, really, under the circumstances. Corsets must be restricting, to say the least." My face caught fire and he said, "My dear Miss St. Claire, I'm a doctor. I know that ladies wear corsets. I just don't approve of them. They're unhealthy."

I made no comment. I wasn't about to discuss corsets with him.

43

"Think you can make it through the woods?" he asked.

"Of course," I answered. "When we lived in Sussex, I used to spend hours tramping through the woods."

It was an exaggeration to be sure, but for some perverse reason, I didn't want this overbearing man to think of me as a prim little spinster with my nose stuck constantly in a book.

"Is that a fact?"

"It is, so don't concern yourself on my account," I answered.

"Fine. In that case, we can cut across this field and save a little more time."

Taking my hand, he helped me up a steep incline, and there was the field, lush and green and stretching before us like an oasis.

Feasting my eyes on it, I said, "This is better than that dusty old road."

I wanted to take my shoes and stockings off and run barefoot through that cool, thick grass like the children in our old village used to do. I, of course, had never run barefoot and I didn't know what could have possessed me to even think such a silly thing.

Sheep were grazing on the hillside and the pastoral scene was so beautiful that I paused to let my senses take it all in. Breathing deeply, I filled my lungs with the fresh clean country air. I smelled the fragrance of the grass, heard the plaintive *baa* of a lamb calling to its mother, and then I looked up and saw the shepherd.

His coarse woolen robe had a hood that partially concealed his face, but I recognized him immediately.

Dark eyes bored into mine, and then the stranger

who had haunted my footsteps in London turned from me to the man standing at my side. No movement, no gesture of recognition did they make, but their eyes locked, and after a moment the shepherd's lips began to curve in a knowing smile that chilled me to the bone.

Just then a playful breeze blew my hat off and landed it in a sticker bush. Dr. McAllister retrieved it, but a piece of its ribbon remained behind, snagged on a thorn. "Sorry, I'm afraid it tore," he said, and then added with a chuckle, "the birds will make use of the ribbon though."

I took the hat from him without comment. I had more things to worry about than ribbons.

He walked ahead of me then and when I didn't immediately follow, he called back, "Come along, Miss St. Claire. We'll rest when we reach the woods."

I hurried after him and when the shepherd and his flock were out of sight, I said, "I've seen that man before. Who is he?"

"What man?"

"The man we just passed, the shepherd. He acted like he knew you."

"I didn't see any shepherd," he said.

I don't know what I had expected to hear, but I certainly hadn't expected him to lie about it. "He stared at you and you stared right back at him," I said. "Why are you denying it?"

He shrugged impatiently. "Look, I was trying to get my bearings. I didn't see a shepherd, but I'll take your word that there was one. As for him knowing me, everybody knows me. I'm the town doctor for God's sake."

I didn't like it at all. I had seen this dark man in London. I might even have seen him in York, for the man who had passed me on the street when I was pursued by rowdies had a similar build, although I had not seen his face. Now he was here in Northumberland and it would be ludicrous to call it coincidence. Why was he following me? And why would Dr. McAllister lie about him?

Or, is my traveling companion really Dr. McAllister? This new thought unnerved me, and my fertile imagination took over.

He doesn't act like a doctor. He doesn't look like a doctor and no doctor would consort with a barmaid the way this man did.

I had lagged behind and he turned and regarded me with an expression that could have passed for concern, or at least the pretense of it. "You're in pain. What's wrong, Miss St. Claire?"

"I have a terrible headache," I said.

The pain was excruciating. It had come upon me all of a sudden and took precedence now over all the unanswered questions I had been pondering.

Taking my arm, he led me over to a large tree. "Sit down. Rest your head against the trunk. I'll be right back."

I couldn't think. I could only feel and my head felt like it was being hammered by a heavy mallet. The ground rose up to meet me and then something blessedly cool was pressing against my temples and strong hands were kneading the back of my neck.

A drop of icy cold water slid down the front of my dress and I shuddered.

"Sorry," Dr. McAllister said as he continued pressing

his water-soaked handkerchief against my temples.

The pain subsided, and I suddenly became aware that I was being cradled in the man's lap. "I'm better now," I said, trying to rise.

He helped me to a sitting position and reaching into the inside pocket of his coat he withdrew a white envelope.

"I'm going to mix this with water. It should be hot water, but the stream is all we have. I want you to drink it, though."

I looked inside the envelope and saw a small quantity of what looked like dried leaves.

"It's an herbal tea," he said. "It won't taste very good cold, but it'll help your headache."

When he returned from the stream, he had the envelope cupped in his hand. I automatically drew back and he said, "It won't hurt you."

Before I could protest, he was holding the makeshift cup to my lips and I had swallowed the contents.

Taking out his watch, he felt my pulse and said, "I want you to lean your head back and rest for fifteen minutes. I'm going to retrace our steps and ask that shepherd you saw for directions."

Several minutes later my headache had miraculously disappeared and my unanswered questions immediately resurfaced. Was he asking for directions, or did he have something else to discuss with the shepherd?

Acting on a sudden impulse, I decided to find out. I'd march right up to them and demand to know what was going on. Why was the dark-complected one following me and why would McAllister, or whoever he was, say he hadn't seen him?

47

I headed back the way we had come, but just as I reached the foot of the hill, I collided with Philip McAllister.

"What are you doing? Didn't I tell you to rest?"

I looked over his shoulder at an empty field. "Did you see the shepherd?"

"No. There's no one here."

"No sheep," I said.

He looked at me strangely. "Sheep?"

My eyes swept the field. It looked different. The grass wasn't as green and the trees were much taller. "Are you sure this is the same spot?" I asked.

"Of course." And motioning toward the bush, he said, "There's your ribbon still stuck on a thorn."

The sun was setting when we entered Thornton Wood and my first glimpse of it affected me strangely. Set against the backdrop of a blazing pink and orange sky, the legendary forest took on the appearance of a charcoal sketch, the trees blackened and dark shadows smudging its waters.

Strangely familiar, I felt I knew this place. Had I come here once in a dream, perhaps?

Cloaked in a tomblike silence, the glen seemed enchanted, other-worldly—ominous, but also sad and I knew in that moment without a shadow of a doubt that I would come back here again and again, for Thornton Wood had something to tell me.

Dr. McAllister, however, was not concerned with my fancies. "Give me your hand, Miss St. Claire. We must hurry. Night falls suddenly in the woods."

Despite my corset, long skirt, and uncomfortable shoes, I was determined to keep up with the relentless

Dr. McAllister. This, to my great satisfaction, I some-how managed to do and consequently, we emerged from the woods just as dusk was descending on Thornton Manor.

"There it is," Dr. McAllister said, and looking up, I saw a large grey stone mansion.

If Thornton Wood had intrigued me, Thornton Manor merely repelled me. Standing like a dismal fortress at the edge of the forest, it was an unfriendly house, its long narrow windows giving it the appearance of a dragon with a thousand eyes.

Dr. McAllister's boyhood description fit it well and I said, "You were right. Thornton Manor does look like a dragon."

It was dusk now, and I tried to tell myself the house would look fine in the morning, but I didn't believe it.

"It's no better inside," he said, and then surprised me by grabbing my shoulders and staring intently into my eyes. "Take my advice and leave as soon as possible."

Shadows gave his handsome face a sinister look and I shrugged out of his grasp. "I make my own decisions, Dr. McAllister."

"Do you? Do any of us?"

Then he added as an afterthought, "Just don't believe everything you hear, Miss St. Claire."

That said, he strode up to Thornton Manor's massive double doors and lifted the knocker.

A pinched-faced old butler answered and we were ushered into a cavernous great hall. The walls were embellished with faded tapestries, priceless heirlooms, no doubt, but they did nothing to dispel the dark and gloomy mood the room evoked.

"Tell Sir Evan we must see him at once."

Dr. McAllister's tone was abrupt and I felt a little embarrassed for the servant.

"Sir Evan is dressing for dinner, Dr. McAllister."

"Damn it, Farnsworth. This is an emergency. Get your master down here immediately."

"As you say, sir."

Farnsworth moved on silent feet, and like a wraith, he appeared to literally float up the staircase.

I was annoyed by the doctor's rudeness. "The poor man was only doing his duty," I said.

"Save your sympathy, Miss St. Claire. This house has little need for it."

"McAllister?"

Following the voice, I looked up to find a man standing on the balcony.

My companion said, "*Dr.* McAllister, and Miss St. Claire, Sir Evan."

The man descended then and as he drew closer I saw that Sir Evan was a strikingly handsome man with hair the palest of silver and very intense slate-grey eyes. He was as tall as Philip McAllister, but not as brawny and although his shock of silver hair made him appear older, I didn't think he could be more than forty-five.

"There's been an accident," Philip was saying. "About three miles down the road. No one was injured, but you'll need to send some of your men down to rescue the coachman."

Farnsworth was standing beside his master and Sir Evan turned to him. "Have several of the hands ride down and give assistance."

"I see you rescued our governess, doctor," Sir Evan said, and then turned to me. "Allow me to introduce

myself, Miss St. Claire, I am Sir Evan Thornton." He
favored me with a gracious smile and then added, "Am
I to understand you had to walk three miles?"

"I'm pleased to meet you, Sir Evan," I said. "And yes,
we did have to walk, but I'm very grateful to Dr. Mc-
Allister for assisting me."

"As am I," he said, casting cold grey eyes on the
younger man.

Philip made no comment. Why did I suddenly think
of him as *Philip?* I wondered. Was it because alongside
Sir Evan Thornton, Philip McAllister seemed young
and brusque, maybe even a little uncouth?

Perhaps this house and its obviously cultured and
sophisticated master were painful reminders that the
McAllisters had been crofters and were beholden to
the Thorntons.

"You will, of course, stay the night," Sir Evan was
saying to Dr. McAllister.

Philip mumbled his thanks and Sir Evan had servants show us to our rooms.

"Dinner is at eight," he said.

I was shown to a modest room, larger and more
comfortably furnished than servants' quarters, but similarly unpretentious. Not grand enough for guests, it
was typical of rooms reserved for housekeepers and
governesses.

I was tired and since I had no trunk to unpack and
nothing else to do, I stretched out on the narrow bed
and thought about this strange and disturbing day.

Why did I keep seeing that dark-complected man?
Philip McAllister had seen him, too, and yet he had
denied it. Why?

None of it made sense, and I almost wanted to believe I had imagined it. But, I certainly hadn't imagined Dr. Philip McAllister, I thought, and what an enigma he had turned out to be!

A rake, an uncouth, opinionated bore, and yet our trek through Thornton Wood had revealed another side of Dr. McAllister's personality: that of the dedicated and forward-thinking physician.

He had spoken of his patients and it was obvious that he cared a great deal about them. He was involved in research, too, for he was experimenting with medicines obtained from plants and herbs.

Many of his specimens were from Thornton Wood, he'd said, but others he had discovered in the wild Highlands of Scotland.

Recalling the bitter dose he'd forced on me, I made a face. It had cured my headache though, and for that I had certainly been grateful.

A soft knock interrupted my thoughts and when I opened the door I found my trunk had arrived.

"Please, bring it right in," I said to the young lad who stood outside.

I was relieved, for now I would be able to change my clothes and present a more favorable appearance at dinner this evening.

It didn't take me long to unpack, and scanning the meager array of gowns that hung in my wardrobe, I tried to decide what to wear.

Did the Thorntons dress formally for dinner? I wondered. If so, I hoped I would not be expected to dine with the family often for I had only one formal gown. It was four years old and had never been worn.

I took it out and laid it across the bed. It was out of fashion now, but the workmanship was exquisite.

Every seam, every intricate puff and pleat had been expertly and painstakingly sewn by hand with minute, perfect little stitches. It was a loving piece of art, and small wonder, for my mother had made it.

Tears welled up in my eyes when I recalled how hard she had worked on it and how she had looked forward to seeing me wear it to Caroline Wynfield's wedding. The invitation, of course, had never arrived.

The material was crushed velvet in a rich, ruby red. Holding the gown up to me, I stood before the mirror. Four long years slipped away and I heard my mother's voice once again.

You're going to look lovely in it, Olivia. See how the color accents your coal black hair and beautiful dark eyes. We won't spoil it with ruffles and bows, maybe we could use puffing.

Yes, I think puffing would be very chic, very French, and we'll use double darts to show off your tiny waist. Oh, Olivia I just know you're going to meet someone wonderful at this wedding—someone cultured and kind, someone who will give you all the things I never could. . . .

Poor Mama, I thought. She always treated me like a misplaced aristocrat.

My thoughts were interrupted again by another soft knock and after hanging the gown back in the wardrobe, I opened the door to a woman whom I identified immediately as Thornton Manor's housekeeper.

Middle-aged and plain, she wore her position in her demeanor, which was authoritative rather than servile, and in the black serge gown with its long tight sleeves and crisply starched white collar.

"I'm Mrs. Cathcart, the housekeeper," she said. "I'm sorry I wasn't here when you arrived."

I was glad to see her. If anyone could tell me what was expected at Thornton Manor, it would be the housekeeper.

"Please come in," I said. "I'm Olivia St. Claire and I'm very happy to meet you."

"You're so young," she commented.

I wondered if she was disappointed. Perhaps she had hoped for someone closer to her own age. "I'm not very young. I'm twenty-two."

She smiled. "From a vantage point of fifty-three, that's young, my dear."

"Sir Evan informed me that dinner was at eight and I was wondering how I should dress. I don't have many formal clothes," I added.

"The family does dress for dinner, but I shouldn't think they would expect you to do so."

Was she putting me in my place? I wondered.

"We've never had a governess here before," she explained. "I usually take my meals in my room and I was going to invite you to join me."

I didn't want to start out on the wrong foot, so I said, "That would be ever so nice. I imagine Sir Evan wants to introduce me to the family tonight, but I hope you'll ask me again."

"Of course, but we'll have to go along with whatever Sir Evan decides. I imagine you'll be wanting to freshen up before dinner. I'll send one of the maids up with hot water."

"Thank you, Mrs. Cathcart, and thank you for welcoming me to Thornton Manor," I said. "I'm looking forward to meeting Vanessa and I just know I'm going to be happy here."

She gave me a very strange look. "I hope so, Miss St. Claire."

After she left, I looked through my wardrobe again. Mentally discarding the ruby velvet, I settled for a pearl grey taffeta with a high neck and a lace yoke. It had a modest bustle and no train and had been my standby for church recitals and such.

A talkative young maid arrived with the hot water and more gossip than I cared to hear.

"You're the talk of the kitchen, Miss. Everybody is surprised at how young and pretty you are."

There it is, I thought, another reference to my youth.

"Perhaps Sir Evan prefers a younger teacher for his daughter," I said.

"I'm sure he does, Miss."

Concerned that she might have misconstrued my meaning, I said, "Girls Miss Vanessa's age often relate better to younger women."

She nodded and I added, "I'm anxious to meet my pupil. Does she usually dine with the family?"

"When she's not locked in her room, she does."

I thought it best to drop that subject, but she had already dismissed it and taking a stack of towels from her cart, she placed them beside the washbowl. "The coachman told cook you had to walk through the woods."

"Yes, the coach broke down and Dr. McAllister was concerned that it might be attacked by bandits."

"Aye, there's funny things been goin' on around here, Miss. A girl disappeared from the village a couple of months ago."

So, there was legitimate cause for concern, I thought. "In that case, I'm glad I listened to Dr. McAllister."

She started to say something and then changed her mind. Lifting her pail, she poured scalding water into my pitcher and as the steam rose up in our faces, she said a little ominously, "Can't trust nobody, Miss."

The steam made me cough and I covered my mouth with my hand.

Her eyes widened and she stared at the ugly red mark. "I'll be getting back to the kitchen now, Miss. Cook'll be needing me," she said.

When she had gone, I tried to recapture my enthusiasm, but a vague feeling of unease had settled over me and I found myself contemplating the new life I had chosen with sudden grave misgivings.

Chapter Five

Surveying myself in the full-length mirror, I felt vaguely dissatisfied. Grey was definitely not my color, and this melt-into-the-woodwork, prim and proper little grey dress had "old maid" written all over it.

For some obscure reason, Gracie the barmaid's face suddenly flashed before my eyes and without thinking, I reached up and yanked the dress open.

Four or five little grey buttons shot across the room and I knew I'd never have time to sew them back on. It would have to be the ruby velvet now.

Stepping out of one gown and into the other, I hooked myself up quickly and returned to the mirror. This time the woman who stared back at me looked and felt entirely different.

The gown's crimson color highlighted my face, making my eyes appear larger, and my hair even blacker.

Its lush velvet fabric felt soft and sensuous and I rubbed my hands over the nap, luxuriating in the fantasies it evoked. . . .

The courtly man that my mother predicted I would meet at Caroline's wedding. He would carry me off to his castle and we would live happily ever after. . . .

I was just putting on my gloves when a sharp knock made me jump like a startled cat and then a familiar male voice called out, "Miss St. Claire. It's Philip McAllister. May I escort you downstairs?"

Feeling self-conscious and a little ridiculous, I opened the door. "Thank you," I said. "I would probably have lost my way."

He had changed into fresh clothes, too, but his attire was informal and I wondered if I was making a fool of myself.

Assessing me with bold, blue eyes, he smiled warmly and said, "You look charming, Miss St. Claire. Bright colors become you."

"Thank you," I replied stiffly.

Although I had altered my opinion of him, I still couldn't forget his conduct with the barmaid at the inn.

He offered me his arm and together we descended Thornton Manor's regal staircase.

Farnsworth stood waiting in the hall and giving the young doctor a sullen look, he said, "Sir Evan and the family are in the withdrawing room."

"Thank you," Philip answered and then added, "don't bother. I remember the way."

The old butler ignored him and leading us to the room, announced us. I took a moment to glance quickly at the other women and was relieved to see that they were in formal clothes.

Sir Evan, looking very handsome, greeted us warmly and then taking my arm, he said, "Come, Miss St. Claire. Let me introduce you to my mother."

Leading me over to a woman with silver hair the exact shade of her son's, he presented me. "Mother, this is our new governess, Miss St. Claire."

A handsome woman in her sixties, she looked me over with cold, rather haughty eyes.

"I am pleased to meet you, Lady Thornton." I spoke formally, trying to gain her approval.

She acknowledged the introduction and then turned anxiously to her son, "Where's Vanessa?"

A look of impatience passed briefly over his handsome face, but he covered it quickly, and turning to me explained. "My daughter is inclined to be tardy, Miss St. Claire, but with your help I'm sure she'll improve."

I was introduced next to a Miss Hamilton, Lady Thornton's companion and nurse. Middle-aged, tall, and big-boned she had rather sharp, unattractive features. "I understand you were recommended by Amanda Truesdale," she said.

"Yes, do you know Mrs. Truesdale?" I asked, thinking perhaps that was how she had attained her own position, but her answer took me by surprise.

"Amanda and I were girlhood friends," she said curtly.

I was about to make some polite comment about Mrs. Truesdale when Dr. McAllister, who had been speaking to Sir Evan said, "Good God, here's Vanessa now."

59

All eyes turned toward the door. Lady Thornton gasped, and tugging on her son's arm, said, "Perhaps Vanessa could have her dinner with Mrs. Cathcart tonight."

He ignored the suggestion and marching purposefully toward the outrageous-looking girl, he took her firmly by the arm and led her into the center of the group.

"Vanessa's a little late," he said in a cold, carefully controlled voice. "No doubt it took her a long time to dress tonight, but this is my daughter, Miss St. Claire, and as you can see, you have your work cut out for you."

"I'm happy to meet you, Vanessa," I said in a perfectly natural voice, and conscious of her father's presence, she curtsied and repeated my name in a sarcastic manner. "Miss St. Claire."

At her best, she could never have been an attractive child, but decked out in someone's obviously discarded hoop-skirted ballgown, she looked ridiculous and utterly pathetic.

Bony, childish shoulders peeped out from the lavender gown's low neckline. They were covered with freckles, as was her face, and the bright red hair that went along with them was frizzy and unmanageable.

I felt a deep rush of sympathy for her, but later at the dinner table when I had removed my gloves, her face suddenly took on a shrewish, calculating look, and pointing to me, she shrieked, "Look at her hand. That's a devil's mark!" Her eyes glittered with malicious glee. "She's a witch. I'll not have her for a teacher. Send her away, Papa. I won't have her here!"

I did not try to hide the ugly birthmark and all eyes in the room riveted themselves on it. Sir Evan's face turned bloodred. He stood up and I thought for a moment he was going to strike her, but he only glared at his daughter's defiant face and said, "Go to your room, you wicked girl, and don't expect to come out until you have apologized to Miss St. Claire."

Half tripping over the long gown, she ran out of the dining room, but once in the corridor, she shouted back, "Witches should burn!"

Lady Thornton had gone very white and her eyes rolled back in her head. Dr. McAllister was at her side immediately. He rubbed her hands and dipping a napkin in the water glass, pressed it to her temples.

"Thank you, I'm all right now," she assured him and turning to her son, said, "It's nothing, Evan. Please let us continue with dinner."

Polite conversation resumed and Dr. McAllister, who was seated next to me, whispered, "Take my advice and leave."

"I am not a quitter," I whispered back and indeed I had no intention of quitting then. Vanessa Thornton might not be what I had expected, but she was a challenge and one I hoped with patience to overcome.

Ah, what grand illusions the naive doth court!

After dinner Dr. McAllister went to speak to Mr. Glace about getting an early start in the morning and Sir Evan took me aside and apologized for his daughter's behaviour.

"The child has been upset ever since her mother's death four years ago. Frankly, Miss St. Claire, I'm at a loss as to how to handle Vanessa." His silver hair glistened in the lamplight and his handsome face looked boyishly vulnerable. "I might as well tell you," he confided. "Vanessa has been dismissed from three schools. That's why Mrs. Truesdale's offer, coming unsolicited the way it did, seemed like such a godsend to me. I certainly wouldn't want you to be unhappy here, but I'm sure with a little time, things will work out." He threw up his hands in a gesture of defeat. "My mother can't cope with any of it, as you saw for yourself tonight. You're just what Vanessa needs, what all of us at Thornton Manor need, Miss St. Claire, someone fresh and young, someone who will bring a little sunshine to these grey old walls. Please say you'll give us a chance."

How could I do otherwise? My heart went out to the man. "I'll do my best, Sir Evan. I give you my word on that."

"Wonderful," he said. "And if I might offer a word of caution about Dr. McAllister. He has somewhat of an unsavory reputation where women are concerned."

"I'm not surprised," I said.

Bidding him goodnight, I retired to my room, but instead of going to bed, I undressed and busied myself rearranging drawers and putting small toilet articles away. Presently I heard heavy footsteps at the end of the hall and I quickly doused the light.

"Miss St. Claire. It's Philip McAllister. Are you asleep?"

Can't he see the room is dark? Surely he doesn't expect me to come to the door in my nightclothes. Or does he? I certainly wouldn't put it past him, I thought, but after Sir Evan's warning there was no way I was going to open that door.

"I just wanted to say goodnight."

In the dark, his disembodied voice sounded low and intimate coming into my bedroom.

"I gather Sir Evan has talked you into staying, so I won't try to convince you to leave, but when you get settled, come to my office in the village. I'd like to examine you and check up on those headaches of yours. And, Miss St. Claire, don't believe everything you hear, especially from Sir Evan. Goodnight, and take care."

Oh, what a womanizer, I thought. *He'd like to examine me.* I'll just bet he would! Thank God Sir Evan confirmed my suspicions.

I didn't move a muscle until I heard his door close and even then, I was afraid to turn up the lamp. He might consider it an invitation to come back!

Lying in a suspended state between wakefulness and sleep, my mind drifted aimlessly and a sea of faces paraded themselves before my closed eyes. Mrs. Truesdale's, followed by the hatchet-faced Miss Hamilton. Could there be a connection between their friendship and my offer to come to Thornton Manor?

They faded, and the mysterious young man who had been a cabbie in London and a shepherd in Thornton Wood stared back at me with dark, haunting eyes. Who was he? And why had Philip denied seeing him?

Vanessa Thornton's plain, childish face appeared next. I watched in horror as she laughed with fiendish glee and removed her mask. Was she a changeling? Or just a pathetic little girl?

Sonia, Rashev, Sir Evan, and Philip McAllister, I saw them all. The last thing that floated before me was not a person, though, it was a huge vat, a kind of cistern or tub used for dyeing. Hadn't I seen one someplace before? But I was too tired to think, and blessed oblivion beckoned, so I surrendered my mind as well as my exhausted body to sleep.

"Miss St. Claire, Olivia! Open this door."

The insistent voice penetrated my slumbering brain. Dr. McAllister again! He must be mad. Hadn't I made it perfectly clear I was not like his compliant little barmaid?

He was pounding on the door so hard I was afraid he was going to break it down. This man's behaviour is outrageous, I thought, all the while struggling to disentangle myself from the bedclothes.

There was a thud and then a splintering sound. Where are the servants? Confused, I stumbled around the unfamiliar pitch-dark room. Where was the lamp?

"Olivia, wake up. The house is on fire!"

The incendiary words were followed by another tremendous crash. The unmistakable stench of smoke assaulted my nostrils and I realized it was true. The house *was* on fire.

In a vain attempt to scream, I swallowed a mouthful of smoke that billowed in from the hall.

"Olivia, where are you?"

Philip, thank God! I thought. He was already in the room.

"Here," I cried in between coughs.

Strong arms grabbed hold of me. "Put the blanket over your head and cover your mouth," he commanded.

Tugging the heavy blanket free, I draped it over me like a tent. Philip's arm went around my waist and together we moved through the doorway.

"Mrs. Cathcart," Philip shouted and the housekeeper answered.

"I'm here, doctor."

"Take my hand," he told her. "We'll use the back stairs. What about Farnsworth? Is his room on this floor?"

"No. His room is downstairs. We're the only ones."

"Good. Keep your mouths covered and don't talk," he said.

The three of us moved slowly forward. I don't know what made me look back, but what I saw made me gasp. The lower end of the corridor was engulfed in flames and it was obvious we had escaped just in time. My room was probably an inferno and everything I owned was surely gone.

The brightness of the fire at the other end of the hall lit our way and helped us find the staircase. Several male servants were already on their way up the steps.

"Stay back," Philip told them. "There's no one else up here. Nothing can be saved, so don't risk your lives."

They assisted us down the steps and we ran out of the house. A great deal of shouting and confusion followed and several seconds later the entire household had been aroused.

Occupants poured out of the manor house and joined us on the lawn. After Sir Evan was assured that no one was left in the burning wing, he dispatched several stablehands to the barn to bring out the portable pump and attach hoses to it.

The fire, which was confined to the second floor of the servants' wing, was nonetheless severe. Flames could now be seen through the windows and I shuddered to think what would have happened if Dr. McAllister had not been there.

Servants huddled on the ground in their nightclothes and I heard one of them make reference to my birthmark. The family, who resided in another section of the house, were all fully dressed, as was Dr. McAllister.

"Thank God you were there," Miss Cathcart was saying to him. "How did you discover the fire?"

"I was awake and smelled smoke."

"What time was that?" she asked.

Pulling out his watch, he said, "It's four o'clock now, so I'd say around three-thirty."

I was shocked. I had no idea it was so late. Had he taken time out to dress? I wondered. Or, had he never gone to bed at all?

By daybreak, the fire had been extinguished. Servants were allowed to return to their quarters to retrieve valuables, but as a precautionary measure no one was allowed on the second floor.

It was soon ascertained that smoke and water had done extensive damage to the whole wing and Sir Evan decreed that it would be closed off until the necessary repairs could be made. All concerned would be relocated, he announced.

Wearing a gown borrowed from one of the servants who was about my size, I reported for an early breakfast with the family at Sir Evan's request.

Dr. McAllister was not present. He and Mr. Glace had left Thornton Manor as soon as the fire had been extinguished, and Vanessa, too, was noticeably absent.

Lady Thornton looked very pale, and Miss Hamilton fussed over her, insisting that she must eat a little something from the sideboard's lavish buffet.

Sir Evan took me aside and explained that he was moving Vanessa and me to Amberwood, an estate on the other side of the woods.

"It belongs to my first wife's father," he explained. "Lord Fenwick is in Ireland now and won't be back for several months. By that time, Thornton Manor will be repaired. Besides," he added, "Vanessa and I need to be separated for awhile. I think you'll have more success with her that way."

Then he graciously insisted that Thornton Manor would replace everything I had lost in the fire. "We have a seamstress right here on the premises," he told me. "Miss O'Shay will have you in a new wardrobe in no time at all, Miss St. Claire. I have instructed her to begin at once. She will take measurements and begin sewing for you immediately."

"Just a few serviceable gowns will be sufficient," I insisted. "I didn't really own many."

"Nonsense. We shall do better than that. And, if I remember correctly, you lost a red dinner gown. Very charming it was, too, and quite becoming."

I bit my lip. It hurt to think the gown my mother had made was gone.

"I shall have Miss O'Shay make several dinner gowns," he said, and when I opened my mouth to protest, he added, "I want you to assume a position equal to Miss Hamilton's. She is my mother's companion and confidant. I hope that you will become Vanessa's companion and confidant."

Depressed over the loss of Mama's gown and the

upsetting event that precipitated it, tears welled up in my eyes, and I said, "Vanessa doesn't like me. She. . . ."

"Vanessa is a headstrong and foolish child, but give her some time, Miss St. Claire. You are a warm and vibrant woman. She will like you, I promise. No one could help it."

Surprised and flattered by his words, I blushed. Having Sir Evan as a champion was indeed a pleasing and rather heady experience.

He appeared to study me and then suggested in a lighter vein, "I think blue would be becoming. Certainly another red, and perhaps a vivid yellow."

Then taking my arm in an intimate gesture, he led me over to the buffet.

Miss Hamilton, having attended to Lady Thornton, was heaping her own plate with food. "Have you determined how the fire started, Sir Evan?" she asked.

His expression was a guarded one. "Not yet, Miss Hamilton. Miss Cathcart will be questioning the servants to make sure no carelessness was involved."

"Smoking can cause a fire," she said simply.

He gave her a blank look.

"Dr. McAllister smokes a pipe. I saw him with it." Her small eyes narrowed and almost disappeared. "I was in the kitchen fixing Lady Thornton a glass of warm milk. She couldn't get to sleep last night, and I saw Dr. McAllister come back from the barn after speaking to Mr. Glace. He was smoking it then and I think he had been drinking, too."

Philip McAllister was impetuous and unconventional, but he had saved my life and I didn't like Miss Hamilton's sly insinuation. However, I had thought it odd that even he would have the nerve to pound on a lady's door so late at night. Could he have been drinking?

"We mustn't jump to conclusions," Sir Evan said.

Miss Hamilton looked embarrassed and I was glad Sir Evan had put her in her place. The woman disturbed me. I don't know why, but I just didn't like her and something told me the feeling was mutual.

We joined Lady Thornton at the table and Sir Evan said, "Mother, I've decided to make use of Amberwood while Thornton Manor is being repaired. Lord Fenwick won't mind. In fact, if he were here, he would insist. So, I want you and Miss Hamilton to move in there with Vanessa."

Lady Thornton nodded her head. "I think that would be an excellent idea, Evan. The change will do Vanessa good."

"Fine," he said. "Then the four of you can leave today."

Lady Thornton frowned. "The four of us?"

"Of course, Miss St. Claire will be going, too. She's Vanessa's governess, Mother."

"But, I thought. . . . I mean, I didn't think . . ."

She had gone very white and she was staring at me like she was terrified.

"I can't go," she said. "I'm too ill. Send Miss Cathcart instead."

He looked annoyed. "Suit yourself then, Mother."

She doesn't want to go because of me, I thought. She was perfectly willing at first. I remembered our initial meeting the night before. I had taken her to be a person in command of herself, even a little arrogant, when we had been introduced, but then her personality had abruptly changed and she had turned into a frightened old woman.

Glancing down at my hand, I told myself that Lady Thornton was an intelligent, cultured woman. She would hardly be taken in by some lurid old wives' tale. Or, would she?

Chapter Six

Mrs. Cathcart, Vanessa, and I left for Amberwood late that same afternoon.

Vanessa was sullen and it was obvious that she was not happy about this new arrangement.

"How far is it to Amberwood?" I asked as the three of us settled ourselves into the carriage.

"A two-hour drive," Mrs. Cathcart answered. "But you can walk it in an hour if you cut through the woods."

So, the field where I had seen the shepherd belongs to Amberwood, I thought.

"Are there caretakers at the house?" I inquired.

"Oh, my dear, Lord Fenwick is a very wealthy man. He keeps a full staff of servants at all of his estates." Speaking in a confidential tone, she added, "He's very generous, too. Why, Nanny Grey, Amberwood's housekeeper, was formerly Lady Violette's nursemaid. But did Lord Fenwick dismiss her after his daughter grew up? No indeed! He promoted Nanny to housekeeper and she's been running Amberwood ever since. She's treated like a member of the family, too," she added.

Recalling that Miss Cathcart took her meals alone in her room, I gathered that such was not the case at Thornton Manor.

"A fine gentleman, Lord Fenwick is, but a lonely one," she said. "You see, he never fully recovered from his daughter's death."

Since Lady Violette had also been Sir Evan's first wife, I thought it best not to pursue this subject in Vanessa's presence. Mrs. Cathcart's information was encouraging, though. The servants at Amberwood would surely know something about the shepherd and I wasn't above questioning them.

"Amberwood is a lovely house," Mrs. Cathcart was saying. "Much newer than Thornton Manor."

Vanessa suddenly spoke up. "What do you, a housekeeper, know? Thornton Manor is a historic monument. The Thorntons were ruling Northumberland when the Fenwicks were their Saxon slaves."

"Mrs. Cathcart was merely making a statement, Vanessa," I said. "And the Saxons were never the Angles' slaves. The two tribes settled in different parts of England, but since you're interested in Old English history, we'll make that a priority for study this year. Now, will you please apologize to Mrs. Cathcart for your rudeness?"

I was sitting next to Vanessa and the face she turned toward me was more demon than child. Somehow, I managed to keep calm, although I must confess for a split second, I was afraid of her. Then almost immediately her expression changed to that of a shy little girl. "I'm sorry," she said stiffly.

Is the child unbalanced? I wondered, and then chastised myself for the thought. My mother would be ashamed of me. I was supposed to be a governess and Vanessa Thornton was a lonely little girl with only one parent. Surely, I could relate to that!

Mrs. Cathcart was pleasant and seemed willing to overlook Vanessa's outburst, but though we both tried to include the girl in our conversation, she made no effort to cooperate. After awhile she went to sleep, effectively discouraging any further attempts at communication.

I wanted to hear more about Amberwood, but the subject seemed to be a sore spot with Vanessa and I hesitated to bring it up in case she only pretended to be asleep.

Presently, having exhausted small talk, Mrs. Cathcart and I both succumbed to the motion of the carriage and dozed, and so it was that I caught my first glimpse of Amberwood: through sleep-drugged eyes.

My blurred vision gave it a hazy, fairytale quality like a painting by Renoir.

"What a beautiful house," I exclaimed.

Mrs. Cathcart's eyes popped open and she said, "Are we here? Yes, of course we are. I must have nodded off for a few moments. Forgive me, Miss St. Claire."

Vanessa turned sulky eyes on the house. "I won't sleep in the nursery," she announced.

"There's no nursery," Mrs. Cathcart said.

"Miss Hamilton told me Lord Fenwick had a nursery added on when he thought he was going to have a

73

grandchild," Vanessa cried. "I won't sleep in a dead baby's room."

Her eyes bulged and I could see another tantrum in the making. "Vanessa, no one is going to force you to sleep anywhere you don't want to sleep. Now come along, let's go inside," I said.

The footman was assisting us from the carriage when a white-haired little woman came running out of the house. Grabbing Mrs. Cathcart by the hand, she said, "Oh, my dear. I'm so glad to see you. Thank God you're safe. Sir Evan told us about the fire."

Casting a benign smile in my direction, Mrs. Cathcart said, "If this young woman hadn't arrived, I would have been alone up there and it might have been a different story."

She introduced us then and I said, "I'm pleased to meet you, Miss Grey. Thank you for taking us in."

"Call me Nanny. Everybody does, and don't thank me, child. I love company." Still smiling, she turned to Vanessa and shook her head. "Little Miss Vanessa. Why, I can't believe it. You're almost a young lady."

Little Miss Vanessa looked like she was about to say something impolite, so I fixed her with one of my mother's no-nonsense stares, and much to my surprise, she swallowed her retort.

We entered Amberwood, a beautiful Georgian manor house built most likely sometime in the middle of the eighteenth century. The handsome front door, flanked on either side by long oval windows, opened to reveal a richly furnished entry hall. Persian carpets in vibrant hues were scattered over the highly polished, dark wood floors. The room's stark white walls were relieved by rococo panels of magnificent plaster work. Depicting mythological and biblical scenes, each panel was a work of art.

I was introduced to Cummings, the butler, a rotund little man in his sixties with a shiny bald head and a twinkle in his bright blue eyes. Cummings, as far removed from Farnsworth as Amberwood was from Thornton Manor, made me feel welcome and privileged to be staying in this gracious house.

Vanessa's trunk and the two small traveling bags belonging to Mrs. Cathcart and myself were brought in. We were grateful to Miss O'Shay and her assistants, who had taken our measurements and in a matter of hours produced two sets of undergarments and one plain gown apiece for us.

"Let me show you to your rooms," Nanny Grey said. "Then we'll have tea and some of cook's little cakes. Mrs. Bodine is famous for them."

"I hate sweets. I just like tea," Vanessa said. "And besides, I don't feel well. I think I'll just stay in my room until dinner."

"I'm sorry to hear that," I said. "It's such a lovely afternoon and Mrs. Cathcart tells me Amberwood has a garden with a maze. I thought we might explore it together."

"My head hurts. I want to lie down."

"Of course. You get into bed and I'll unpack your trunk."

Her eyes flashed. "No, I want you to leave so I can go to sleep."

"Very well. I'll call you in time for dinner."

Give me patience, I thought, silently begging my mother to show me the way.

I saw Vanessa settled in bed and then returned to

my own room to freshen up before tea. Despite the fire and the challenge that Vanessa presented, I felt elated. Coming to Amberwood had miraculously lifted my spirits. The house was magnificent, and yet there was a serenity and warmth about it that made one feel comfortable and completely at home.

The plasterwork that I had so admired in the entry hall was repeated throughout the house. Delicate white garlands and fans embellished the pale green walls of my bedroom and the vaulted ceiling in the upstairs hall was decorated with graceful vines and clusters of flowers.

My sparsely furnished, utilitarian room at Thornton Manor flashed before my eyes. It contrasted sharply with this airy, gardenlike room with its floral, rose-coloured bedspread, matching drapes, and comfortable upholstered chairs.

This was a guest room and I realized I was being offered it only because of Vanessa, but I would enjoy it no less, and after washing the road dust from my face and hands, I smoothed my hair and hurried downstairs for tea.

Sitting in the handsome blue and white drawing room, I was secretly relieved that Vanessa was not present, for I was enjoying myself in the company of these pleasant older women.

"Amberwood is a perfectly beautiful house," I remarked and Mrs. Cathcart smiled.

"Didn't I tell you? I know Miss Vanessa took exception, but honestly, I meant to cast no aspersions on Thornton Manor. I know about its history, but the house is a museum. Amberwood is a home." She stirred her tea and eyed me with growing respect. "You handled her remarkably well, if I may say so, Miss St. Claire."

"Poor child. Has she been acting up again?" Nanny Grey asked.

Miss Cathcart rolled her eyes at me. "I'm afraid so, but I think Sir Evan has chosen wisely this time. Miss St. Claire is young and perhaps that is what Vanessa needs."

Nanny Grey turned to me. "Take heart, my dear. Our Violette was spoiled and hard to manage, too. I'm referring to Lord Fenwick's late daughter," she explained. "Lady Fenwick and the long-awaited heir to Amberwood both died in childbirth when little Violette was six and that's when Lord Fenwick brought Genevieve here as governess."

She gave the name its French pronunciation, *John-Vi-Ev*, trilling the beautiful syllables over her lips and pausing a moment, as if the name brought back fond memories, before continuing.

"She was young, like you, and French," she added. "And it wasn't only Lady Violette who fell in love with her. We all did. Genevieve worked a miracle and you will, too, my dear. Just have patience."

"Thank you," I said. "I want so much to help Vanessa." Then I turned to Mrs. Cathcart. "Has she always been difficult?"

"Yes, but more so after her mother's death and worse after Sir Evan remarried. She's extremely jealous of him. She's even jealous of his first wife. That's why she doesn't like Amberwood."

I thought it best to change the subject. Sir Evan

might not appreciate my discussing his daughter with the housekeepers.

"The stucco work at Amberwood is magnificent," I observed. "I've never seen anything like it."

Nanny Grey smiled. "Nor are you likely to, my dear, unless you travel to Ireland. This was all done by the famous Irish stuccodore, Robert West. He and his brother, John West, were masters of the art. Lord Fenwick's great-grandfather, who built this house, brought Robert West over here to work on Amberwood. When we've finished our tea, I'll show you through the house. There's a most unusual pattern in the small salon."

The scrollwork in the small salon was certainly beautiful and most unusual, but it was overshadowed by the painting that hung over the mantelpiece.

The young woman was so breathtakingly beautiful that I could not tear my eyes away from the portrait. Pale blond hair and the face of a Botticelli angel gave the subject an ethereal look, but her gorgeous violet-coloured eyes and come-hither smile dispelled any angelic illusion. This was no saintly ascetic. This was a warm and vibrant young woman.

"That's our Violette," Nanny Grey said in a hushed, almost reverent tone of voice.

"Were her eyes really that shade?" I asked, for I had never seen violet eyes before.

"Oh yes," Nanny Grey said. "She was christened Rachel Louise, but her father changed her name to Violette because of her eyes. And, of course, the colour was more pronounced when she wore one of the lilac shades."

It was then that I noticed the low-cut lavender gown

that bared her beautiful shoulders. Something vague tugged at my memory, but it escaped me when Mrs. Cathcart spoke.

"Sir Evan was terribly in love with her, they say. That's not hard to understand now, is it?"

"Not at all," I said. "Nor Vanessa's jealousy."

I returned to the portrait, focusing again on those beautiful white shoulders. My mind immediately played back a memory of small bony shoulders covered with freckles.

Could this gown and the faded lavender gown that Vanessa had worn last night be one and the same?

Recalling Sir Evan's shocked face and his mother's attempt to control his anger, it seemed likely.

"Such a lovely gown," I said.

Nanny Grey smiled. "Aye, she wore it the night her engagement to Sir Evan was announced." The old lady shook her head. "Ah, the parties, the balls that took place in this house after Violette's come-out. She had lots of suitors, as you can well imagine, but of course, it was preordained that she should marry Sir Evan. They'd been promised since they were children."

Such an archaeic custom, I thought, but wasn't it a blessing they had fallen in love?

"Begging your pardon, Miss St. Claire." Cummings, the butler, stood in the doorway. "Miss Vanessa said to tell you she'd be in the garden."

"Thank you, Cummings. I'll go outside with her," I said to the others.

"Cummings will show you the way," Nanny Grey said. "We dine at eight."

"Wonderful. I shall have time for a nap," Mrs. Cathcart said.

Nanny Grey smiled. "My sentiments exactly. I usually rest before dinner."

"Then we shall leave you young ones to the great outdoors," Mrs. Cathcart said as I followed Cummings out of the room.

I found Vanessa sitting on a stone bench. "Headache better?" I asked.

"Completely gone," she answered. "I feel fine and I remembered what you said about the maze."

"Good. I guess we'll have no trouble finding it." I paused and looked around the immaculately kept grounds. "Let's take a walk and look for it."

She stood up and we strolled companionably down the flagstone walkway.

"How was tea?" she asked.

"Very nice and Mrs. Bodine's cakes were delicious. Oh, I forgot, you don't like sweets."

"Yes I do. I love them. It's tea I don't like."

I was sure she had said the opposite, but I didn't pursue the subject.

"Did Nanny Grey show you the house?" she asked.

"Some of it. I was interested in the ornamental plaster work."

"Oh, that. Did you see the picture of my father's first wife?"

I tried to act nonchalant. "There was a portrait, I believe."

"She was only married to him a year when she died, she and her baby. My mother was married to him for ten years."

"I'd like to see a picture of your mother, Vanessa. What was her name and is there a portrait of her at Thornton Manor?"

"No. She was Lady Thornton, you know, and so was his third wife, the one who died last year. His first wife was Lady Violette. That's because she already had a title when she married Papa. My mother's name was Esther," she added. "And his third wife's name was Diana. My mother was really beautiful," she stressed.

"I'm sure she was, Vanessa, and I'm sure your father loved her very much. Do you resemble her?"

"Yes. I'm beautiful, too," she added, tossing her head at me.

"Well, I'm sure you will be when you're a grown-up lady," I said diplomatically. "But it's much more important to be good."

"No, it's not. My mother was good, but my father didn't love her. He loved Lady Violette and she was a bitch."

"Vanessa! We don't use that kind of language and I don't ever want to hear you talk like that again."

"How old are you?" she asked, switching the subject with very little effort.

"Twenty-two."

"You're only eight years older than I am. When I'm twenty, you'll be twenty-eight. Then we can be friends."

"We can be friends right now, and I hope we will be."

"There's the maze," she shouted. "See it over there?"

Looking out over the grounds, I could see a clump of tall boxwoods at the far end of the lawn.

"Let's run," she said, and grabbing my hand, pulled me down the stone steps.

"I am not in my dotage yet," I cried, sprinting ahead

81

of her. It was fun, and laughing helplessly, I collapsed on a stone bench outside the maze.

A few seconds later, she arrived, flushed and with her unruly red hair sticking out all over her head. Wearing her demon's face, she glared at me. Her voice dripping with sarcasm, she said, "So, you won. After all, you're the teacher. You can't be beaten at anything. Right?"

Refusing to be goaded, I answered her calmly. "Sit down and rest a minute, Vanessa. It was only a game."

We rested in silence for a few minutes and then all traces of anger gone, she stood up. "Well, what are we waiting for? Aren't we going to explore the maze?"

"Of course."

"You first," she said, stepping back and allowing me to enter ahead of her. "The trick is to always stay to the left. I read that in a book," she added, as she followed me through the narrow opening.

There had been a maze on the grounds of Wynfield Towers, but it was much smaller than this one. "I think we should switch directions every other time," I said.

"Oh, well then, you must know. After all, you are the teacher, so you must be right, or is it left, Miss St. Claire?"

Already a giant wall of thick boxwoods loomed up before us. "We'll have to backtrack," I said.

I turned around and Vanessa was gone. "Vanessa," I called. "I think we should stay together. This is more complicated than I thought."

A shrill, disembodied voice answered me. "Oh, you'll do better by yourself. I'll just wander around on my own. You're not afraid, are you? After all, what could happen? Only, I did read in that same book that a man in Germany got lost in a maze and starved to death. But you'll figure it out. You're a teacher, right? Or is it left?"

She laughed hysterically at her repeated joke and I said, "Stay where you are, Vanessa. I'll find you and we'll get out of this maze together."

"I'm already out," she shouted. "Good-bye, Miss St. Claire . . ."

"Vanessa," I called, but all was silence. She's punishing me for winning the race, I thought. She couldn't have found her way out already. She must be hiding close by. I came to another opening. Which way should I turn?

"Vanessa," I called.

Still no answer. If she jumps out at me, I shall scream and make a fool of myself, I thought. Entering each opening on my left seemed to be working. I was going deeper and deeper into the maze, of course, but I should be able to come out on the other side.

"Vanessa. Are you all right?" I waited a moment and then said, "Don't you think this has gone far enough? It could be fun if we find our way out together. Just answer and I'll follow your voice."

When she didn't respond, I turned the next corner and ran into a dead end. Frustrated, I circled my way back and met with another row of hedges cutting off my path.

Discouraged and feeling hemmed in, I sat down on the ground. How long had I been wandering around in circles? And looking up at the sky I wondered if it was growing dark, or if those were rain clouds I saw. Dear God, I thought, had Vanessa found her way out and just left me here?

I thought about the man in Germany. It was just a story, of course. Or could somebody really get lost in one of these things?

A loud clap of thunder brought me to my feet, and looking up, I saw a bolt of lightning streak across the sky. Galvanized into action, I scurried for the nearest opening.

It proved to be another dead end, and feeling trapped, I gave way to panic.

"Help," I cried hysterically, but the thunder drowned me out.

I almost welcomed the intermittent flashes of light, for without them I could see nothing. The boxwoods were easily twelve feet high and like tall, dark giants I felt them closing in on me.

"Help," I cried again, but I was wasting my breath. The maze was at the far end of the garden. No one in the house could possibly hear me.

A particularly sharp clap made me jump and I wondered if the boxwoods attracted lightning like trees did.

The rain began then, big, pelting drops that soaked me to the skin. The ground turned to mud, making me slip and land in a puddle of water.

Feeling my way blindly, I squeezed through the wet shrubbery, only to find myself facing yet another wall of thick boxwoods.

A flash of brilliant light illuminated the whole area, revealing for a split second a shadowy figure at the far end of the section where I stood. Somebody was in the maze with me!

"Vanessa," I started to shout and then the word died in my throat. It hadn't been Vanessa.

The figure was taller and . . . Oh dear God, I thought. It had been wearing a hood!

Chapter Seven

Turning in the opposite direction, I ran like the devil himself was after me.

And he is, I thought, for surely no normal human being could appear out of nowhere the way this man did.

My heart was pounding and raw fear sharpened my senses. Oblivious now to the storm, I welcomed the lightning, for it helped me to see. I thought of nothing but getting out of the maze and escaping the dark man who had dogged my footsteps ever since I left Sussex.

If he is waiting for me around the bend, I shall drop dead of fright, I thought, but still I kept running.

Once again, the whole sky lit up and this time I saw that I had reached the end of the maze. Tears of relief streamed down my rain-splashed face and a spray of water showered over me as I squeezed through the final opening.

With my lungs ready to burst, I forced myself to keep running. He could be right behind me, I told myself.

Now I was lost. I had come out on the other side of the maze and even though the rain had slacked off, a mist hung on the air, making it impossible for me to find the house.

I could be going away from the house and into the woods, I thought, stopping to lean up against a large tree to catch my breath.

I heard hoof beats and suddenly, like phantoms from hell, a huge horse and its shadowy rider burst through the mist.

Screaming hysterically, I broke into another run, but there was no escape for me now. A long, strong arm reached down and I was scooped up like a rag doll and deposited on the horse's back.

"Stop screaming. What is the matter with you?" he shouted, reigning the horse in.

Astonished, I stared into the face of Dr. McAllister.

"Let me go," I cried. "You were in the maze. I saw you."

"In the maze? Are you crazy? I just rode through the woods in this downpour."

He wore no hood and instinctively I knew it was the shepherd, and not Philip McAllister, who had been in the maze with me. But why should Philip appear at the same time? Was there some connection between the two of them?

"What were you doing in the maze in the middle of a thunder storm?" he demanded.

"And what are you doing here?" I countered.

"Making a call, Miss St. Claire. I'm a doctor, remember? I just delivered a baby to one of Amberwood's tenants."

He started to laugh. "I'm sorry, but you do look a little comical. Whatever possessed you to go into the maze alone?"

"I wasn't alone," I said. "Vanessa was with me, but she ran off and left me there."

He immediately grew serious. "Didn't I tell you to leave? Vanessa is not to be trusted and neither is the honourable Sir Evan Thornton."

"Vanessa is a child, Dr. McAllister, and I grant you, a mischievous one, but I do not intend to turn tail and run. Sir Evan has hired me to help Vanessa and that is what I intend to do."

"Sir Evan and his daughter are both crazy, and I'm beginning to think you are, too. Now hold on tight, I'm taking you back to Amberwood."

He closed his legs around the huge animal and the horse took off like it had wings. I was terrified, but he held me tightly against him. Sucking in my breath, I swore I would not give him the satisfaction of hearing me scream.

"Water-soaked, but safe," he said when the horse stopped and I could see that we were in front of Amberwood. "I hope you weren't frightened," he said. "Someone brave enough to work for Sir Evan and go into a maze with Vanessa shouldn't be afraid of a brisk little ride."

"Not at all," I said, as he lowered me to the ground. "Thank you for bringing me home."

"Oh, I'm coming in. I want to have a look at those

scratches on your arms and I want to give you some medicine to ward off a cold."

I didn't want any fuss made. All I wanted was to sneak upstairs, get out of my wet clothes, and take a bath.

"The first thing I prescribe is a hot bath," he said, dismounting and taking me by the arm.

"I'd already decided to do that, doctor," I said sharply.

Cummings opened the door.

"Has Miss Vanessa come back?" I asked.

"Yes, miss. She went right upstairs. Said she didn't feel well and didn't want any supper."

I breathed a sigh of relief and turned to the doctor. "Thank you again and goodnight, Dr. McAllister." Before he could answer, I picked up my sodden skirts and made a run for the stairs.

Once safely in my room, I rang for a servant and was surprised when my ring was answered in a matter of seconds.

Opening the door, I found two stalwart young maids standing in the hall, each of them holding a large pail of steaming water. "Dr. McAllister says you're to get into a hot tub, miss," one of them said.

They entered and I closed the door quickly before he, too, should appear and think to be admitted.

"Thank you. You may go now," I said when they had filled the tub, which was stationed in a small bathing chamber off the bedroom.

"Dr. McAllister says we're to wait, Mum, until you're done, sos we can tell him to come on up."

I said, "What? You'll do no such thing." And then, knowing Dr. McAllister, I thought it prudent to add,

"You may tell the doctor I'll be down to see him when I have finished."

They left and I sank down into the hot soapy water. Every part of my body ached; my arms from the scratches that covered them, my ribs from being scooped up and thrown on a horse like a sack of potatoes, and my legs from rubbing against the horse's flanks.

If only I could collapse in the bed and not have to think about Dr. McAllister or Vanessa or that blasted shepherd, I thought. But no, he has to insist on playing doctor and wasting my time when I should be having a talk with Vanessa and getting to the bottom of her irresponsible behaviour.

Stepping out of the tub, I threw on my clothes and hurried downstairs to make short work of Philip McAllister, M.D. More appropriate initials for him would be B.P. for *Big Pest*, I decided.

Cummings was standing in the hall and he said, "Dr. McAllister's in the kitchen, miss. I'll take you there."

I followed the butler down a long corridor and into another part of the house where the large homey kitchen was located.

Dr. McAllister was seated before the fire, drinking from a large glass that probably contained whiskey with Nanny Grey, the cook, and several maids dancing attendance on him.

They all looked up as I entered.

"Oh, Miss St. Claire," Nanny Gray said. "The doctor was telling us about your experience. You shouldn't have come downstairs."

"No, she shouldn't," he said. "And, I want you to see

to it, Nanny, that she goes up to her room as soon as I've finished with her."

"I'm perfectly all right," I said, trying and failing to smother a sneeze.

He gave Nanny a sly look. "What is a doctor to do with a patient like this?"

"Just give me the medicine," I said, "and I'll go right upstairs."

Reaching into his medical bag, he brought out a white envelope and a small jar. "First we'll tend to those scrapes." The ointment was soothing and his large fingers were surprisingly gentle in applying it. "Put it on again tomorrow," he said, his eyes traveling down my body. "What about your legs?"

"My limbs were covered by my gown," I said emphatically.

"Well, if you see any more wounds, just cover them with the ointment." He reached for the envelope then and said, "Mrs. Bodine will make you a cup of herbal tea. That should take care of your cold."

The tea he had given me in the woods had worked like a charm and I was thinking that I wouldn't mind having some of it on hand. "Is it the same tea you gave me for a headache?" I asked.

"Certainly not. Would you take a purgative for a sore toe?"

The maids snickered and I blushed. He really was the most disgusting man!

Handing the envelope to Mrs. Bodine, he said, "I'll be getting back before I catch cold myself."

"We'll see that Miss St. Claire goes straight to bed, doctor," Nanny Grey said. Then she turned to me, "We don't want you getting sick, my dear. And as for Miss

Vanessa, she should be punished for what she did."

Philip McAllister frowned. "Just watch her," he said, holding me in a steady stare.

I thanked him and he left by the kitchen door.

How had Vanessa found her way out of the maze so quickly?

The question had bothered me all night, and very early the next morning when only the servants were up and about the house, I paid a return visit to the sight of the previous night's adventure.

My suspicions were confirmed when I found a thin but sturdy length of rope tied to one of the boxwoods and hidden inside the shrubbery.

What a diabolical mind the child has, I thought. This was no spur-of-the-moment, childish prank. She had lured me there with a smiling face and I, like a fool, had thought I was winning her over.

Untying the rope, I coiled it over my arm and walked purposefully back to the house.

"Good morning, miss."

The disembodied voice caused me to jump and look anxiously around.

An elderly, rosy-cheeked man stood up, spade in hand, and fixed me with a sheepish grin. "I'm after doing some planting over here in the flower bed," he explained, tipping his hat. "Name's Farley, miss. I'm the gardener."

"I'm Miss Vanessa's governess," I said.

"Aye, you're Miss St. Claire. Cook told me," he added.

I complimented him on Amberwood's gardens and he beamed with pleasure.

"Wait til summer, miss. These flower beds'll be a riot of colour. Lord Fenwick is most fond of his garden," he added, "especially the roses."

"They were my mother's favorite, and I am partial to them, too."

"Are ye, now? Well, ye have a treat in store for ye at Amberwood then, miss. Old Farley's raised some unusual ones. Ever seen a lilac rose?" he asked.

"No, I don't believe I have."

He pointed to a row of bushes. "Them's the Lady Violette roses, miss. Took me many a year to produce that colour. They'll be bloomin' come June and you'll see for yourself what I mean." He shook his head a little sadly. "Tragic thing, Lady Violette dying in childbirth. Like to kill the master, her husband, too, for that matter. They say the shock turned Sir Evan's hair white overnight."

"Were you here then?" I asked.

"No, miss. Lord Fenwick brought me over from Dublin a couple of years later. I was groundskeeper at Trinity College and his lordship heard about my experiments with hybrids. He wanted me to develop a lilac rose in his daughter's memory." Then, taking on the guise of a cocky Irish imp, he added, "So, I said I'd give him five years."

I smiled. "And that was how long ago?"

"Twenty years, give or take a month," he said with a chuckle.

"Then you must know everyone on the estate," I commented.

"Just about, miss."

"There is a shepherd I keep seeing—a young dark-complected man. Wears a hood. Do you know him?"

"No, miss, but there's some new tenants. Perhaps he's one of them."

"You've never seen anyone like that around here?" I persisted.

"No, miss."

"Then, he must be one of the new tenants," I said.

Bidding the gardener a good day, I vowed to put the shepherd out of my mind. Farley had provided me with a logical explanation. I must either accept it or conclude that I had imagined the man and with all my other problems, that was something I was not prepared to do.

Entering the house through the conservatory's side door, I saw a small figure carrying an enormous tray hurry down the corridor.

"Just a minute, please," I said. Startled, the child froze in her tracks.

When she turned around, I saw that she was about twelve years old, a scrawny, sallow-faced child who reminded me of a frightened rabbit.

"You're the tweeny, aren't you?" I said, for she could be nothing else.

"Aye, mum. Name's Becky."

The covered dishes rattled as she attempted to hold on to the loaded tray. I steadied it and said, "Put the tray down on the hall table for a minute, Becky."

She set it down and came back, rubbing her thin little arms. "Just who is this tray for?" I asked.

"Miss Vanessa, mum. I was dustin' outside her room and she come out and give me instructions to tell cook what to fix. She said I was to say Miss St. Claire ordered it, mum."

"I see. Well, I am Miss St. Claire, Becky, and I am

about to give you some new instructions."

"Yes, mum."

"I want you to take that tray back to the kitchen and eat it yourself. Tell Mrs. Bodine I said so. And then, I want you to tell her to prepare a pot of tea and some toast for Miss Vanessa."

"Aye, mum. Thank ye, mum."

She bobbed another curtsy and hurried over to retrieve the tray. She seemed to have acquired additional strength, for she lifted it with ease and was hurrying to the kitchen as I mounted the stairs.

I stood outside Vanessa's door and knocked just once.

"Come in, you lazy girl."

She was seated at the dressing table, her back to me as I entered.

"If that food's not hot, I'm going to slap your face for you. Didn't I tell you to hurry? I'm hungry."

"That's too bad, but I rescinded your order," I said, and she whirled around and stared open-mouthed at me.

I threw the rope on the bed. "Anybody who cheats can escape a maze."

"I don't know what you're talking about," she said.

"I think you do, and until you're ready to discuss it, you will remain in your room and be served the meals that I order for you."

Giving her no chance to answer, I left the room and closed the door.

I had a pleasant breakfast with the two housekeepers and then returned to the garden to work on my lesson plans. I figured to let Vanessa sulk in her room until after lunch and then I would return and have a talk with her.

She was turning out to be more of a problem than I had anticipated. I hadn't liked her attitude toward the tweeny and I wouldn't have put it past Vanessa to have carried out her threat to slap poor Becky, had she been given the opportunity.

Common sense told me to go back to London and seek another post. The child had more deeply rooted problems than I was equipped to deal with, and besides, hadn't the Gypsy warned me about the Prince of Darkness?

I was convinced now she meant the shepherd, and after seeing him in the maze, why did I still hesitate?

My thoughts turned then to Sir Evan Thornton. A proud man and a powerful one, and yet his slate-grey eyes had held a mute appeal when he had asked me to stay. How could I go back on my word?

Lost in my daydream, I was startled when Sir Evan, himself, suddenly materialized and came walking toward me.

"Good afternoon. Cummings said you were out here." He looked around the garden. "Where's Vanessa?"

I hesitated. "She's in her room."

The warm smile abruptly left his face. "Punished, I'll wager."

I took a deep breath. "I'm afraid so, Sir Evan."

His grey eyes turned to charcoal. "What did she do this time?"

Now was my chance to turn back, but I made a hasty decision and sealed my fate. "I'd rather not say, Sir Evan. Please let me handle things in my own way."

"Very admirable, but probably foolish, Miss St. Claire. Nevertheless, I shall bow to your wishes."

That settled, he cast aside his stern-father role and gazing at me with eyes that had reverted to slate, he said, "I brought Miss O'Shay with me. She's been working on your gowns, but she requires a fitting."

I didn't know what to say. What about Mrs. Cathcart's gowns? I wondered. Was she to have a fitting, too?

"Very well," I said. "Where shall I find her?"

"Come along. I'll take you to the sewing room."

He's being kind, I thought. Surely a man of Sir Even's sophistication and background could not be interested in his daughter's governess.

Remembering the portrait of the beautiful girl who had been Sir Evan's first wife and recalling Vanessa's description of her own mother, I blushed at the thought of such a vain and ridiculous notion.

He led me down a long corridor to another wing of the house.

"This is Nanny Grey's domain," he said. "My father-in-law converted this wing into an apartment for her when she took over as housekeeper at Amberwood."

"How generous of him," I remarked.

"Oh, Lord Fenwick's a generous man, and a wealthy one," he added. "This land once belonged to Thornton Manor, but a gambling ancestor lost it in the early part of the last century. Our families were rivals then, but my father and Lord Fenwick became friends, and the marriage of their children united the two houses."

Recalling the bleakness and austerity of Thornton Manor, I could see how such a marriage would be advantageous for the Thorntons.

I followed him up a back staircase to a large room equipped with a cutting table and a treadle sewing machine. I had never seen one before and I wondered what my mother would have thought of such equipment.

The seamstress was waiting for us, and Sir Evan said, "I'll be across the hall in Nanny Grey's sitting room, Miss O'Shay. I want to see the gowns on Miss St. Claire when you have fitted them."

I couldn't believe he intended to supervise the fittings, and the very thought of it embarrassed me. "I don't think that will be necessary, Sir Evan . . ."

He ignored me, and in a voice that left no doubt he was the lord and master, addressed the seamstress. "You may call me in, Miss O'Shay, after the first fitting, but show Miss St. Claire the red gown now."

I was shocked when the woman opened a large box and brought out the ruby velvet gown that my mother had made.

"But, that's impossible. My gown was burnt up in the fire," I said.

Sir Evan and Miss O'Shay exchanged glances, and the seamstress smiled. "Thank you, my dear. Your gown was damaged, but not completely destroyed. Sir Evan explained that your mother had made it. He said the gown had great sentimental value and he requested that I copy it exactly."

Sir Evan's eyes were warm and compassionate. "It's not your mother's work," he said, "but it is her design. Please accept the gown on behalf of Miss O'Shay and myself."

I was touched by his sensitivity. "It's beautiful and I'm very grateful," I said.

Sir Evan left the room then, and Miss O'Shay opened another box and brought out a sheet-covered gown. Placing it over my arms, she said, "I forgot my marking chalk. Try this on and I'll be right back."

Slipping out of my dress, I removed the sheet and gasped. There had to be some mistake. This was a ball gown fit for a queen! Some countess or duchess must have commissioned it and Miss O'Shay had accidentally brought it here.

Made of shimmering white satin, the gown had an off-the-shoulder neckline, tiny puffed sleeves, and a fashionable, long train. Exquisite red satin roses that were themselves a work of art adorned the neckline and the bustle in the back.

While I was standing there, staring down at the gown, Miss O'Shay returned. "Not ready yet? Here let me help you."

"This has to be a mistake," I said. "I have no use for a ball gown."

She shrugged. "Sir Evan commissioned it. Put it on and then you can discuss the situation with him."

She held the dress out and I stepped into it.

"Oh, yes," she said when she had buttoned me up the back and stood in front of me. "I wanted to make the roses pink, but Sir Evan said red. He was right. Red is your colour."

Before I could protest, she had called his name and almost immediately he was in the room, staring at me with a strange expression on his face.

"Really, Sir Evan, I cannot accept this gown." His eyes darkened in anger and I stammered. "Please sir, I am grateful, but I have no use for a ball gown."

His expression immediately changed. "Is that all?

Well, let me be the judge of that, Miss St. Claire. We give balls at Thornton Manor and as my daughter's companion, you will be attending them." Then turning abruptly to Miss O'Shay, he said, "The gown should be taken in at the waist."

"You're right." Her nimble fingers took in the side seams and secured them with pins."

He smiled. "Perfect, Miss O'Shay."

"Thank you, Sir Evan, and may I say that you were also right about using red for the roses. Such a luscious shade," she added. "I call it gypsy red."

"Not gypsy," he said with distaste. "It should be called regal red."

"Yes, of course, the queen's own colour."

I might have been a dress form for all they included me in the conversation. "The gown is handsome, Sir Evan, but don't you think it's a little ornate to be worn by your daughter's governess?" I asked.

"No, I do not," he answered.

Sir Evan and Miss O'Shay faced me, but I faced the door. It was partially open and I thought I saw someone standing in the hall. As I watched, whoever it was very stealthily closed the door.

I didn't know how to react to Sir Evan's generosity. After the ball gown had been fitted, there were two dinner gowns to be tried on. One was a watered silk in Indigo blue and the other was a bright yellow satin trimmed in black lace.

I had never worn such vibrant colours, but the mirror told me they were becoming. Even the three day dresses that Miss O'Shay had made were attractive, and not one of them was black, gray, or dark blue.

Inwardly, I wrestled with my conscience. Was it proper to accept all this?

"The fire was covered by insurance," Sir Evan said. "Surely you will allow me to be fair and make up for your losses."

He wants me to assume a position comparable to Miss Hamilton's and she is included in all the family's functions, I told myself. Sir Evan is a cultured, refined gentleman. He would never consort with a barmaid or embarrass a lady by making reference to corsets and purgatives like that disgusting Philip McAllister.

Pushing all my inhibitions aside, I thanked him and after changing into my drab little morning gown, I met him downstairs.

We closeted ourselves in Lord Fenwick's study so I could show Sir Evan my lesson plans and go over the curriculum I had mapped out for Vanessa.

"Excellent," he said when I had finished. "Now, won't you tell me why she's being punished?"

"I'd rather not. I'm confident Vanessa and I can work things out on our own."

"Perhaps, but promise me if she goes too far, you'll consult with me."

I was about to answer when we were interrupted by Cummings. The butler's usually cheerful face was grave, and he said to Sir Evan, "Begging your pardon, sir, but Nanny Grey's gone to market and one of the servants has discovered a mishap in one of the rooms. Could you come and have a look?"

Sir Evan looked puzzled and I couldn't imagine that Cummings would consult the master of Thornton Manor about some little domestic crisis at Amberwood. Nevertheless, Sir Evan excused himself and left the room with the butler.

Several minutes later, the study door burst open and Sir Evan, his face mottled with rage, said, "Get Vanessa down here immediately, Miss St. Claire."

Chapter Eight

I paled at the sight of his anger and I was almost afraid
to expose Vanessa to it. "What has she done?"

"Go to the small salon and you'll see. And don't
bother getting her. I'll get her myself!"

He was out the door and up the steps before I could
move. Oh, dear God. It must be something terrible, I
thought, but I collected my wits and hurried down the
corridor to see for myself.

Becky and another servant were standing outside
the door, and seeing me, the tweeny said, "Please
mum. I didn't do it. I swear on my mother's grave, I
didn't do it."

I opened the door and instinctively my eyes moved
to the portrait that dominated the room.

Someone had taken something black and scribbled
all over the painting. The face, the neck, the lovely

lilac dress, all were marred by ugly black marks.

A shrill voice pierced my ears. "Becky did it, I tell you. I saw her and if you go to her room, you'll find a black crayon!"

I went back to the hall. Vanessa and her father were facing each other like twin demons and I have never been so terrified in my life.

The tweeny had buried her face in the older servant's apron and her thin shoulders shook with massive sobs.

"Let us go to the study," I said calmly, focusing my attention on Sir Evan, whom I hardly recognized. His eyes had turned as black as the marks on the portrait and his heightened colour made me fear he might have a stroke.

He took a deep breath and said, "Yes, we'll go to the study."

Holding his daughter's arm in what must have been a painful grip, he practically dragged her down the corridor. I exchanged glances with the adult servant and mutely shook my head, signaling to her that they should not follow.

By the time we had entered the study and closed the door, both father and daughter appeared to have calmed down, but I sensed that Sir Evan's anger, though for the moment contained, still smoldered like a brush fire under the surface.

"I shall be taking Vanessa back to Thornton Wood with me," he said, and in spite of her vicious attack on Becky, I felt sorry for the girl.

She's sick, I thought, and no amount of punishment is going to make her well.

"Could we speak alone?" I asked her father.

"That won't be necessary, Miss St. Claire. I'll handle this myself."

His voice was completely cold and I knew there was no way that I could reach him.

"I would appreciate it," he added, "if you would have a servant take the portrait down and wrap a cloth around it. I'll be taking it with me." Then turning to his daughter, he said, "You'd better pray that it can be repaired, Vanessa."

Several days later, I received a note from Sir Evan. He apologized for losing his temper in my presence. The portrait was in London, being repaired, he said, and Vanessa had admitted that she, and not Becky, had damaged it.

He thought it best to keep Vanessa at Thornton Manor for the time being and he said I was to consider myself on a sabbatical for the next few weeks.

Vanessa would be ready to resume her studies by the first of the month, he assured me, and we would work out a schedule whereby I would come to Thornton Manor to tutor her until the manor house was repaired and I could move back in.

I was delighted to remain at Amberwood; nevertheless, I thought it strange. Surely, there was room in the undamaged wing for another person.

I used my free time to prepare more lesson plans and when I realized I had scheduled myself as far ahead as Christmas, I put away my books and gave myself a holiday for the next two weeks.

Nanny Grey, dear soul that she was, encouraged me to get out of the house, and she even came up with a unique mode of transportation for me to use.

"Do you ride a bicycle, dear?" she asked one morning over breakfast.

"No. Unfortunately, my mother didn't approve of young ladies riding them. Not that it would have mattered. We couldn't have afforded one anyway."

"I used to feel that way, but I've changed my mind," she said. "Why should young gentlemen have all the fun?" She peered at me over her glasses and her eyes twinkled with mischief. "There's a bicycle in the barn. It belonged to one of the grooms, but he ran off and left it there. If you could learn to ride it, it would be a wonderful way to see the countryside."

And I might get to meet some of the tenants, I thought. Then I could find out something about the shepherd.

"That's a wonderful idea," I said. "I suppose one would have to learn balance, but I could practice."

"Of course, and a smart young woman like yourself'll catch on in no time a'tall," she said.

I lacked Nanny's confidence, as several days later I applied Dr. McAllister's salve to an ever-increasing series of scrapes and scratches.

"It's your long dress," Nanny said, and I hiked it up as far as decency would allow.

It still got in the way and this old-fashioned little woman who still wore a lace cap on her silver hair said, "Don't they have something for cycling called knockerbickers?"

"Knickerbockers," I said, "but I don't have any."

"I shouldn't think they'd be hard to make from an old skirt, and there's a sewing machine upstairs."

I spent the afternoon in the sewing room using a sewing machine for the very first time, but I fashioned myself a pair of knickerbockers and I learned to ride the bicycle.

I must have presented an incongruous picture to Amberwood's tenants as I pedaled along their country lanes in my outlandish getup. They thought me odd, I'm sure, but then I was a governess and when too much book learning got stuffed inside a young woman's head, it addled her brains.

That had been the viewpoint of our villagers back in Sussex, so I was surprised when my cycling about the Northumberland countryside in makeshift knickerbockers earned me little more than an occasional raised eyebrow.

Never once in my excursions, though, did I come across the shepherd and if the truth were known, I was enjoying myself too much to bother about him.

One beautiful morning when April had given way to May I decided to leave my bicycle home and explore the woods.

I had Mrs. Bodine pack me a picnic lunch, and, feeling like an adventurous lad in my cycling clothes, I set out to fulfill a wish from my childhood.

Feasting my eyes on nature's untouched garden, I felt myself in Paradise. With no human to prune and control them, bushes, vines, trees and other plants grew in abundance, and with haphazard grace, they spilled over one another in a lush display of wild, natural beauty.

A gentle, meandering stream ran through the center and to keep from getting lost, I decided to follow it. Amberwood and Thornton Manor stood at opposite ends of the woods and Mrs. Cathcart had said the distance between them could be covered in a hour's walk. Not that I planned on doing any visiting, but Thornton Manor was a goal to reach for.

I ate my lunch by a particularly beautiful spot. The stream had widened at this point and the land had sharply risen to form a grassy bank that overlooked it.

Spreading Mrs. Bodine's fine linen tablecloth under a shady tree, I laid out my lunch of crusty bread, cheese, and fruit and looked out over the stream. Feeling like I was looking at the world through a veil where all imperfections are concealed, I rubbed my eyes. The woods had taken on the enchantment of *A Midsummer Night's Dream* and I almost expected playful Puck to be hiding behind the tree.

What are you doing here?

The childish voice took me by surprise, but before I could speak, another voice answered.

Taking a walk.

This is my woods, and you need my permission to walk through it.

Amused, I stood up and looked around, but the children were nowhere to be seen.

I'll let you through though, 'cause you're only a girl.

Is that so? Well, I can do anything boys can do.

Where are the little devils? I thought.

Can you climb over that ridge?

Why should I?

Because there's a house deep in the woods on the other side. There's no trail, but I know how to find it.

Show me.

Shielding my eyes, I looked up, thinking they might be hiding in the tree, but I didn't see anybody.

"Hello," I called, but no one answered.

They must have run off, I thought, a little disappointed. They'd sounded young and I enjoyed the company of children.

I finished my lunch, but continued to sit under the tree, for I felt nauseous. A second later, a terrible pain exploded in my head. It was just like the headache I'd gotten when I had arrived in Thornton Wood with Dr. McAllister and I knew I would have to break down and ask that officious man to give me a supply of his medication to keep on hand.

It was three o'clock before I felt well enough to move on and by that time it was too late to do anything but turn back the way I had come. But I shall come again, I promised myself. If there really is a house in the woods, I want to see it, too.

Colin, one of Amberwood's grooms, drove me into town. The village was small and quaint with a smattering of shops close to the square.

"Doctor's office is over there," Colin said, pointing to a rather ramshackle-looking old house next door to a livery stable.

"I shan't be long," I told him, as he handed me down from the open carriage.

He smiled. "I'll call for ye lass in a couple of hours."

"A couple of hours!" I repeated.

"Aye, the doc's a busy mon."

Entering the office, I found myself in a crowded waiting room. A glance out the window at the empty carriage told me that the groom was already on his way to the village pub, so I sat down to wait.

"Don't put your sticky fingers on the lady's gown," a woman admonished her toddler.

"He's fine," I said as the little fellow drew back in alarm.

"Dr. McAllister gave him a stick of licorice," she said. "It's his brother the doc's tending to now. Stepped on a nail playing in the barn. My husband said to leave him be, but I hauled him up here to see the doctor."

"That was very wise," I said.

"Aye, lost one of me brothers after he stepped on a nail and he was a growed man. Foamed at the mouth, just like a dog," she added.

"Should'a rubbed his foot with horse manure."

We jerked our heads around in unison to the old man who sat behind us.

The harried-looking woman sitting next to him gave us an embarrassed look. "Hush up, Pa."

"Kills the 'fection," he retorted.

"Pay him no mind," she said, tapping her finger on her head by way of explanation.

The door to the examining room opened and a boy of about twelve hopped back into the waiting room. "The doc wants to see you, Ma," he said. She got up and went inside the office and he broke off a piece of licorice and handed it to his little brother. "Here, I'll share with ye."

The mother came back and the woman's thin face wore a bright smile. "The doc says Willie's goin to be all right and I can pay for the medicine with eggs."

She left with her sons and the woman behind us said, "Ye're next, Pa."

"Ain't tykin me clothes off."

She got him up, pointed him toward the door, and he shuffled into the office.

"He's a cross to bear," she told me, "but he's my pa

and Dr. McAllister's medicine's helped his rheumatism so much. Ye wouldn't believe how much better he is."

I looked around the office. These people looked on Philip McAllister as a saint and at Thornton Manor he was considered a devil. Which one was he?

I looked at my watch and sighed. The groom had been right. I wouldn't get out of here for another hour. I hoped the horse knew his way home because after two hours in a pub, I imagined Colin going around in circles.

The cantankerous old man with rheumatism came out and when the next patient failed to appear, Dr. McAllister stepped out of his office and stood in the waiting room.

"Next patient," he said, and an old woman who had been dozing in a chair shuffled to her feet.

A look of surprise crossed his face when he spotted me and then he smiled. He looked very professional and quite handsome in his white doctor's coat, but I wasn't here to see Philip McAllister and if he thought so, he was a damn fool.

There I go, I thought, using language that would have horrified my mother, but the man's arrogance made me bristle.

"I've come for headache medicine," I said when the waiting room had emptied out and I, the last patient, stood in the doctor's office.

"And how often have you gotten these headaches?" he asked.

"Just once, but it was an excruciating headache like the one I had when you were with me. The tea worked so well, I would like to have a supply to keep on hand."

"This isn't a store and I'm not in the business of selling tea. Now sit down and open your blouse," he said, putting his stethoscope into his ears and coming out from behind his desk.

I reluctantly complied, feeling more uncomfortable than I have ever felt in my whole life. There was something intimate and erotic about the situation and although his attitude was cooly professional, I felt disturbed.

His raw masculinity aroused feelings in me that I found shocking. Was I no better than Gracie?

"Your heart's fine," he said, putting down his stethoscope and returning to his desk.

I buttoned my blouse. "Of course. Now, if you will just give me the medicine, I'll be happy to pay your fee, doctor."

"I'm going to give you the medication," he said. "But, only enough for one dose. If you get another severe headache, I want you to come back."

Drat the man, I thought, watching him measure a small quantity out of one of the apothecary jars on his desk.

"Thank you," I said, putting the envelope in my purse. "Now, what do I owe you, doctor?"

He smiled. "No charge, but you could do me a favor."

"What is it?"

"Attend May Day with me. Remember, I told you the fair was Thorton Wood's only claim to fame."

He looked very appealing, and recalling that he had rescued me from the broken-down coach, rescued me from the fire, and even rescued me after I'd been lost in the maze, I could hardly refuse.

"Thank you, Dr. McAllister. I'll be happy to go."

"Wonderful," he said. "I'll pick you up at Amber-wood Saturday morning at nine o'clock."

I left the office in a very disturbed mood. Had I consented to go to the fair out of gratitude? Or was it because almost against my will, I was finding myself attracted to Philip McAllister?

Once outside, I looked up and down the street, but Colin was nowhere to be seen. Wonderful, I thought. I can hardly go to the pub and drag him out.

"Good afternoon, Miss St. Claire." The young girl smiled and said, "Remember me, mum? I'm Maggie, upstairs maid at Thornton Manor. I brung you water the day you arrived."

Ah, yes, the talkative one, I thought.

"It's nice to see you, Maggie," I said. "How is everything at Thornton Manor?"

"Not so good, mum. Miss Vanessa's in disgrace, locked in her room, she is, and Lady Thornton's nerves are so bad, cook says Miss Hamilton's afraid her ladyship's going into decline."

"Dear me," I said. "Have they called the doctor?"

"Oh, Sir Evan wouldn't call Dr. McAllister, mum."

"The villagers seem to think highly of him," I said.

"I know, mum, but strange things have been goin on." She looked around and lowered her voice. "Sir Evan's last wife was. . . . Well, she saw Dr. McAllister a lot. Some say they were more than doctor and patient, if you know what I mean. Then she started bothering him all the time. Some say he got tired of her and right after that she took sick and died."

Gossips can't exist without an audience, my mother used to say. "I don't put much stock in rumors, Maggie."

"All the same, there was Lutie Winslow, the barmaid at the pub. Lutie was sweet on Dr. McAllister, too, they say and she just up and disappeared one night. Ain't never been seen since."

Good Lord, what else? I thought.

Giving my long skirt a quick glance, she said, "Did you come to town on your bicycle, mum?"

No secrets from Maggie, I thought. "No, Colin, one of the grooms, drove me, but I'm afraid he's still in the pub and I don't know how I'll ever get him out."

"Stay here," she said, and marching herself up to the pub's door, she stuck her head inside and in a voice that threatened to shatter every glass in the saloon, she yelled, "Put that mug'a ale down ya bloody fool and get on home. It's supper time!"

In a matter of seconds, the pub was emptied and the startled expressions on the men's faces bore witness to the fact that each one thought his own irate woman had summoned him.

They scattered in all directions like leaves in a windstorm and Colin was left facing Maggie with a sheepish grin on his face. "Ye didn't have to do that, Maggie. I was on me way out."

She gave him a exasperated look. "I know you like a book, Colin James." Then she turned to me. "Colin and me will be getting married one of these days, Miss St. Claire. That is if the big oaf can stay out of the pub."

"Ah Maggie, I ain't been in there for a month," he said.

Maggie was on an errand for the seamstress, she told us, and Colin asked me if we could wait and give her a lift home. She wasn't gone long and the three of us left in the carriage for the open road.

The House in Thornton Wood

We dropped Maggie off at the manor's private road and after waving goodbye, I said to Colin, "I understand Dr. McAllister isn't received at Thornton Manor. How do people feel about him at Amberwood?"

I counted on the drink loosening his tongue, but he would only say, "He don't gouge the poor. That much I know. Never had a doctor at Thornton Wood before. Folk had to go all the way into Thirsk. Maybe the Thorntons don't like it cause he's one of us."

I couldn't dismiss Maggie's words so casually, though. *Where there is smoke, there is fire*, my mother used to say. And, how could I forget the Gypsy's warning? Was Philip MacAllister the Prince of Darkness?

Chapter Nine

Several times that week, I tried to compose a note to Dr. McAllister.

Dear Dr. McAllister,

I regret that I will be unable to accompany you to the Fair on Saturday. . . .

I never got any farther than the first sentence. What could I say? He'd be sure to see through any excuse I might offer and then his enormous ego would convince him that I, poor little spinster that I am, was just too timid to expose myself to his masculine charm.

Maybe it will rain and the fair will be cancelled, I thought, but Saturday morning dawned bright and beautiful.

I hadn't mentioned the outing to Nanny Grey. Since I wasn't certain I would go, it had seemed pointless, but now we faced each other over the breakfast table and I was forced to speak.

"I saw Dr. McAllister in the village. He said there's to be a fair in Thornton Wood today."

She sipped her tea and smiled. "I'm sorry, dear. I'm a little old for fairs—so much noise, and too much walking for me, but perhaps Mrs. Cathcart would go with you. Why don't you ask her? Colin can take her a note."

"Dr. McAllister offered to show me around the fair," I said.

She lowered her eyes and thoughtfully stirred her tea. "Be careful, dear. Philip McAllister wasn't raised as a gentleman, you know. His family were crofters and after he began treating Sir Evan's wife there was some talk. I don't know how much truth there was to it, but she *was* seen meeting the doctor in the woods."

Seemingly uncomfortable with gossip, she quickly added, "Lord Fenwick always admired the young man for his ambition, though. Philip literally pulled himself up by his bootstraps." Then, pursing her lips and continuing to stir her tea, she said in words my mother might have used, "Still and all, breeding shows, and we cannot hold a man to standards that he has not been raised to observe."

I was reminded of Philip's words to me in the coach. *You probably believe class distinctions are sacrosanct.*

And who is more conscious of them, I thought, than those of us who serve the ruling class?

I made no comment, though, and Nanny dropped the subject, satisfied, I'm sure, that she had done her duty by reminding me that Philip McAllister might be a physician, but in the small town of Thornton Wood he would remain first and foremost a crofter's son.

I was wearing a new pink muslin afternoon dress and Nanny complimented me on it. Miss O'Shay had finished my gowns and they had arrived several days before, carefully packed in long boxes lined with tissue paper. I had mixed feelings about them. Never before had I owned such a lavish wardrobe, but I couldn't help associating the gowns with Vanessa's violent vandalism.

I hadn't told Sir Evan, but I was certain it was Vanessa who had been standing in the hall watching me as the gowns had been fitted. But why take out her frustration on the portrait of a dead woman?

We finished breakfast, and shortly thereafter, Philip arrived, looking very dashing in a light blue suit and what looked like a brand new straw hat. The Prince of Wales had made them fashionable and now every man in England was wearing them.

He removed it in my presence and said, "Why Miss St. Claire, you look positively ravishing in pink. You'll be the prettiest girl at the fair and I'll be the envy of every man there."

"Don't talk nonsense," I said. "At my age, I'm hardly considered a girl."

We left the house and as he helped me up into his open carriage, he pursued the subject. "Haven't reached thirty yet, have you?"

"Certainly not!"

"Twenty-nine?" he offered, getting in himself and sitting beside me.

"It's rude to fish for a lady's age," I said, "but I'll tell you anyway. I'm twenty-two."

He smiled and reached for the reins. "That's not old. I'm thirty-two."

"But you're a man. Society looks on women in a different light."

"Society," he said with a mocking laugh. "You pay too much attention to what society says. All those rules and regulations: They restrict your mind like that corset you wear restricts your body. Haven't you ever wanted to be free to follow your own instincts?"

"Life is more orderly when there are limits to individual freedom," I said. It sounded pompous and I felt a need to justify myself. "However, I'll have you know, Dr. McAllister, that I am not a slave to convention. What I disagree with, I disregard."

His eye was on the road, but his mouth curved into a smile. "Yes, I heard you had taken to riding a bicycle and wearing trousers."

I wondered how he knew about it, but I wouldn't give him the satisfaction of asking. "You sound like you disapprove."

"Not at all. I think it's healthy and since you're flouting convention these days, Miss St. Claire, couldn't we drop the formalities and call each other Philip and Olivia?"

"Of course."

"Good. I hate formality," he said.

As we entered the village, I felt my excitement grow. There was something magical and a little decadent about fairs, with their circuslike atmosphere, exotic performers, and lively music.

We left the carriage in the livery stable and walked to the village square.

It was everything I had remembered and more; the

119

crowds, the noise, the music and the barkers. A strolling fiddler was serenading an embarrassed young couple who gazed at each other with stars in their eyes. "Love, sweet, sweet love," he sang and they laughed and blushed.

Vendors shouted and held up their wares. A woman selling flowers spotted Philip and said, "Buy your lady a flower for her hair."

Philip stopped and, pointing to a beautiful china-pink rose, said, "I'll take that one. It matches your dress," he told me and then abruptly added, "Take your hat off. I'll pin it in your hair."

Feeling a little foolish, I removed my hat and he very carefully arranged the flower in my hair.

The woman smiled and winked her eye at him. "Your sweetheart is even prettier now, gov'ner."

I stuck a hairpin in the flower and pretended not to hear.

"Let's watch the jugglers," I said. "And oh, look, Philip! There's a fire-eater, and over there—isn't that a carousel?"

He laughed. "We'll see everything, I promise you."

"Good. I've only been to one fair and we had to leave before I got a chance to see anything."

"Why was that?"

"My mother was afraid of Gypsies," I explained. "A small band of them were at the fair and as soon as Mama laid eyes on that caravan, she took me home. She was very protective," I added. "I guess she was afraid they might steal me."

"Are you afraid of Gypsies, too?" he asked. "Because there's a blue caravan parked over there on the hill."

I shook my head emphatically. "No. Mr. Glace and

I stayed at a Gypsy campsite the first time the coach broke down. They were very kind and if they are the same ones, I'd like to thank them."

We watched the jugglers and the fire-eater, who made me nervous, but Philip said the man only pretended to swallow the flames. We ate meat pies and lemon sticks and rode the carousel twice.

"Are you dizzy?" he asked when the ride was over.

"Not really, but I'd like to walk up the hill and talk to the Gypsies, if you don't mind. I'm sure that's Rashev's caravan."

"Fine, but I won't have my fortune told."

"Why? Are you afraid to know the future?"

"I make my own future," he said in his gruff, matter-of-fact way. "That's all poppycock."

I didn't tell him I had had my fortune told and it had been a very disturbing experience.

Rashev was standing outside and when he saw me, he ran around to the back of the wagon. By the time we had reached the top of the hill, Sonia was waiting for us.

Philip snickered. "Now she'll tell you 'the spirits' told her you were coming."

Scanning my face with anxious eyes, Sonia said, "The spirits are uneasy. You must let me read your palm."

Philip gave me a knowing smile and said, "I'll sit under that tree and wait for you."

I followed Sonia to the back of the caravan where a small tent had been set up.

"You left before we had a chance to thank you for your hospitality," I said. "I would like to pay your son for fixing the wheel."

"No pay," she said emphatically, opening the tent's flap and beckoning to me. I hesitated a moment and then entered.

It was dark inside, but she lit a candle and then I could see that there was a table and on it rested a large crystal ball.

"Sit down," she said. "I will read your palm first, and then I will consult the crystal."

The candle flickered, casting shadows over the tent, and an eerie feeling washed over me. Her face took on that fanatical glow again as she reached for my hand.

Rubbing her fingers over my birthmark, she said, "Powerful forces are at work. I have had many dreams about you, but I do not understand their meaning." Her eyes grew glassy and she said, "I keep seeing a large copper vat."

I gasped. "I see that, too, in my own dreams. What does it mean?"

"I don't know, but evil is connected with it. You must be very careful where you put your trust."

Turning my palm over, she said, "You have a double lifeline, you know. One is very faint, and very short."

"What does that mean?"

She shrugged. "I'm not sure. Perhaps you are two people. Some of us are, you know."

Was I? At times I had thought there was another person inside of me, a wild, unconventional person who was at war with my other self.

Suddenly dropping my hand, the Gypsy said, "Let me consult the crystal now." She stared intently into the shimmering ball for several seconds and then her eyes widened. "I see a young person. She is unhappy and very disturbed. I see two men. One dark, one light."

The young person is Vanessa, I thought, and the light man would have to be Sir Evan, but is the dark one the shepherd or Philip?

"The dark man," I said. "Is he the man who is waiting outside?"

"I cannot see their faces clearly, but I think so," she answered.

"There is another man," I said. "I keep seeing him, but then he disappears. He's darker than the man outside and he wears the clothes of a shepherd."

A horrified expression crossed the Gypsy's face and her knuckles turned white as she gripped the edge of the table. "You see a shepherd?" she gasped.

"Yes. I think he's following me."

She was slipping into a trance and I tried to pull her back. "Please," I cried in a shrill voice. "Tell me where I can find this shepherd."

But it was too late. Sonia's eyes had taken on a faraway look, her body had stiffened and in a flat, unnatural voice, she chanted, "Tongues of fire, light the pyre. The tide will turn and the devil will burn."

An eerie chill permeated the air and I felt an unseen presence enter the tent. Time stood still and my own body stiffened, not so much in fear, though I suppose I was afraid, but more in wonder because instinctively I knew that something out of the ordinary had taken place here.

A second or so later, the temperature in the tent returned to normal. Sonia went limp and her eyes, no longer glassy, looked into mine. "You felt the presence?" I nodded, and she said, "You are in great danger. I can help you, but we must keep in touch."

123

I said, "But how?"

"Go to the woods. I will meet you there."

"But, how will I know where to find you and how will I know when you'll be there?"

"You will know."

She stood up and held the flap open for me. "Your young man is waiting," she said. "Tell him nothing, and be very, very careful."

Philip took my arm as we walked down the hill. "Did she tell you you would meet a prince?"

I looked at him sharply, but his face betrayed no guile.

"Well, isn't that what they always tell young women, that they're going to travel and meet a fairy-tale prince?"

I forced myself to smile. "I suppose so."

"You seem subdued," he said. "Did she upset you? What did she say?"

I had to tell him something. "She said I have a double lifeline and that one line is very short and faint."

He gave me a skeptical look. "And what is that supposed to mean?"

"She wasn't sure. Perhaps I am two people."

We had reached the bottom of the hill and he stopped and faced me with a wicked grin. "I could have told you that. Miss St. Claire is a prim little spinster who follows all society's silly rules, but then there's Olivia," he added softly and before I could stop him, he had reached over and pulled several hairpins out of my hair.

I should have stopped him immediately, but he held me captive with eyes that seemed to caress my face.

"You have beautiful hair, Olivia. Please, wear it down like the country girls . . . just for today."

I should have rolled it right back up into a proper knot, but I didn't. "It's May Day," I heard myself say. "I suppose we can both pretend to be peasants."

He laughed and grabbed my hand. "I've never stopped being a *peasant*, as you well know, but if you're game, I'll show you how we *peasants* enjoy a fair."

Looking back, I don't think I have ever had so much fun. An outdoor cafe had been set up near the bandstand with an open space in the center for dancing. We ate fish and drank cider and I think Philip was surprised when I emptied the glass.

"You're not going to get tipsy, are you?"

"Certainly not. I've had cider before."

He smiled and shook his head. "Not Northumberland cider, though."

I did laugh a lot and once or twice when I was watching the dancers weave in and out of their squares, I felt a little strange, but the feeling quickly passed and when Philip asked me to dance, I gave him my hand.

I didn't expect it to be a waltz, though, and when he held out his arms, I hesitated a moment.

"What's the matter, Miss St. Claire? Do you find the waltz a little too wicked?"

"Certainly not," I said, although I knew some clergymen objected to the dance. I had only waltzed once and that had been at a wedding reception Mama and I had attended in Sussex. The tempo had been rather slow, which was fortunate, because my partner had been a rather elderly man.

This was a Viennese waltz, though, *Tales from the Vienna Woods*, and there was nothing slow about either the tempo or my partner. I was whisked practically off my feet as we twirled around and around in a circle. He was a marvelous dancer, I must admit, and even though I didn't know what I was doing, he led me so well and held me so tightly that I could hardly make a mistake.

When the dance was over, I was embarrassed to see that we were the only couple left on the floor. Those who had been watching applauded and there were some good-natured shouts. "Fine steppin, Doc," and "Best couple on the floor."

"Please, let's leave. I'm dying of embarrassment," I said.

He laughed. "Oh Lord. The proper Miss St. Claire is back." Then, reaching for my hand, he whispered, "Let's run off and leave her here. The potato race is about to start and I want to enter it."

I stood on the sidelines and laughed till my sides ached at the sight of Philip hopping around in a potato sack. He finished next-to-last and blamed it all on the undersized sack he'd been given.

"That thing would only hold about five potatoes. Everybody else had a bigger sack."

"Everybody else was shorter than you, Philip. That's why their sacks looked longer. Yours only came up to your knees." And I started laughing all over again at the hilarious picture he had made.

"Next time I bring my own sack," he said.

It was dusk and the fair was closing when we

wended our way back to the livery stable.

He said, "It's been a wonderful day, Olivia. There won't be another fair for a year, but we could go for a buggy ride one day. Thornton Wood is a beautiful village and I'd like to show you more of it."

"I will be going back to Thornton Manor soon, and I don't know exactly what my duties will entail."

"Surely, you'll have a day off now and then," he said.

Why was I afraid to commit myself? I had enjoyed the day and also his company.

"Thank you, Philip. Yes, I would love to see more of Thornton Wood."

He tucked my arm in his and said smugly. "Good. I knew Olivia would win."

We had arrived at the livery stable and I waited while he settled up with the groom.

When we were in the buggy and on our way out of town, I said, "Whatever did you mean when you said you knew Olivia would win?"

He flicked the reins and gave me that wicked grin again. "Didn't the Gypsy say you were two people?"

I should never have told him, I thought. "Not really. She said she didn't know why I had a double lifeline."

He shrugged. "Well, I believe it, and I like Olivia much better than Miss St. Claire. I think you do, too, but you're afraid to admit it," he said.

I changed the subject. "May I ask you a personal question, Philip?"

"Certainly."

"How did you happen to go to medical school?"

"You mean, how could I afford to go to medical school."

"I didn't say that."

"No, but I'll tell you anyway." He leaned back and let the horse have his head. "My father died because there was no doctor in Thornton Wood. The Thorntons didn't want a doctor here. Don't ask me why. I suppose devils don't require the services of a doctor."

His sensuous mouth stiffened and bitter lines that time had erased suddenly reappeared. "My father was gored by a bull. He bled to death before Evan Thornton thought it necessary to summon the doctor from Thirsk."

"I'm sorry, Philip, but surely it was unintentional on Sir Evan's part."

He gave me a sick smile. "I beg your pardon, Miss St. Claire. I know you find it hard to believe, but some masters consider a tenant farmer an expendable commodity. Anyway," he continued, "that answers the *why*. The *how* I owe to your host."

"My host?"

"You're staying at Amberwood. Isn't Lord Fenwick your host?"

"I suppose so, although I've never met the man, but you mean to say that it was Lord Fenwick who sponsored you?"

"Exactly, and I guess you'll be surprised to hear that I'm grateful to him. Oil and water don't mix, and I haven't much use for aristocrats as a whole, but Lord Fenwick is an exception."

We mounted the winding drive into Amberwood. A carriage stood in front of the entrance and we stopped behind it. "I believe that's Sir Evan's carriage," I said.

"You're right, and now I suppose you will turn back into Miss St. Claire, so if you don't mind, I would like to say good-bye to Olivia."

Before I knew what was happening, he had reached over and pressed his lips to mine. I had never been kissed by a man before and I was not prepared for the feelings it aroused in me. The sensation was pleasant and I did not pull away. He must have taken my compliance for something more, for he increased the pressure on my lips and my whole body began to tingle and I felt like sparks were exploding between us.

This time I did pull away and, giving him an outraged look, I said, "I'll have you know, Dr. McAllister, I am not Gracie."

He looked puzzled and I supposed he had already forgotten the foolish barmaid's name.

In that same instant, the door to Amberwood burst open and Sir Evan and the butler appeared. Sir Evan's eyes were grey smoldering embers and I wondered if he could have seen us through the window.

He walked swiftly up to the buggy and held out his hand to me. "I was just leaving," he said. "But now that you're back, Miss St. Claire, we can go inside."

Looking up at Philip, he added, "Don't bother getting down, McAllister. I'll assist Miss St. Claire."

Chapter Ten

I followed Sir Evan into the study. My lips still burned from Philip's kiss and I was mortified to think that Sir Evan might have seen us.

Eyeing me critically, he said, "Sit down, Miss St. Claire."

Now he's going to dismiss me, I thought, feeling like an errant child about to be expelled from school.

I took a seat, but he stood, facing me. He was staring at my hair and I suddenly remembered that it was loose and hanging down my back. Nervously, I began to twist it up into a knot, but he held up his hand and studied me for a moment.

"You look different with your hair down, rather like a beautiful senorita. Have you any Spanish blood, Miss St. Claire?"

I said, "No, just English and French."

"French, of course. I knew there was something Latin about you."

He seemed more friendly and I thought perhaps he hadn't seen the kiss, but then he leveled those smoldering grey eyes at me and said, "I was distressed when Nanny Grey told me you'd gone out with McAllister. I thought I had warned you about him."

I said, "I went to him for some headache medicine, and he asked me to go to the fair with him. After all, he had rescued me from the fire. I didn't see any harm in it."

His eyes widened. "Did you take the medication he prescribed?"

"No, I just wanted to have it in reserve."

Sir Evan closed the door and, taking a chair behind the massive desk in front of me, he continued in a voice that was low and confidential. "Dr. McAllister's medicine is derived from plants and herbs that grow here in the woods and farther north, in the highlands of Scotland. Some of these plants cause hallucinations. Do you know what that means, Miss St. Claire?"

I said, "I've read about primitive people using such things in religious ceremonies and such."

"Then I must tell you that unbeknownst to me, my late wife, Lady Diana Thornton, became a patient of this so-called *doctor*. Shortly after he began prescribing medication for her, Lady Thornton began hallucinating and, several months later, my wife was dead!"

I said, "But surely this was investigated and if it had been shown that she died of poison. . . ."

He said, "My wife did not die of poison, Miss St. Claire. Lady Thornton lost her mind and killed herself!"

His words hung in the air between us and I finally

131

recovered enough to say, "Oh, Sir Evan, I'm so sorry."

He said, "Her suicide has been kept a secret and I must ask that you let it remain so."

"You have my word, but Sir Evan, you have no proof that Philip McAllister was the cause of this."

His eyes took on the intensity of a zealot and he said, "Exactly. And that is why I cannot accuse him, but heed the warning, Miss St. Claire, and bear in mind that two young women from the village have been missing and they were also patients of Dr. McAllister."

While I was mentally digesting these three shocking disclosures, his mood suddenly changed. No longer somber, he gave me a debonair smile. "Now, I shall tell you why I came to see you."

Still recovering from the effects of what I had just been told, I marvelled at the way he and Vanessa could switch moods and become entirely different people in the blink of an eye.

"I hope you have come to tell me that Vanessa is better," I said, but he dismissed his daughter with a wave of his hand.

"This is not about Vanessa. I came to tell you that Lord Fenwick is coming home and I will be giving a grand ball in his honour."

"Shall I be returning to Thornton Manor, then?"

He seemed impatient with the question. "No, that has nothing to do with this. Lord Fenwick is a gracious man. He will welcome your presence at Amberwood, but I shall require your assistance with preparations for the ball."

"But I know nothing about giving balls."

"You are schooled in proper English, are you not?"

"Yes."

"And you have a fine hand for penmanship."

"I believe so."

"Then you shall help me make the arrangements. These things take time and much preparation, Miss St. Claire. The ball shall not be given until the autumn. All of London retreats to the country for the summer, anyway." His eyes glittered with anticipation. "It's been a long time since Thornton Manor has done any proper entertaining."

"But what about Vanessa's lessons?" I insisted. "Sir Evan, I accepted this position expecting to be a governess."

Speaking with the patience of one explaining things to a child, he said, "And you shall be Vanessa's governess, Miss St. Claire. Vanessa is not an ordinary pupil, as I'm sure you are aware. A child with her nervous temperament cannot be subjected to the normal schedule of lessons." He paused a moment and frowned. "What is it? Twenty, twenty-four hours of study a week?" I nodded and he continued. "And so we must improvise and gradually acclimate Vanessa to longer and longer sessions."

"I find no fault with that."

"Good. Then we can begin by having you come to Thornton Manor two or three days a week. You can spend an hour or so with Vanessa and the rest of the time, you can work with me on preparations for the ball."

I felt like I was being pressured into assuming a position that I was not qualified for, but he gave me an imploring look and said, "I realize this is asking a lot of you, Miss St. Claire, but I would be most grateful for your assistance. My mother is not well. I can't expect any help from her and I want to honor my father-in-law by giving this ball. I need a gracious lady to stand beside me and act as hostess. I would like that lady to be you, Olivia. Won't you help me?"

Again, what could I say? The man had been more than generous. I was being treated like one of the family and the prospect of actually attending the ball and acting as Sir Evan's hostess was beyond any of my wildest dreams.

"I would be honoured, Sir Evan," I said.

That night I lay in bed, going over the events of a day that had combined many contrasting experiences. I didn't think I should ever forget the fun I'd had at the fair with Philip, or the strange incident in the tent when Sonia was telling my fortune. Who was the shepherd, I wondered, and why did Sonia act so strange when I mentioned him?

Philip's parting kiss had left me weak and aroused emotions in me that I never dreamed I possessed. Was I, in fact, two people?

And then Sir Evan's strange story had filled me with doubts that gnawed at my very soul. Was Philip the Prince of Darkness I had been warned about? Or had Sir Evan read more into his wife's illness than the facts allowed?

Philip, on the other hand, had mentioned disturbing things about Sir Evan. Why would Sir Evan object to having a doctor in Thornton Wood? I wondered, and if he had, indeed, delayed sending to Thirsk for a physician, I could understand why Philip would hold Sir Evan accountable for his father's death.

And finally, the day had brought the unlikely request that I should stand beside Sir Evan and assume the role of his hostess at a grand ball. What did it mean? Remembering the way he had looked at me in the study and conscious of the fact that he had referred to me as *beautiful*, I shuddered to think. Could both Philip McAllister and Sir Evan Thornton be capable of offering me indecent proposals?

Several days later my intuition told me that Sonia wanted me to come to the woods. The feeling was so strong that it frightened me. Was it possible that the Gypsy could communicate with me through my mind? Evidently Sonia thought so, for she had told me that I would *know* when she needed to see me.

I recalled the first time I had met the Gypsy woman. She had told me then that I had the gift of sight. Had she recognized that I had powers that were latent, but similar to her own? And wasn't it strange, I thought, that both of us saw the same copper vat in our dreams?

I had no idea where she wanted us to meet, but I remembered the two children saying that there was an abandoned house on the other side of the forest. I had better dress for climbing, I decided, so I put on my cycling clothes.

On my way out the front door, I noticed a stout walking stick protruding from the umbrella stand and I took it along with me.

It was a beautiful sunny day, but as I entered the woods, its tall trees blocked out the sun, letting in only enough light to bathe the forest in sepia tones. It added an eerie, almost mystical quality to the woods, and again, I felt like I was stepping into a dreamworld.

I looked for the place where I had stopped to eat

my lunch and where I had heard the children, but I couldn't find it.

Following what I thought to be the same trail, I came upon a similar spot, but the tree on its bank was much taller than the one I had sat under a week ago. At any rate, I reminded myself, according to the children, the house was on the other side of the hill.

I started the climb and more than once I mentally thanked Lord Fenwick for the use of his walking stick and myself for having the good sense to wear my cycling clothes. Imagine trying to negotiate this steep hill in a corset and long dress!

I managed to reach the top without falling, though, and it was with a sense of accomplishment that I looked down on the stream and the path that I had left behind.

This part of the forest was thick and there was no well-worn trail to guide my way, but I felt a strong compulsion to bear to the east, and again I let my intuition be my guide.

Sometime later, I still saw no sign of a house and I was beginning to wonder if I had been going around in circles.

Tired and frustrated, I sat down on the forest's mossy floor to rest and it was then that I heard the children's voices.

There isn't any house up here. You told a lie.

I did not. I'm a king and kings don't lie.

You're not a king.

Well, I will be one when I grow up and if you're not nice to me, I won't let you be my queen.

Their childish banter lightened my spirits, and now I knew I wasn't hopelessly lost after all.

Will your queen wear a crown?

Yes, and it'll be a big crown, too—only not as big as the king's.

What will my crown be made out of?

Gold, with diamonds and pearls.

I want some emeralds on it, too.

Oh, all right, emeralds, too. Now, would you like to see the house? We can pretend it's our castle.

All right.

See that clump of tall bushes down there? Come on, I'll race you.

I struggled to my feet and followed the sound of their laughter. They must have flown, for I saw the clump of bushes, but not a sign of the children.

This must surely be the thickest part of the forest, I thought, and keeping my eyes closed for protection, I struggled through all the tangled vines that had attached themselves to the bushes.

The prickly vines snapped at my face and hands, but I kept ploughing through them and when I opened my eyes, I found that I was in a clearing and in its center, surrounded by a profusion of purple heather, stood a little house.

There was a fairy-tale quality about it and picking my way through the heather, I approached the cottage and rapped on the door. It swing open at my touch. I entered cautiously and called out, "Hello," but there was no answer.

The children are probably hiding, I thought, but where is the Gypsy?

The house smelled musty and cobwebs hung over the few pieces of broken furniture that remained. There was a table, a long bench, and a rocking chair.

My skin prickled as the rocker creaked and slowly began to move in a ghostly rhythm, back and forth, back and forth. I almost turned and ran, but then I noticed that the cobwebs were moving, too, and I realized that it was the wind coming through the open door.

"Please come out, children," I said, closing the door. "I know you're here."

I sat down on the bench and waited. They must have heard the door close and thought I had left.

Promise you won't tell anybody about the house.

I promise. I'll never tell because then they wouldn't let me come up here.

You won't tell about me, either?

No, never.

Because if you do, they'll send me away and then you'll never get to be queen.

I won't tell, honest.

Do you swear before the king?

Yes, your majesty. I swear before the king.

I said, "Please come out and let me see you. I won't tell, either. I promise."

All was silence. I was a little disappointed. They sounded like such charming, imaginative children. I wanted to ask them, too, to lead me back to the lower part of the woods.

I stood up and looked out the window. There was no sign of Sonia, either. So much for my intuition. I called out to the children one more time and when they didn't answer me, I gave up.

I had just stepped outside when someone called my name. It was Sonia. She was standing at the entrance to the clearing and for some reason I got the impression she had been there all along.

I was a little irritated and I said, "You saw me arrive. Why didn't you come in the house?"

She gave me a mysterious smile. "I wanted to give you some time alone. Did you see anything?"

"No, but I heard the children. They were hiding from me. Did you see them leave?"

She shook her head. "There are no children, miss."

"I heard them, I tell you. They were the same children I heard last week down by the stream."

Her dark eyes held a triumphant gleam and she said, "It is time we talk."

"Let's go inside the house then," I said, and she followed me.

"What do you see?" she asked when we were inside the house.

My patience was wearing thin. "I see an old house, full of cobwebs. What do you see?"

She gave me that mysterious smile again. "I just needed to hear your answer."

Suddenly, I felt afraid. What was I doing in this old abandoned house in the middle of a forest?

Rashev could be hiding outside. I could have walked into a trap.

"Do not be afraid," she said. "You are in danger, that is true, but not from my son or me. I am your friend. You must trust me."

I stared at her with shocked eyes. "You read my mind."

"Yes, and you read mine when I told you to come here. You have the sight. I knew it the first time we met. You are a medium and the spirits are using you. I don't know why, though."

I felt a headache coming on and I put my hand up to my forehead. "I don't understand any of this," I said.

Sonia put her arm around me. "Let me help you. I don't understand all of this yet, but I will try. You must confide in me, though."

"I have a terrible headache," I said in a weak voice.

"I know. That is because you have just returned from another time." Then taking off her shawl, she spread it on the floor and said, "Lie down and rest. We'll talk when you feel better."

When I woke up, Sonia was sitting in front of me with her eyes closed. I hoped she hadn't gone into a trance because I needed some answers. What had she meant by saying I had just returned from another time?

I sat up and she immediately opened her eyes. "Feeling better?"

"A little. The pain is just . . ."

"Just a dull ache. I know. I've had them, too."

I brushed the hair out of my eyes and said, "What does it all mean?"

"I wish I knew, miss, but perhaps we can help each other. Tell me, when did you start getting these headaches?"

"The first day I arrived in Thornton Wood. Dr. McAllister and I were hiking to Thornton Manor because the coach had broken down on the road. We crossed an open field. That's when I saw the shepherd. He was tending a flock of sheep. We walked on a little way and suddenly my head felt like it was exploding. Dr.

McAllister gave me some herbal tea and the headache went away."

"Have you been back to that spot since you saw the shepherd and the flock of sheep?"

"We went back a few minutes later, but the shepherd was gone and so were the sheep."

The Gypsy's dark eyes stared intently into mine. "Think carefully, miss. Did everything look the same the second time?"

I said, "No. Everything looked different, but it was the same spot because a thorny bush had snagged a ribbon off my hat and the ribbon was still there."

"And when was the next time you got the headache?"

"Last week in the woods when I heard the children for the first time."

"Where were you?"

"Sitting on a bank by the stream."

"And did you visit that spot again today?"

"I couldn't find it. I thought I had, but it looked . . . different," I finished weakly.

I didn't want to believe what she was trying to tell me. "People can't slip back in time," I said.

She nodded her head very slowly. "Some of us can."

"But why? How?"

"I don't know. For some reason, the spirits have chosen you to be their medium. What you heard today was spoken here, but sometime in the past. I want you to tell me word for word, if possible, what you heard."

I repeated the children's conversation and she said, "From now on, write down everything you see and hear from the past. We'll meet here again and you will tell it to me."

Suddenly grabbing my hand, she ran her fingers over the bright red mark. "This birthmark has branded you with the tongues of fire. You have been exposed to the flames once and you may be exposed to them again. Be very careful. Witches and sorcerers have traditionally been burned to death. Someone wants you out of Thornton Wood. You escaped one fire, miss. You might not escape another."

She followed the warning with that eerie chant, "Tongues of fire, light the pyre. The tide will turn and the devil will burn!"

Chapter Eleven

That evening, wrapped in the warmth and graciousness of Amberwood, a house I now thought of as
home, the Gypsy, the woods, and the enchanted cottage all seemed unreal.

Summer nights were cool in this northernmost tip of
England. There was a fire in the grate and it added to
the cozy feeling the house engendered in me.

Nanny had put down her knitting, and following her
custom was reading a chapter from the Bible. Surely,
I thought, there are no such things as spirits or visions
or voices from the past. Sonia was a Gypsy and Gypsies
thrived on the occult, but I was an educated, modern
woman.

There was a rational explanation for everything, I
had been taught to believe, so Sir Evan's confidential

143

disclosure that his wife had been subject to hallucinations disturbed me greatly.

I had taken Philip's herbal medications twice; once for a headache and the second time to ward off pneumonia, or so I had been told. Could that account for my strange encounters with the children in the woods? Had I, too, been the victim of a hallucination?

Nanny closed the Bible and laid it back on the table. "I'm so glad Sir Evan is allowing you to remain at Amberwood, Olivia. I don't know how I shall bear it when you move back to Thornton Manor."

"Nor I, Nanny dear. You have made me so welcome. I love you and I love Amberwood. I know it sounds foolish, but from the very beginning, I felt like I belonged here."

"Bless you, child. You've brightened a lonely old woman's days. Genevieve and I used to sit together like this after Lady Violette had been tucked into bed." She brushed a frail hand over her eyes. "I miss them both to this very day. Poor Lady Violette, cut off in the prime of life, and Genevieve, just disappearing that very night. I never could understand why she didn't say good-bye to me."

"Perhaps she was too grief-stricken. She and Lady Violette were very close, were they not?"

"Oh yes, Genevieve was like an older sister to Lady Violette. There was nothing she wouldn't do for her." Nanny paused a moment and said, "I still hope, Olivia, that you and Vanessa can forge a similar relationship."

I wasn't very optimistic on that score, so I nodded, but took the opportunity to satisfy my curiosity on another matter. Recalling how my mother had been dismissed by the Wynfields after Caroline outgrew the need for a governess, I wondered how Genevieve had managed to remain at Amberwood even after Lady Violette's marriage.

"What did Genevieve do here at Amberwood after Lady Violette grew up?" I asked.

"She acted as Lord Fenwick's secretary," Nanny said. The old lady smiled wistfully. "That was his lordship's idea. He knew his daughter would be heartbroken if Genevieve left, so he offered Genevieve another position. He did the same thing with me, you know. Not that Lord Fenwick didn't need a housekeeper or a secretary, but a less sensitive man would have just hired new people and forgotten all about us."

Like the Wynfields, I thought. "Lord Fenwick must be a wonderful person."

"Oh, he is, but you'll see for yourself. He's coming home soon."

"Yes, I know. Sir Evan mentioned it." I hadn't told Nanny about my new duties and I wasn't ready to do so, not yet, at least.

I was still unsure of my own reaction to Sir Evan's suggestion. Somehow it didn't seem to parallel Genevieve's situation, for after all, my duties as a governess were still very definitely required. Yet, Sir Evan seemed anxious to relegate my teaching position to second place.

"When are you to resume teaching Vanessa?" Nanny asked.

"Day after tomorrow," I replied. "Will it be all right for Colin to drive me over? I would love to walk or ride the bicycle, but I have quite a few books to take with me."

"Don't even consider walking or cycling, my dear.

Colin will drive whenever you need to go to Thornton Manor. Besides," she said with a twinkle in her eye. "He's sweet on one of the maids over there and this will give him an opportunity to see her."

"I know," I said. "Her name's Maggie."

Nanny nodded. "Aye, she's a good gel, but a bit of a gossip. She keeps Colin on a short leash, though. He's an Irishman," she added, "and they have a weakness for the bottle, you know, but after he met Maggie, Colin turned his back on the pubs."

I tried not to smile. "Then we'll surely have to keep exposing him to Maggie's good influence."

It was when Colin was driving me over to Thornton Manor and I was recalling Nanny's conversation that I was struck by a strange coincidence. Genevieve had mysteriously disappeared from Thornton Wood over twenty years ago and now history was repeating itself. Could there be a connection between the long ago disappearance of Lady Violette's governess and the recently missing girls from the village?

We entered the driveway and Thornton Manor came into view. The house seemed twice as dark and ugly as I had remembered. Although Mrs. Cathcart greeted me at the door, her pleasant personality failed to dispel the gloom that hung like a shroud over Thornton Manor's decaying body.

The house repelled me just as strongly as Amberwood drew me to it. Light and dark, good and evil; I couldn't separate those images from the two houses. And yet, I could not substantiate my feelings.

We went upstairs to Mrs. Cathcart's small room and she served me a cup of tea. "Sir Evan is calling on tenants right now," she said. "He advised me to instruct you to spend the morning on Vanessa's lessons. He should be back by lunchtime, he said, and then you will begin working with him."

I detected a note of disapproval in her voice and it made me feel uncomfortable.

"Sir Evan doesn't think Vanessa is up to a full course of study just yet. That's why he wants her to resume her lessons on a part-time basis for now."

Mrs. Cathcart pursed her lips. "I see."

"How is Vanessa?" I asked.

She shrugged. "I haven't seen much of her. Lady Thornton has not been well and Vanessa has been spending most of her time in her grandmother's room."

"Poor girl," I said.

"I saw the portrait," she remarked. "Sir Evan was furious with Vanessa and I don't much blame him."

"It's been repaired," I told her. "Sir Evan brought it back to Amberwood several days ago. The artist did a wonderful job. No one would ever know it had been damaged."

"Thank God for that," she said. "Lord Fenwick would never forgive Sir Evan if anything happened to that painting." She smiled ever so slightly. "And that would not bode well for Sir Evan's chances of inheriting Amberwood."

"I remember now. You told me Lord Fenwick has no heirs."

"Only some very distant cousins and I believe they're on Lady Fenwick's side. Of course, the bargain would have been sealed if Vanessa had cooperated."

"What do you mean?"

"Well, it's pretty obvious she hates Amberwood and

Lady Violette. That could hardly endear her to Lord Fenwick. You see...." Mrs. Cathcart lowered her voice, and I knew she could not resist indulging in a little gossip. "Sir Evan wanted Lord Fenwick to look on Vanessa as a grandchild, but the minx put on one of her acts every time he took her over there. Confidentially, I think her mother put her up to it."

"Why would she do that?" I asked.

"I suppose she was jealous of Lady Violette. Sir Evan was madly in love with her, you know, and they say his hair turned white overnight when she died."

She continued to speak in low, confidential tones and it was obvious she was enjoying herself. "Naturally, Sir Evan hoped for a male heir, but neither the second nor the third Lady Thornton could give him one. The child that died was male, you know," she added.

Mrs. Cathcart stirred her tea and looked thoughtful. "I'd say as long as Vanessa is Sir Evan's only heir, those distant cousins still have a chance for Amberwood."

Gossip always made me feel uncomfortable, for my mother put herself above it and I could almost hear her say, *Wagging tongues like wagging tails belong in the barnyard, not in the parlour.*

I put down my cup and said, "Thank you for the tea, Mrs. Cathcart. I think it's time I met with Vanessa. Could you have someone send for her?"

She rang and a few moments later, Maggie appeared.

She smiled when she saw me. "Good morning, Miss St. Claire. It's good to see you back."

"Thank you, Maggie. I'm here to start lessons with

Miss Vanessa. Could you ask her to meet me in the garden?"

I sat on a stone bench, facing the house, so I saw Vanessa before she saw me.

Her wild red hair was constrained by a thick braid that hung down her back and in her blue-and-white pinafore, she looked like a perfectly normal schoolgirl.

And that is what she is, I told myself. The child is highstrung and she desperately wants her father's attention. It is your job to teach her that there are acceptable ways of getting that attention.

"Good morning," I called out cheerfully.

She looked disinterested, but joined me.

"It's good to see you, Vanessa. I'm so glad we're going to start our lessons," I said, maybe a little too heartily.

"You don't have to pretend you're glad to see me, Miss St. Claire."

"Oh, but I am, Vanessa. I'm your teacher, and I want to be your friend. Can't we put the past behind us?"

She shrugged her shoulders. "I suppose so."

"Good, then it's forgotten. Your father wants us to have lessons several mornings a week. And, since it's such a beautiful day, I thought it would be nice to study out here this morning. Would you like that?"

"I guess."

I tried to keep her indifference from dampening my spirits, but it wasn't easy. "What subject would you like to start with?"

Again, she shrugged.

"Well, what is your favorite subject, then?"

She said, "History. I'd like to know about the Saxons

149

and the Angles. We talked about them once. Do you remember?"

It was a start, and I was grateful for it. "Indeed I do remember," I said and reaching into my sack, I brought out a thick volume entitled, "An Early History of England."

I had her read the first chapter and then I asked questions and we discussed it. She had a sharp mind, and a strong will, which I suspected would always lead her to take the opposing view, but teaching Vanessa would never be dull.

"Let's read the second chapter," she said when we had all but exhausted discussion on the first. I was tempted, but just then Maggie came outside and told us that Sir Evan had requested that Vanessa and I join the family for lunch in the dining room.

We followed Maggie back to the house and linking her arm in mine, Vanessa said, "Let's study the second chapter after lunch."

"Your father has some other work for me to do after lunch," I said. "But I would like you to read the second and third chapters before our next lesson. Jot down notes and any questions you have and we'll discuss them the next time we meet."

"And when will that be?"

"Probably the middle of the week. I need to discuss the schedule with your father."

"What other work does he have for you to do?"

"I don't know exactly," I said.

She disengaged her arm from mine and I wished with all my heart that Sir Evan had not asked me to work with him on the ball.

Sir Evan, Lady Thornton, Miss Hamilton, and a gentleman who was a stranger to me were gathered in the small salon off the dining room. Sir Evan greeted us with a smile. "Good afternoon, Miss St. Claire, Vanessa. Did you have a good lesson?"

"Oh quite," I said. "Vanessa is very interested in history."

Vanessa made no comment and joining her grandmother on the settee, she leaned over and whispered something in Lady Thornton's ear.

Sir Evan introduced the stranger to me. He was Thornton Manor's overseer, a Mr. Clyde Bancroft. "Mr. Bancroft was managing Thornton Manor before I was born," Sir Evan said.

"That's stretching the truth a wee bit," Bancroft said. "I think Sir Evan was about two when his father hired me."

He was a big, florid-faced man whose white hair had probably been red in his youth.

At that point, Farnsworth glided into the room and announced that luncheon was served.

Sir Evan and his mother took their customary places at the head and foot of the table. Vanessa was seated at her grandmother's right and I was between Vanessa and Sir Evan, with Miss Hamilton and Mr. Bancroft across from us.

I would have preferred having Vanessa seated next to her father because I sensed her resentment at my position at the table.

Miss Hamilton's sharp eye took the situation in and she glared openly at me. "Are you enjoying your holiday at Amberwood, Miss St. Claire?"

I ignored the *holiday* reference. "I've been busy preparing lesson plans and mapping out a course of study for Vanessa," I said.

"Indeed. I heard you attended our village fair with Dr. McAllister last week."

I willed myself not to blush. "Yes, I did."

"One has to beware of pickpockets at fairs," Mr. Bancroft said. "The Gypsies usually follow them."

Sir Evan's eyes flashed. "Blasted heathens. I thought they'd been run out of Thornton Wood years ago."

Eyes glittering with excitement, Vanessa turned and faced me. "The villagers don't like the Gypsies. They think they're all sorcerers and witches. They burned one of them up once and left his body in the woods," she told me and giggled.

"Vanessa," Sir Evan said coldly. "That's hardly fit conversation for the table. Now apologize or leave the room. You're upsetting your grandmother."

Poor Lady Thornton did look ill and Vanessa hung her head and mumbled, "I'm sorry."

Sir Evan quickly changed the subject. "Lord Fenwick will be coming home soon and I've decided that Thornton Manor will host a ball in his honor. Miss St. Claire will be helping me with the arrangements."

Miss Hamilton's beady little eyes bored into mine, but she made no comment.

Lady Thornton seemed to come to life, though, and she said, "But Evan, the contractors are still working on the house, and it hasn't been . . ."

She let the sentence trail off as her son regarded her with defiant eyes. "The ball won't take place until the autumn, Mother. The contractors will be finished by then."

I didn't think the contractors were the cause of Lady

Thornton's concern. Sir Evan's wife had not been dead a year yet, and officially, the house was still in mourning.

Mr. Bancroft rescued the conversation by switching the subject to horses. "We have a new foal in the stable," he announced. "Born last night and a right pretty little filly she is, too."

"I want to see her," Vanessa said.

Mr. Bancroft looked pleased. "Visitors are welcome, lassie. Just bring a lump of sugar for the proud mother."

Again, I marvelled at Vanessa's mood swings. She was excited now, but it was the excitement of a normal little girl, not the abnormal and macabre excitement she had manifested when talking about the gypsies.

"You must come to the stable, too, Miss St. Claire," Mr. Bancroft said. "Just peek in and have a look at the little lady before you leave."

"Thank you, I will," I told him.

I spent the afternoon closeted with Sir Evan in his study. Arrangements had to be made to hire several coaches in York to convey the guests coming up from London to Thornton Manor.

Sir Evan had me write a letter to his solicitor in London to that effect. He also instructed him to hire London musicians to play for the ball. I wrote to the stationer, also in London, and ordered the invitations. Sir Evan presented me with a hastily scrawled list of names and a thick book of addresses, which I was to compile into a guest list.

I was beginning to understand why a frequent entertainer like Mrs. Truesdale's duchess would require the services of a social secretary.

When the clock chimed four, Sir Evan said, "Good Lord, it's tea time. You must think me a slave driver, Miss St. Claire." Giving me an apologetic smile, he took the pen out of my hand. "Come, the family will have gathered for tea."

I wasn't anxious to be exposed to the family again and I said, "I really must be getting back to Amberwood, Sir Evan."

He took my arm in a firm grip. "Have your tea and then Colin can drive you back."

We joined the others in the drawing room, where Lady Thornton poured the tea and Farnsworth floated about the room with a tray holding an elaborate assortment of dainty cakes.

Teacup in hand, Miss Hamilton sought me out. "You must stop at the stable to see the foal before you go back to Amberwood, Miss St. Claire. Or will you be staying overnight to work late with Sir Evan?"

I didn't like the way she posed the question and I informed her, "Colin will be driving me back to Amberwood after tea, Miss Hamilton."

"Mr. Bancroft took us down to the stable to see the new filly after luncheon," Vanessa said. Then turning to her father, she gave him a pleading look. "Can it be my horse, Papa?"

"If your schoolwork is up to Miss St. Claire's standards," he answered.

I saw the quick flash of anger in her eyes, but her lips smiled sweetly. "Of course. I must always strive to please Miss St. Claire, mustn't I?"

Lady Thornton joined us then and told Sir Evan that

while Mr. Bancroft was showing them the foal, he had been called away to settle an urgent matter at one of the tenant farms. "I believe he went to the Donovan place," she said.

Sir Evan scowled. "I'd better go over there. Bancroft's getting old and soft. Those Irish troublemakers'll walk all over him."

Then without a trace of rancor, he turned to me and smiled. "Sorry about this, but have your tea and I'll see you on Friday."

Sir Evan left and Lady Thornton turned to me and said, "Could I have a word with you, Miss St. Claire?"

"Certainly, Lady Thornton."

I was surprised, for Lady Thornton usually avoided engaging me in conversation.

"We'll use the morning room," she said and I followed her to a bright, informal-looking room done in shades of blue and yellow.

We sat across from each other on twin love seats and Lady Thornton nervously picked at the fringe on her shawl. "The situation here is not working out, Miss St. Claire and I think it would be wise if you left Thornton Wood and returned to London."

Shocked, I said, "But Sir Evan . . ."

She interrupted me coldly. "I am aware that my son wishes you to remain, but I am concerned for my granddaughter's sake and for your own, Miss St. Claire. Sir Evan has been under a tremendous strain since his wife's death. I am afraid he is not thinking too clearly at the moment."

"Sir Evan hired me, Lady Thornton and if you think there is a problem, why don't you discuss it with him?" I asked.

155

"Because I am discussing it with you, miss. I am willing to make you a handsome offer if you will say nothing to my son and just disappear from Thornton Wood."

"I'm sorry, Lady Thornton. I can't do that. Please, talk over your concerns with Sir Evan and if he feels as you do, I will leave Thornton Wood, and no one will have to bribe me to do so." I stood up then and held out my hands to her. "Please understand, I, too, have Vanessa's best interests at heart."

Riveting her eyes on my ugly birthmark, she shrank away from me. "You are either a fool or a demon in disguise," she said.

Her words upset me so much that I turned and ran out of the room. Walking past the parlour, I was relieved to notice that it was empty, for tears of humiliation were already burning my eyes.

I returned to Mrs. Cathcart's sitting room to pick up my purse. I did not expect to see the housekeeper, for at this time of day, she would most likely be supervising the help in their preparations for the dinner hour.

Then, I left the house and when I didn't see Colin or the carriage in the driveway, I decided to walk down to the stable.

He wasn't there either, but I went inside and paid my respects to the new arrival. The little foal was beautiful and the mother nuzzled my hand and seemed proud that I had come to admire her baby.

While I was petting the foal and crooning softly to the mother, the barn door suddenly banged shut. Startled, both horses shied away from me.

I hurried over to open the door, for the interior of

the barn looked dark and scary now, but no matter how hard I pushed, it would not budge.

A wave of panic washed over me. Had the door locked? Or was someone holding it on the other side?

It was then that I smelled the smoke. "Somebody, help. Let me out!" I screamed.

Chapter Twelve

The Gypsy's ominous words rang in my ears.

You escaped one fire, miss. You might not escape another.

Pounding on the door, I shouted at the top of my lungs, "Help, fire! Help!"

Suddenly the door gave way. The unexpected release caught me off balance and pitched me forward. Sprawled unceremoniously on the ground, I looked up into Colin's startled face.

"Miss St. Claire! Are you all right?"

I stood up and spoke in a frantic voice. "Something's burning in there, Colin."

Racing inside the stable, he shouted back over his shoulder. "Stay there, miss. I'll see to it."

Badly shaken, I stood at the entrance and watched Colin shove a smoking barrel outside.

Picking up a bucket of water from the ground, he doused it over the small fire. "Somebody threw a lighted match in there," he said. Colin's usually placid face wore an angry scowl. "And I know who did it, too."

"Who?" I asked, but he was already running behind the stable and in a matter of seconds, he returned, dragging a terrified youth by the collar.

"Smoking again, were you?" Colin shouted and the lad cringed.

"I warn't smokin, honest."

"I'll be reportin' ye to Sir Evan and you know what that means."

"No, no, please. I didn't do it."

"Bloody little liar. You threw the match in that barrel, didn't you?"

"No, honest. I ain't been smokin'. I swear on me mother's grave."

"Colin, please. Let him go," I said.

The child broke away and flung himself down on the ground at my feet. "Oh miss, don't let him report me to the master. I swear I warn't smokin'."

"Colin, I forbid it. Now get the carriage and take me back to Amberwood," I said.

Colin threw up his hands in a gesture of defeat, and, giving the prostrate lad a scathing look, he said, "Don't ye ever be smokin' in that stable again, or I'll hand ye over to Sir Evan for true."

I didn't calm down until I was in the carriage and leaving Thornton Manor behind. Convinced that the stableboy was telling the truth, I was left to wonder who had tossed the lighted match into the barrel?

"There be Dr. McAllister."

Colin's words cut through my thoughts like a scythe and following his gaze, I saw the doctor's closed carriage speeding ahead of us down the lane.

"Where did he come from?" I asked.

"Look like he come from Thornton Manor, miss."

What would Philip be doing at Thornton Manor? I wondered, and immediately that question was followed by another more ominous one.

Why was it that Philip always seemed to be around when disaster threatened?

Colin was still ruminating on the stableboy's supposed transgression. "That lad should'a had a good whaling, miss. One of these days he's going to burn up the stable and then I don't know what Sir Evan'll do to him."

"Sir Evan must be very strict," I said. "The lad acted like he was terrified."

"Aye, Sir Evan's a hard master, that's for true. Wouldn't want to be working for him meself, but this time the lad deserved a punishment."

Had the fire resulted from a careless act on the stableboy's part? Or had it been deliberately set by someone who wanted to frighten me?

I couldn't help remembering Vanessa's cruel little trick in the maze. And today, she had taken an unnatural delight in recounting that tale about the Gypsy who had burned to death. Was her ugly little story meant to foreshadow what happened in the stable?

And then there is Lady Thornton, I thought. Did I force her hand when I refused to be bribed into leaving Thornton Manor?

"Look at that sunset!" Colin exclaimed.

Jolted out of my meanderings, I looked to the west

where a bright orange sun was slowly sinking behind the mountain. Splashes of brilliant pink fanned out over the sky and formed a backdrop against the deep purple hills.

"This is beautiful country," I remarked.

"Aye. Reminds me of home, it does, but Ireland's a poor, sick land and there's no place there for a young man to get ahead."

"How did you come to Northumberland?" I asked.

"Lord Fenwick brought me over. A fine man, he is, though he be British and Protestant."

I was anxious to meet the legendary Lord Fenwick, for I had heard nothing but good things about him from everyone in Thornton Wood. And so it seemed prophetic that we should arrive at Amberwood to be told that the master had come home.

He was a tall, ruddy-complexioned man with a bald head and a bushy white mustauche. His forceful personality dominated the room and I found myself a little in awe of him.

"Olivia St. Claire, Vanessa's new governess," Nanny said as she presented me to him.

I inclined my head. "I am honoured to meet you, your lordship."

He took my hand. "And I you, my dear. Nanny has been telling me all about you. She says you remind her of Genevieve, my late daughter's governess, and that is high praise, indeed."

"Nanny is very kind," I said.

We chatted for several minutes and then Lord Fenwick went to consult with his overseer.

"Should I dress for dinner tonight?" I asked Nanny when he had left the room.

"Please do. His lordship is quite conscious of the proprieties. I dress for dinner myself whenever he is in residence, but tonight will be special because Sir Evan and his mother will be joining us."

Rifling through my wardrobe, I brought out the copy of the gown my mother had made and laid it across the bed. Poor Mama, I mused, she thought it would catch me an aristocratic husband.

I put the gown on and staring at my reflection in the mirror, I played a childish game of *What If*.

What if I had gone to Caroline's wedding four years ago the way Mama had planned? And, what if Sir Evan had been one of the guests? Would he still have married Diana, or . . .

The thought was so outrageous that I found myself unable to articulate it, and picking up my black wool shawl, I hurried downstairs.

Lord Fenwick and his guests were gathered in the small salon next to the dining room. Lord Fenwick and Sir Evan stood by the mantelpiece under the portrait of the lovely Lady Violette. All traces of the ugly black marks had been obliterated from the painting and the iris-eyed beauty appeared to be smiling down on her husband and father as they chatted.

Lady Thornton was seated on the loveseat next to Nanny with the ever-present Nurse Hamilton by her side. Sir Evan's mother looked up as I entered the room and for a split second, the expression on her face was such that an evil aura might have hovered around me like a dark and ominous cloud. A second later, the horrified look was masked by Lady Thornton's usual bland expression.

Greetings were exchanged all around and I had just accepted a glass of sherry from the maid when another guest, and one I had not expected to see, put in an appearance.

Philip McAllister, looking ruggedly handsome, but a little uncomfortable in evening clothes, was warmly greeted by Lord Fenwick.

Sir Evan's face registered surprise and then annoyance, but he quickly recovered himself and shook hands with the new arrival.

Cummings announced that dinner was served and Lord Fenwick offered his arm to Lady Thornton.

Philip smiled and started to approach me, but Sir Evan placed his hand possessively on my arm and, casting a steely eye in Philip's direction, he said, "Allow me to escort you to the dining room, Miss St. Claire."

Philip recovered himself and, extending an arm to both Miss Hamilton and Nanny Grey, he followed us in to dinner.

Such was Lord Fenwick's warmth and cordiality that he managed to put all of us at ease. Glancing hurriedly about the table I wasn't surprised to see that Lady Thornton did not appear quite so anxious, nor the disagreeable Miss Hamilton quite so malevolent.

"It's good to be home," Lord Fenwick declared. "Ireland is a beautiful land, but an Englishman is never completely happy unless he's in England." Then, raising his glass, he proposed a toast. "To England," he said in a strong, vibrant voice.

We drank and Sir Evan said, "You've been sorely

missed in Thornton Wood, your lordship."

The older man smiled and looked around the table. "Nonsense. You've all gotten along admirably without me, but I want to thank you for taking care of Amberwood and its tenants in my absence." Then turning directly to Sir Evan, he added, "Thank you for sending Bancroft over to help out when my overseer broke his leg. That was kind and I appreciate it, Evan."

"Think nothing of it," Sir Evan replied. "How is your man doing?"

"Fine, and I have Philip to thank for that." Glancing over at Dr. McAllister, Lord Fenwick smiled. "James hasn't stopped singing your praises. 'That young doctor got me on me feet in no time a'tall,' " he said, imitating the overseer's soft brogue. Eyeing the young doctor with affection, he added, "You're doing a proper job here, Philip. The tenants are healthy and we haven't lost one mother or babe to childbirth since you started practicing medicine in Thornton Wood."

Lord Fenwick's expression sobered and I imagined he was thinking of the daughter and grandson he had lost in childbirth many years ago.

"A healthy diet breeds healthy bodies," Philip said. "Your tenants are well-fed, sir. They aren't the ones I see often in my office."

Sir Evan's eyes darkened in anger and I wondered if Philip was implying that Thornton Manor's tenants were not as fortunate as Amberwood's.

It was common knowledge that some landlords allowed their tenants to produce more crops for their own consumption than others. Was Sir Evan less generous than Lord Fenwick in this regard? I wondered.

As if sensing the sensitive turn the conversation

might be taking, Lord Fenwick deftly changed the subject, and, addressing himself to Lady Thornton, he said, "I'm sorry Vanessa wasn't feeling well enough to come tonight. Sir Evan tells me the child has a cold."

"She was much better when we left," Lady Thornton said, "but Miss Hamilton thought the night air might not be good for her."

"Very wise. I'm sure she'll feel better in the morning and now that Vanessa has an interesting young teacher, I'm sure she'll be anxious to resume her lessons."

Sir Evan smiled across the table at me. "Very true, your lordship. Miss St. Claire has sparked Vanessa's interest in history. She's looking forward to her lessons, now."

Nanny Grey winked her eye at me and said, "I could have predicted that, Sir Evan."

Miss Hamilton turned a fawning smile in Sir Evan's direction. "It might not be wise to put too much pressure on her, though. Vanessa is delicate and too vigorous a course of study could be deleterious to her health."

Sir Evan gave her an annoyed look. "We'll see, Miss Hamilton. Miss St. Claire and I will discuss the matter."

Miss Hamilton's face turned an unattractive beet red and she fixed me with a hateful look.

"Where did you teach before coming to Northumberland?" she asked smugly.

"Nowhere. Vanessa is my first pupil," I answered. "But I received my teacher's training from my mother, Jenny St. Claire, who was a very fine governess. She taught Lady Caroline Wynfield for ten years and Lord

Anne Knoll

Wynfield retired my mother with a pension when Lady Caroline grew up."

Lord Fenwick chimed in. "I knew Lord Wynfield and wasn't that his daughter's wedding that you attended in my place, Evan?"

"Yes, you were in Ireland at the time," Sir Evan replied.

My little game of *What If* hadn't been so far-fetched after all, I mused. If I had gone to the wedding I would have met Sir Evan Thornton four years ago. The coincidence intrigued me and made me wonder if one way or the other fate had decreed that I should come to Thornton Manor.

After dinner when the gentlemen were smoking their cigars and the ladies had retired to the drawing room, Nanny asked how the renovations at Thornton Manor were coming along.

"Very slowly," Lady Thornton said. "The workmen claim their tools keep disappearing and it hampers their progress."

Nanny looked thoughtful. "The Gypsies have come back to Thornton Wood. Perhaps they are stealing the tools."

Nanny's words aroused my curiosity. "What do you mean, they've come back?" I asked her. "Haven't they always been here?"

"Not for a long time," she answered. "They were frightened away many years ago after an unfortunate incident that happened in the woods."

Vanessa's story must have been true then, I thought.

Lady Thornton paled and Miss Hamilton quickly asserted that the workmen were probably only pretending their equipment was missing. "That's just an excuse for their own tardiness," she said.

The gentlemen joined us then and Miss Hamilton made a show of fussing over her patient. "You look exhausted, your ladyship."

Sir Evan glanced over at me and then at Philip McAllister. A demonic look suddenly flashed across his face and for a split second I was reminded of Vanessa, but then it was gone and once again the sophisticated and urbane gentleman took over. "You'll have to excuse us, sir," he told Lord Fenwick. "My mother has not been well."

Lord Fenwick looked at Lady Thornton with concern. "I'm sorry to hear that, my dear."

Sir Evan offered Lady Thornton his arm and turning back to Lord Fenwick he said, "Thank you, sir, for a wonderful evening."

"My pleasure," Lord Fenwick replied.

Bowing his head to the rest of us, Sir Evan bade us a good evening, and then capturing me with his eyes, added, "I shall expect you at Thornton Manor on Friday, Miss St. Claire."

Lord Fenwick left the room with his departing guests and Philip turned to me. "Lady Thornton seemed fine at dinner. Did something upset her afterwards?"

"I think my presence upsets Lady Thornton," I answered.

"Nonsense," Nanny countered. "I'm afraid it was my fault. I shouldn't have mentioned the Gypsies. Some people are rather terrified of them, you know."

Recalling my own mother's reaction to the sight of a Gypsy caravan, I had to agree that Nanny's explanation was probably the logical one.

Lord Fenwick returned to the drawing room and shortly thereafter Nanny and I made our excuses and retired, leaving the gentlemen to discuss whatever it is that gentlemen discuss in the absence of ladies.

This time I did not question the force that drew me like a magnet to the house in the woods. Would I hear the children again? I wondered. I still found it hard to believe that their voices were only echos from the past as Sonia had said, but the Gypsy had predicted there would be another fire and already that had happened, so I had to respect her opinion. I wanted to ask her, too, why the Gypsies had decided to return to Thornton Wood after such a long absence.

The sky was overcast and storm clouds cast shadows over the forest, but in spite of the weather, I set out bravely for the little house deep in the woods.

Like a homing pigeon, I traveled by instinct, discarding one path for another without knowing the reason why. When I came upon the clearing, I looked around, but there was no sign of Sonia.

That the children were not real gave me an eerie feeling and I hesitated before opening the door.

"Hello," I called, purely out of habit. But of course there was no answer.

Gathering up my courage, I entered the house and closed the door behind me.

Where have you been? I've been waiting for hours.

The man's voice caught me off guard and I froze, unable to move.

I had a hard time getting away.

The woman sounded breathless, like she had been running.

The House in Thornton Wood

I saw you. You were with him.

I didn't invite him. He just came to the house. Was I to turn him away?

You were smiling and flirting with him. I was up in the tree watching you.

You have no right to spy on me.

Who has a better right?

His voice turned bitter. *Look at you, all dressed up in ruffles and lace. Tea party clothes! I don't know you anymore.*

This is the latest style. I have a right to wear pretty things.

Your beautiful hair, all crimped and curled like a fancy wig. That hard gold necklace like a dog collar around your throat.

What do you know about it? This is how ladies dress. I'm fifteen now and I'm a fashionable lady.

I thought you were my queen.

He sounded so wounded that my heart ached for him.

Remember the necklace and the crown I made out of wild flowers for you to wear? You were so beautiful in them. I kissed you that day and made you my queen.

His voice faltered and there was a long pause before she answered him, her voice an agony of contrition.

Oh my love, my dear, dear king. I am your queen. Look, I'm taking the pins out of my hair. You want me to take the dress off? Here, I'm taking it off.

Her voice grew very soft.

Please don't be angry, your majesty. I can't bear it when we quarrel. You mean more to me than all the fine jewels and dresses in the world.

More than all the fine gentlemen in the world?

Yes!

Say it, my love. Say you'll love only me.

I'll love only you.

You say that now, but when one of your own kind asks your father for your hand, you'll marry him and you'll forget all about this poor fool who loves you beyond all reason.

No, I won't. I never could.

Prove it to me, my queen. Marry me here and now. The forest will be our chapel and the birds will carry our vows up to heaven. This house that we love will become our castle and we will rule together not as princess and peasant, but as king and queen. Say it my darling, say I take you for my husband.

I take you for my husband.

And I take you for my wife. I will cherish you and love you until the end of time. Oh my darling, now we can love each other without sin. Now we can truly be one. You're not afraid, are you dearest?

No, I'm not afraid. This is the happiest moment of my life. Nothing can part us now. I am your wife and you are my husband.

They were the children, I thought, the king and queen of the forest, only now I heard them as adults pledging their love. Who were they? I wondered, and why should they speak to me?

Chapter Thirteen

Warmth returned to the room, bringing with it an eerie silence and I knew then that Sonia had been right. The voices I had heard were merely echoes from another time.

The forest must be enchanted, I thought, and words once spoken here had remained, frozen in time. Now a powerful force was releasing them for my ears only. But why? What had any of this to do with me?

Startled out of my meanderings by a creaking noise, I looked up to see Sonia standing in the open doorway.

"Did you hear the children again?" she asked.

"Yes, but they were no longer children."

Closing the door, she came and sat beside me on the wooden bench. Her eyes glittering with excitement, she asked, "Can you tell me what they said?"

The conversation must have emblazoned itself on

my mind, for I found myself repeating it word for word.

When I had finished, Sonia stood up and began pacing the floor. "They never referred to each other by name?"

"No."

"Did you recognize either of the voices?"

The question took me by surprise, and though I made a frantic attempt to play the voices back, the sound eluded me. "I don't know," I said.

It had never occurred to me that the voices could belong to living people. The thought was disturbing. Sir Evan claimed that Philip had had affair with his wife, and Nanny Grey had discreetly mentioned rumors about Philip and Diana.

From the conversation I had just overheard, it was obvious that the tormented young man had been his sweetheart's inferior. Recalling that Philip had been a crofter's son, I wondered if the disembodied voices had belonged to Philip and Diana?

Sonia had gotten up from the bench and was kneeling on the floor. Closing her eyes and swaying slowly she began to moan. The sound was unnerving and I felt the hairs stand up on the back of my neck. Digging my nails into the palms of my hands I stiffened and bit my tongue to keep from crying out as she opened her eyes.

The pupils had rolled back inside her head, and horrified, I stared into her all-white, blinded eyes.

Holding her arms out before her in supplication, she spoke in an unnatural, chanting voice, *Come to me, oh spirit brother. Speak to me. Show yourself to me!*

I was badly frightened. I had seen Sonia go into a trance before, but never like this.

The House in Thornton Wood

I was relieved when I saw her go limp and slump to the floor. It was over, and several seconds later she returned from the world of the dead.

Weak, but fully awake, and with her eyes once again normal, she raised her head and looked at me. "I could not reach the spirit. For some reason, he prefers to work only through you."

"But what does this spirit want?" I asked.

"I don't know for sure. I only know you are a very important link. Keep yourself open to these manifestations and record them. I'll help you, but you must tell no one what has transpired here. Keep in touch," she said. "And be careful. You are in great danger."

I shuddered. So far, Sonia's predictions had been right on target.

Reading my thoughts, she added, "You have a very vicious enemy."

"Can't you tell me who it is?"

"I don't know who it is. Just be on your guard and don't trust anyone."

We parted then and I walked slowly back through the woods.

Several times, I thought I heard crackling noises. But I told myself the forest was teeming with birds and small animals. Nevertheless, I felt compelled to keep looking back over my shoulder and the next thing I knew, I had tumbled down a small embankment. Landing in a decidedly unladylike heap, I was further annoyed to be admonished by a familiar male voice.

"Good Lord, Olivia. Why don't you look where you're going?"

Hoping to preserve my dignity, I tried to stand, but my legs had become entangled in my long skirt and in a matter of seconds, Philip McAllister had skittered down the ridge and was helping me to my feet.

"Are you hurt?"

"No. I just couldn't get up for a minute," I said. Feeling like a fool, I wished my rescuer could be anybody, but the good doctor.

"No wonder you couldn't get up. Between your corset and that long skirt, you might as well be wearing a straight jacket. What are you doing in the woods, anyway?"

Ignoring his ungentlmenly allusion to a lady's unmentionables, I deftly turned his question around. "And what are you doing wandering around the woods scaring people to death."

"I'm not *wandering* around the woods and I had no intention of scaring anybody to death. I happen to be searching for a particular plant that I use for medicinal purposes."

"Well, don't let me interrupt you. I'll be going back to Amberwood now."

He gave me an amused smile. "I wouldn't think of letting you out of my sight, Olivia. I'll see you safely home and the next time you decide to take a hike in the woods don't dress yourself up like you're going to a tea party."

His words jolted me back to the little house.

Tea party clothes!

That was the expression I had heard the unidentified young man use. Had Philip McAllister been that young man? I didn't want to think so, and I pushed the thought from my mind.

"Let's sit down by the stream. You look like you could use a rest," he said.

I didn't protest. I had scraped my knee, but I wouldn't dare tell him. He led me over to the same big tree where I had eaten my lunch and where I had heard the children for the first time.

Sonia's suggestion that the voices I heard could belong to living people bothered me and I casually asked him, "Did you come to the woods much when you were a lad?"

"Every chance I got. We used to finish our chores and then head out here."

I was immediately suspicious. "We? Who did you come here with?"

"Other lads. We used to swim in the stream. It was deeper then, or perhaps we were just smaller," he amended with a grin.

Overcome with relief, I smiled. It wasn't Philip then, and for some strange reason that made me feel glad.

"This is a beautiful spot," I said.

His eyes lit up with sudden inspiration. "Why don't we have a picnic? My housekeeper packed me a huge lunch. I was just about to open it when you decided to roll down the hillside."

His outspoken comment tickled my funny bone. "Did I actually roll?"

"Like a barrel," he said, and we both exploded into laughter.

"You always manage to see me at my worst," I complained, wiping my eyes.

He stopped laughing and his expression softened. "I hadn't noticed, Olivia. You always look fine to me." Then he turned quickly toward the hill. "Don't move. I'll be right back," he commanded.

I shouldn't stay, I thought. Philip McAllister is a rake.

Everybody says so, and hadn't I seen it for myself that day at the inn?

I didn't move, though, and a few seconds later he was back, carrying a rather bulky package, which he carefully opened.

"Didn't I tell you Mrs. McCauley packs a hearty lunch? Try some of her bread. She's famous for it in the village."

I was hungrier than I had thought. There was bread and sliced meat, raisin cookies, and a small bottle of apple cider, but only one cup, which we shared.

After we had eaten, I leaned back against the tree and closed my eyes. The enchanted forest must have woven a spell over me for when I felt his lips very gently meet mine, I did not protest. And when he deepened the kiss and held me close, I gave myself up to the thrill of the moment, winding my arms around his neck and kissing him back.

What madness had taken possession of me? Embarrassed and horrified at what I had done, I tried to pull away, but he held me even tighter, raining hot kisses on my face and neck. "I knew you were a warm, passionate woman," he murmured in my ear.

I felt my treacherous body slipping into sweet compliance as he captured my lips again, and then a sudden sharp retort split the air like the crack of a whip.

The next thing I knew, Philip was pushing me down on the ground and I struggled as the full weight of his powerful body descended on mine. "Lie still," he commanded in a harsh whisper.

I could do nothing else and after several minutes had elapsed, he raised himself up and looked around. "The bloody fool. He could have killed us."

"Who?" I said with mounting panic.

"I don't know. Some idiot with a gun. It's illegal to hunt in the forest, but poachers will try anything. Stay down," he said. "I'll be right back."

Moving on silent feet, he disappeared over the hill and I lay on the ground afraid to breathe. A few minutes later, he was back. Reaching for my hand, he raised me to a sitting position and said, "It's all right now. He took off."

"You saw him?"

"No, but I heard him run through the underbrush. I'd have rammed that rifle down his throat if I'd caught him, and he knew it." He walked over and examined the tree. "The bullet's lodged inside the trunk," he said.

I started to shake and he came over and put his arm protectively around me. "It's all right now, Olivia. It was an accident, but I scared him off. He won't try to hunt in these woods again."

Philip took me home, and we parted at Amberwood's gate, but the events of that fateful day stayed in my mind.

Had it really been a stray bullet from a hunter's gun, or had someone fired that rifle on purpose?

Sonia said I had a vicious enemy and Philip seemed to have his share of detractors, too. If it wasn't an accident, which one of us had been the target?

And as for what had preceded the incident, I shuddered to think what might have happened had we not been interrupted.

My own disgraceful reaction to Philip's kisses still shocked me. I had been as compliant and bold as the barmaid at the St. Claire Arms.

Either I was two people as Sonia had said, or the

enchanted forest had cast a spell over me.

And what was I to do about Philip McAllister? When we had parted at Amberwood's gate, he had asked to take me for a buggy ride on Sunday. Too confused and mortified to argue with him, I had agreed, but now I didn't know what I should do.

I was afraid of Philip McAllister, but I was more afraid of myself and the emotions this passionate man had awakened in me.

I had Colin drive me over to Thornton Manor early the next morning. Vanessa must have been looking out the window for she ran out of the house as soon as the carriage pulled into the driveway.

Climbing up inside, she grabbed my hands and held them in a bone-crushing grip. "Oh miss, I'm so glad to see you. I was afraid you wouldn't come."

Her eyes danced with an almost unnatural brightness and her face was flushed with excitement. "Calm down," I said. "We have a lesson today. Why wouldn't I come?"

Mercifully releasing my hands, she plopped herself down beside me and tossed her head. "You don't have to pretend, miss. I know you're leaving Thornton Wood."

"Wherever did you get that idea?"

"I heard my grandmother tell it to Miss Hamilton."

"Lady Thornton is mistaken," I said. "Your father hired me as your teacher, Vanessa, and I shall stay until he asks me to leave."

She thought a moment and then said, "I have something to show you today."

"Something about your studies?"

She gave me a sly look. "No. Something else. It's a secret. I'll show it to you after we have our lesson."

We went inside the house then and Mrs. Cathcart met us in the hall.

I thought her greeting a little restrained, but then I attributed it to the fact that we were in Vanessa's presence.

"Sir Evan has requested that I show you to the classroom, Miss St. Claire," she said.

"Where is it?" Vanessa snapped. "We never had a classroom at Thornton Manor before."

"Your father just had the workmen install it," Mrs. Cathcart answered.

We followed her upstairs to a large, bright room on the third floor.

"How very nice," I said, taking in the shiny blackboard that covered one whole wall, the beautiful world globe that rested on its pedestal, and the two brand new desks that faced each other in the center of the room.

Several large cartons were stacked in a corner, and, following my gaze, Mrs. Cathcart said, "Those are books Sir Evan ordered from London." Giving the room and myself a final, disapproving glance, she added, "I'll be getting back to my other duties now, miss, if there's nothing else you need."

"Thank you, Mrs. Cathcart, but I think Sir Evan has thought of everything."

"I'm sure of it," she said curtly. Then she went downstairs and I was left to wonder what I had done to earn the woman's disapproval, for she certainly was nothing like the charming companion I had known at Amberwood.

Turning to Vanessa, I tried to recapture my enthusiasm. "Shall we open the cartons and have a look at the new books?"

She shrugged. "If you say so."

I ripped a box open, and lifted out one of the heavy volumes. "It's the *Encyclopedia Britannica*!" I exclaimed.

It was a brand new set, handsomely bound in rich brown leather. I had never seen an encyclopedia before and I was thrilled.

"Just think, Vanessa, now we'll have all this knowledge right at our fingertips. Isn't this exciting?" I handed her the volume, and began to leaf through one of the others. "Oh look Vanessa, your encyclopedia even covers history and biographies."

The words had hardly left my mouth when I saw that my own name was engraved in gold on the inside of the volume. The jealous look on Vanessa's face told me that all of the books had been similarly inscribed.

"Let's put them in the bookshelf, shall we?" I suggested.

"Whatever you say, miss. They're your books."

I wished with all my heart that Sir Evan had put the encyclopedias in Vanessa's name. It would have meant so much to her. The set was handsome and obviously quite expensive, and once again, I felt compromised by my employer's generosity.

It was not a good lesson. Vanessa was unresponsive and I felt certain she was brooding about the books. Oh, why couldn't he be more sensitive to his daughter's needs? I wondered.

I was relieved when a young servant girl arrived to inform us that lunch was being served.

"I don't want any lunch," Vanessa told her. "Tell my father I have an upset stomach and I'm going to bed."

The poor girl turned imploring eyes in my direction. "Lor, miss, I gets me tongue-tied around the master, I do. Don't make me give 'im no message."

"Don't worry about it," I said. "I'll inform Sir Evan that Miss Vanessa is not feeling well."

I knew there was nothing physically wrong with Vanessa, but I also knew her temperament. She would never be able to contain herself in her father's presence and both she and I knew it.

"Perhaps a light lunch would settle Miss Vanessa's stomach," I told the servant. "She'll tell you what she wants and you can bring it to her room."

I went downstairs then. I resolved to speak to Sir Evan about Vanessa as soon as we were alone. He ought to be more aware of his daughter's needs and I intended to tell him so. If he thought I was overstepping my bounds and dismissed me, so be it. My leaving Thornton Wood might just be for the best, I decided.

Lady Thornton, Miss Hamilton and now even Mrs. Cathcart had all made it perfectly clear that I was not wanted. And if I left Thorton Wood, I could no longer be used as a pawn in someone's strange and twisted scheme to review the past and seek vengeance for its mistakes.

Sir Evan readily accepted my explanation for Vanessa's absence and I got the impression he was secretly relieved that he wouldn't have to deal with his difficult daughter over luncheon.

Lady Thornton and Miss Hamilton joined us and for my part, I wished I could have been spared their company over lunch. Lady Thornton's trancelike gaze was focused on my birthmark to such a degree that I was made to feel uncomfortable, and since Miss Hamilton was seated directly across the table from me, I was forced to look at her disagreeable face throughout the meal.

"Perhaps I should check on Vanessa. An upset stomach can sometimes be serious," she remarked to Sir Evan.

"That won't be necessary," he said.

I faced the corridor and at that very moment I caught sight of the servant girl, laden down with an overloaded tray. I couldn't help smiling and Miss Hamilton frowned.

"You seem to find Vanessa's illness amusing, Miss St. Claire."

"Not at all," I said. "I'm afraid I was thinking of something else."

She gave me a sarcastic smile. "Some private little joke between you and Vanessa, I dare say."

Sir Evan looked up from his meal. "Miss St. Claire has quite a rapport with Vanessa." Then staring pointedly at his mother, he added, "We are most fortunate that she has agreed to remain at Thornton Manor, for were she to leave, I would have no alternative other than to place Vanessa in an institution."

Lady Thornton paled and I must confess Sir Evan's words shocked me beyond measure. Granted, the child was difficult, but unless there was something about Vanessa that I had not been told, her behaviour hardly warranted such extreme measures.

I didn't get a chance to speak with Sir Evan, for right after lunch, he was called away on estate business, so

I went to the study to finish writing the letters he had dictated the week before.

I was absorbed in my work and so silently did she enter that I didn't realize anyone else was in the room with me until a shadow fell across my paper.

Startled, I looked up and a chill ran down my spine as I gazed into eyes that glittered with an almost deranged excitement.

Placing her finger over her lips and grasping my hand with surprising strength, she whispered, "Come with me, miss. I want to show you the secret room."

Chapter Fourteen

I tried appealing to her in a rational manner. "Vanessa, I must finish these letters."

Giggling, she grabbed the inkwell. "If you don't come, I shall throw ink on your letters."

She was in one of her moods, and challenging her did not seem wise under the circumstances. "All right. What is it that you want to show me?"

Pulling me by the hand, she led me out of the room and down the corridor to a double-bolted door. "There's a hidden staircase in here," she said. "Be careful, it's not used anymore."

I could well understand why. The short treads were extremely high. At one point they curved at what must have been a ninety-degree angle and I almost lost my balance making the turn on the narrow half-step.

The enclosed stairway seemed to go on forever. I

was sure we had passed the second floor and possibly the third. Chiding myself for letting her make a fool of me again, I said, "This is ridiculous, Vanessa. I'm going back."

"No, don't, miss. You might fall and we're almost there."

Glancing down I couldn't believe how high we had climbed. The stairway was treacherous and I hesitated to attempt a retreat.

"A long time ago one of the maids fell down these steps and broke her neck," Vanessa said. "But we'll use the other stairway to go down."

And why hadn't we used it to go up? I thought, but of course I knew. The stairway, like the maze, was Vanessa's way of testing my mettle.

At last we reached the top. "What is this, the fourth floor?" I asked, for the stairway was blind and I knew we had already passed several floors.

"Yes. Are you out of breath?"

"Not really, just out of patience. I have work waiting for me downstairs, Vanessa."

"Then we must hurry, mustn't we? But this won't take long."

Resigned, I followed her down another corridor. Dustcovers shrouded the furniture in the rooms we passed and Vanessa turned her head and smiled at me. "I call this the ghost wing, all those white covers— don't they look spooky, miss?"

"Not really. I don't believe in ghosts," I said.

She gave me a calculating look. "My mother believed in them, and so did my father's third wife."

She paused in front of the only closed door along the corridor, and taking a large key out of her pocket, she said, "Diana had this key made without my father's knowledge. Now I have it and he still doesn't know it exists."

I thought this had gone far enough and I was about to tell her so when she opened the door and I was taken aback by what I saw.

A perfectly beautiful room all done in shades of lavender seemed to beckon to me and I found myself drawn inside almost against my will.

Whisper-soft curtains of gossamer white fluttered like angel wings in the slight draught from the open door. The drapes were of violet silk and the same material had been used for the bed hangings.

I drew back at the sight of a large copper vat in the corner of the room, but it must have been an illusion, for when I looked again, it was gone.

A fragrance of lilacs hung on the air and I breathed in the heavenly scent. "Who's room is this?" I asked.

"My father's first wife." Then opening a closet, she pointed and said, "Look, all her clothes are still here, and in the desk, there are love letters." Before I could reprimand her, she opened the desk and withdrew a piece of notepaper. "Listen, miss.

"My Queen, I shall die if you leave me. I love you beyond life itself. . . ."

"Vanessa!"

It was what I had been about to say and it took me a moment to realize that I hadn't even spoken.

Confused, I looked around the room and there in the doorway stood Lady Thornton. "Go to your room, Vanessa," she commanded.

Vanessa immediately obeyed and I was left alone to justify myself to Sir Evan's mother.

"Your ladyship," I began. "Please don't think—"

She interrupted me. "You know, don't you? That's why you came. I knew it couldn't have been a coincidence."

"Lady Thornton," I pleaded, "please let me explain." But she shrank away in terror. "Go, I beg of you, go. Leave him in peace. I'll give you anything you want, but let it end. For God's sake, let it end."

"I don't know what you're talking about," I said.

She stared with horror-stricken eyes at my disfigured hand. "You're one of them, and you've come to exact payment. Oh please, exact your payment from me, but leave him in peace."

Before I could reach her, she had collapsed and lay in a heap on the floor. I rushed to her side and almost immediately Mrs. Cathcart appeared. Perhaps Vanessa had alerted her to our whereabouts.

We patted Lady Thornton's hands and presently her eyelids fluttered open. Mrs. Cathcart's presence seemed to calm her and she said, "I'm all right now. Just help me up."

When she was on her feet and leaning heavily against Mrs. Cathcart, she turned to me and said, "Swear to me on your mother's grave that you'll say nothing to my son about any of this."

I supposed she thought such an oath to be an iron-clad guarantee, but in my case it wasn't necessary. My dear mother had raised me to respect a confidence. "You have my word, Lady Thornton," I said.

Later that evening, sitting in Amberwood's cozy parlor watching the firelight flicker in the grate, I thought about the strange household at Thornton Manor.

The steady click-click of Nanny's knitting needles and an occasional hiss from the fireplace were the only sounds to break the companionable silence that the three of us had lapsed into.

I was completely comfortable with Lord Fenwick and Nanny Grey. These two very dear people had become like family to me and I couldn't help comparing the gentle, relaxed atmosphere here at Amberwood with the threat of malice that rumbled below the surface at Thornton Manor.

I didn't know what to make of Lady Thornton's irrational allegations this morning.

You know, don't you? she had said.

What in the world did the woman think I knew? And why was she so afraid of me? I had given my word that I would not speak to Sir Evan, and I would not have done so anyway. I did not want him to become angry with Vanessa and I didn't want to hurt the man.

Sir Evan must have loved his first wife very deeply, I thought, for he had turned Lady Violette's room into a shrine. I should die if he found out that I had been gawking at it and that Vanessa had read me a line from one of their love letters.

My train of thought was interrupted when Lord Fenwick suddenly stood up and said, "If you ladies will excuse me, I shall say goodnight. I'll be wanting to get an early start in the morning."

Lord Fenwick had spent so much time in Ireland that he had picked up that country's speech inflections. They gave his voice a charming, down-to-earth quality, and although I knew he was an aristocrat of the first order, I was not intimidated by him. Rather, I thought of his lordship as a grandfatherly figure and since I had never known a grandfather, I found myself drawn to him.

We bade Lord Fenwick an early goodnight and when he had gone, I took the opportunity to confide the distressful incidents of the morning to Nanny.

She listened attentively and then sadly shook her head.

"Poor man. I'm afraid both Sir Evan's mother and his daughter are a trial to him. Sir Evan's whole life literally fell apart when Lady Violette died. Did you know that his hair turned white because of it?"

"I've heard of that, but do you mean it actually happened overnight?"

"Oh yes. It's rare, but a tremendous shock can do that, you know."

"And Lady Thornton," I asked. "Was she always the way she is now?"

"Not at all. That happened after Lady Violette's death, too. In fact, Lady Thornton locked herself in her room and didn't even attend the funeral. If it hadn't been for Miss Hamilton's care, she probably wouldn't have survived."

"Miss Hamilton has been at Thornton Manor for many years, then," I said.

"Oh yes. She came when Sir Evan's father took ill and that was several years before he and Lady Violette married."

"What do you think Lady Thornton meant by all those strange things she said to me?"

"I can't imagine, dear. I'm afraid poor Lady Thornton is not responsible for what she says. And then there's the matter of Vanessa being high-strung."

Nanny shook her head. "Sometimes these things run in families, you know."

"You young people have a beautiful day for a buggy ride," Lord Fenwick remarked to Philip, who had arrived, as promised, to take me out on Sunday afternoon.

I was a little nervous about going. I couldn't forget how I had responded to Philip's kisses in the woods and I resolved not to place myself in such a compromising position again.

"I have a call to make on the other side of the woods, first," Philip said. "The Donovan baby is sick. You don't mind, do you, Olivia?"

"Of course not."

Lord Fenwick was smiling benignly at us and I reminded myself that his lordship heartily approved of Philip McAllister. Perhaps the young doctor was not the ogre I had made him out to be.

It was indeed a beautiful day and as I sat beside Philip in the buggy, I put aside my reservations and chatted away like nothing had occured between us that day in the woods.

We passed a group of Amberwood tenants and their families walking home from a late church service. Dressed in their Sunday best, they greeted us warmly. No question about it, Dr. McAllister seemed to be popular with everyone except the residents of Thornton Manor, I thought.

"Where is the Donovan cottage?" I asked him.

"Not on this side of the woods. The Donovans are Thornton Manor tenants."

That meant a long ride, but it was a warm, sunny

day, the scenery was beautiful, Philip was pleasant and he could hardly seduce me while driving the buggy.

We kept up a steady stream of conversation, most of it rather silly, and at one point it suddenly struck me that we were flirting with each other.

He was an attractive man, but my upbringing had not prepared me to deal with him. His raw masculinity and outspoken opinions shocked me. Nevertheless, it was that very quality that drew me to Philip McAllister, and I wondered if his attraction could have anything to do with the fact that my mother would have disapproved of him.

The thought stunned me, for I had loved my mother dearly and yet she had been so restrictive that at times I had felt a wild desire to rebel.

Philip interrupted my disturbing ruminations. "We're almost there."

The grey spires of Thornton Manor loomed before us, but Philip took a sharp turn to the right. We traveled several more miles down the narrow road and then he reined in the horse.

I had seen some of Amberwood's tenant houses on my cycling jaunts. The small white-washed cottages were as well-kept as the farms that adjoined them and I suppose that was what I was expecting to find here, but the tenant house that lay in the shadow of Thornton Manor looked like a delapidated old shack.

"Not squeamish, are you?" Philip asked as he helped me out of the buggy.

"Certainly not," I said emphatically, but I wasn't prepared for the chickens and piglets that converged on us squawking and squealing as we entered the front yard.

"Shoo," Philip said, waving his medicine bag to scatter them.

The door was open and he called out, "Frank, Kate, it's Doc McAllister."

A short, barrel-chested man appeared and said, "Thank God, you're here, Doc. Herself and three of the little ones have it now, too."

We entered the house and I couldn't believe that so many people lived in such a small space. In answer to her father's request, a girl of about ten herded three younger children outside to play. The man then led us to a small bedroom where the mother, the infant, and three more children lay on cots.

Philip laid his hand on each of the children's heads. "Burning up," he muttered and turning to the man, he said, "Go out to the pump and fill up a bucket. We've got to get their fevers down."

To the woman in the bed, he said, "Kate, are there any clean rags around?"

"In the kitchen," she said, starting to cry. "Lor, Dr. McAllister, I ain't got the strength to get up and find them for ye."

"Don't worry about it, Kate. We'll find what we need. Here, let me take the baby." And reaching down, he lifted a blanket-clad bundle from the woman's arms. Then he turned to me. "Think you can help, Olivia?" he asked. I nodded and he said, "Good. I'll find the rags, and when Frank brings the water, you undress the baby and sponge him down. I'll take care of the others."

The poor little mite felt like he was on fire and I found myself praying that we wouldn't lose him, for he was a thin, sickly little thing.

When Frank Donovan brought in the bucket of water, I bathed the baby's hot little body. When I had finished, Philip rolled another rag into a ball, dipped it in the cool water, and handed it to me.

"Let him suck on this. It'll keep him from dehydrating," he said.

Then he went out to the kitchen and prepared a hot herbal medication, which he poured into cups and administered to the mother and the three older children.

Using an eye dropper, he squeezed some of the warm liquid into the baby's mouth. "The medicine will stop the infection," he said, "but see that his temperature stays down. We don't want him going into convulsions."

It took several sponge baths, but finally the little fellow stayed cool and when he fell asleep, I laid him in his cradle.

The medicine worked wonders on the others, but it was late afternoon before Philip felt the baby was out of danger and it was safe for us to leave.

"What did they have?" I asked when we were back in the buggy and on our way home.

"Grippe. The family's malnourished and susceptible to disease, but the sickness is contagious, so I'm going to give you some medication and before you go to bed tonight, I want you to take it."

"Why are they malnourished?" I asked.

"Because the crops they grow belong to their lord and master and only a small portion is allotted to the tenant."

"I'm sure Sir Evan is not aware of how they are living," I said.

Philip laughed. "You bet he isn't, and he doesn't care. That fine gentleman wouldn't soil his boots walking into the Donovan yard, much less their house. Sir Evan's overseer handles the tenants," he added.

"I shall tell Sir Evan about it."

He sniffed. "Still championing the aristocrats, aren't you?"

"I believe in giving everybody the benefit of the doubt."

"Do you?" he asked, and then his voice mellowed. "But then, you've led a very sheltered life and let me say right here and now, you were wonderful in there, Olivia. Some young ladies would have fainted at the sight *and* the stench, I might add, but you pitched right in and helped. You'd make a fine nurse, or a fine doctor's wife," he added softly.

His words were unsettling. Could it be possible his intentions were honourable? Or was he only toying with me?

What would it be like, I wondered, to be married to Philip McAllister? The thought was intriguing, but a little frightening. This was a man with no inhibitions, and although I had led a sheltered life, I was not completely ignorant. Not that my mother had ever spoken of such things. On the contrary, my mother's views on love were more spiritual than physical.

I felt an arm go around my waist and I stiffened. "We'll wind up in a ditch," I said.

"No we won't. Bessie knows these roads better than I do."

It seemed prudish to protest and when he slyly closed the distance between us, I relaxed and let my head rest on his shoulder.

194

The House in Thornton Wood

I must have dozed off, for when I looked up, the scenery had completely changed. The road had narrowed to little more than a path and open fields had given way to an encroaching forest.

Confused, I sat up straight and looked around. Philip must have turned down off the main road and driven into the woods. Oh, what a vile, underhanded thing to do, I thought, but before I could protest, a flash of bright orange and red caught my eye.

Something was on fire and the blaze was spreading rapidly. Flames licked the ground and traveled in a zigzag pattern, and as they came closer, I saw with horror that it wasn't the woods that were on fire. It was a man! The poor soul had been turned into a human torch and his frantic movements only fanned the flames. "Help him. For God's sake, help him," I screamed.

Philip's hands dug into my shoulders and he shook me. "Stop this, Olivia. Calm down," he commanded.

"The fire. That poor man," I sobbed.

"There is no fire. You fell asleep."

"No, no. I woke up. Oh, help him, please help him."

He slapped me hard and I gasped.

"Look around you," he said softly. "There is no fire. You were dreaming."

Afraid of what I might see, I nevertheless forced myself to look. There was no woods, no charred body, only a peaceful, open field.

Philip kissed my flaming tear-stained cheek. "Poor darling. I'm sorry I had to slap you, but you were hysterical, Olivia. What a dream you must have had!"

My trembling body was encased in Philip's strong arms and I laid my head on his chest and let him comfort me. It was no dream, but I couldn't tell him that. Philip was a man of science and he would never believe what the Gypsy and I both knew to be true.

I had just witnessed another scene from out of the past, like the shepherd and the sheep grazing on the hillside.

Lifting my head, I asked the question though I already knew the answer. "Was this field once part of the woods?"

"Probably. When I was a lad the woods stretched north for another mile or so, but parts of it have since been cleared and turned into farmland."

He stared at me and his blue eyes were full of concern. Rubbing his hand very gently over my cheek, he said, "I'll give you some salve to put on your face."

"It's nothing," I answered.

I was glad I still had some of Philip's headache medicine though, for I knew I would be needing it by the time we got home.

It was dusk when we returned to Amberwood and I was disconcerted to see Sir Evan's carriage in the driveway.

Philip saw it, too, and he said, "Damn. What's that ass doing here?"

My head was killing me and I didn't appreciate his language. "Sir Evan is Lord Fenwick's son-in-law. It's customary for family members to call on one another," I said.

"How convenient for Thornton," he replied brusquely.

Before leaving me at the door, Philip pressed an envelope in my hand. "Add this to a cup of hot water and drink it before you go to bed. Don't forget," he insisted.

My head was pounding and I couldn't wait to get inside the house. "Thank you, Philip. I won't forget."

"May I see you next Sunday?"

"Yes, but I really must go now."

His lip curled. "You're in quite a hurry, Olivia. Don't worry. Thornton won't slip out the back door."

"Thank you for the buggy ride. I'll see you on Sunday." I rubbed two fingers against my temple to ward off the pain.

His jaw tightened. "Don't let me keep you from your lord and master."

Headache forgotten, my own anger flared. "No man is my lord and master," I said, and turning my back on him, I reached for the door handle. Strong hands spun me around and his mouth came down hard on mine.

There was anger and possession in the kiss and when he let me go, he said, "Now you can go inside. And when that fop kisses your hand, you'll remember how a real kiss felt."

Chapter Fifteen

I closed the door and leaned against it. Philip McAllister was overbearing, artless, rude—everything my mother had raised me to abhor in a man and yet his kiss had seared my lips like a branding iron.

"Are you ill, Miss St. Claire?"

I hadn't seen Cummings and I stammered in embarrassment. "J-Just a headache, Cummings. You may tell Lord Fenwick I'll be resting until it's time for dinner."

Once in my room, I took a dose of Philip's headache medicine and stretched out across the bed. The headache was extremely severe and I wondered if it was because the vision had been such a violent one.

That poor man, I thought, and tried to remember what had been said about him. He was a Gypsy and the villagers had suspected him of being a sorcerer.

Vanessa had said that was why he had been burned to death and Sonia had remarked that fire was often used against those who had the sight. Was the vision meant as a warning to me? Or had I been taken back to that horrible scene for another reason?

Too miserable to think about it, I closed my eyes and waited for the medicine to take effect.

An hour later, I woke up and my headache was completely gone. I raised the lamp's wick and looked at the clock. It was seven-thirty.

If I rang for hot water, the tweeny would take forever to bring it up, so I used what was left in the pitcher and gave myself a sponge bath. Then I put on my red velvet dinner gown and went downstairs.

When I reached the bottom of the staircase, I heard Sir Evan's voice in the drawing room and I froze. Philip's opinions were too fresh in my mind and I did not want to see Sir Evan through his disgruntled eyes.

Neither did I want Sir Evan to see on my face that Philip's lips had once again laid claim to me.

I was just about to turn and run back upstairs when Lord Fenwick spoke from the doorway. "Ah, here you are, my dear. I was just about to send Becky upstairs to see to your needs. Cummings said you had a headache. I trust you're feeling better now?"

"Much better, thank you, your lordship."

"Good, then come into the drawing room. Sir Evan is here and we've persuaded him to have dinner with us."

Sir Evan rose and came forward to greet me as I entered the room with Lord Fenwick. "We've missed you, Olivia," he said and kissed my hand.

199

When that fop kisses your hand, you'll remember how a real kiss felt.

The words echoed in my head and I pushed them away.

Nanny, who was seated in her usual spot by the fire looked up from her knitting. "Did you take some of Dr. McAllister's medicine for your headache?" she asked.

I wished she hadn't brought the subject up, but I wasn't going to lie. "Yes, as a matter of fact, I did."

Sir Evan's slate-grey eyes darkened, but he made no comment.

"How was Philip's patient?" Lord Fenwick asked.

"A little better." I answered.

"Who was it? One of Amberwood's tenants?" Nanny asked.

"No, it was one of Sir Evan's tenants. The Donovan family," I said.

Sir Evan looked blank for a moment. "Donovan? Oh, yes, They have a large passel of brats, if I remember correctly."

His cavalier attitude annoyed me and I said, "They have a large family and four of the children were sick. The whole family looked undernourished," I added.

Cummings announced dinner then and the subject was dropped, but later that evening Sir Evan took me aside and said, "I wouldn't want you to think me neglectful or unfeeling, Olivia, but the Donovan crops are poor because Frank Donovan is lazy. However, I shall look into their situation. The family will be taken care of, you can be assured of that."

"Thank you," I said. "The children should not have to suffer for the faults of their father."

A calculating expression suddenly crossed his face

and he said, "A kind and noble thought, and one I hope you shall not forget, Olivia."

I found it a strange remark and I thought of Vanessa who often twisted my words and made me feel that I, and not she, was the one who needed admonishment.

As Sir Evan was leaving that evening, he said, "You needn't come to Thornton Manor tomorrow, Olivia. I shall be busy with estate work, but I shall need you every day for the rest of the week, and don't make any plans for next Sunday, either. Time is of the essence and we are already behind schedule."

He gave no explanation. Obviously, he was referring to the reception in honor of Lord Fenwick. But, in any case, I had no right to question Sir Evan. He was my employer.

In a way I was relieved. Now I had an excuse not to see Philip on Sunday.

Early Monday morning, I set out for the woods. I wasn't going to chance getting caught up in a long skirt and taking another tumble down the hillside, so this time I wore my cycling clothes.

I needed to see Sonia and talk about the vision I'd had yesterday afternoon. Perhaps she could make some sense of it, for I could not.

First there had been the dark-complected man. I had seen him as a cabbie and lately as a shepherd. Then I had heard the voices of the children and those of the young man and woman they had later become. Now I had been shown the burning body of a man professed to be a sorcerer. What connection did these people have to me? Or to one another, for that matter? I wondered.

I climbed the hill with little conscious effort, and at the top, I paused and concentrated on sending Sonia a message to meet me at the little house. I was at a loss to understand how this mental communication between us worked, but there was no doubt in my mind that Sonia would arrive in answer to my summons.

I suppose I should have been afraid to venture into the woods alone, especially after the shooting incident, and in a way, I was, but a force more powerful than fear seemed to draw me like a magnet to the house in Thornton Wood.

There was no path, but I instinctively knew the way. Had there been one once? I wondered, and was I unconsciously following ghostly footprints from the past?

I reached the clearing and when I saw the house it cast its spell on me all over again. Like some enchanted cottage it seemed to have sprung into being by the touch of a magic wand. The heather surrounding it was tall and as I walked through it, the tiny purple- and rose-colored blossoms gave off a fragrance sweeter than any heath I have ever known.

The door sprung open at my touch. "Hello," I called, but expected no answer.

Closing the door, I sat down to wait and several minutes later, the sound of a woman's laughter filled the room.

I was hiding in the heather, you goose. Did you think I wasn't coming?

Why do you torment me? I thought you'd changed your mind.

Ah, my sweet love. I was only teasing. Don't be so melancholy.

The House in Thornton Wood

I was born to be melancholy. We all were. What do we have to be happy about?

You have me, your majesty.

Do I? Do I really have you, or are you only making a fool of me?

Why do you do this? You know I love you. Haven't I proved it?

We haven't been together for a week.

You know how hard it is for me to get away.

I know, I know, but you don't miss me the way I miss you. You're all I have. The others are all gone now and I only stay because of you. You know how I hate it here. My only happiness is in this little house with you.

It's my only happiness, too. Oh, let's not quarrel. I want you to love me. Please, my darling, make love to me.

Quietly I slipped out the door. There was something tragic and beautiful here and I could no longer justify eavesdropping on their love.

Sonia was standing at the edge of the clearing. "You look upset," she said. "What did you hear?"

"Their meetings were clandestine. They were very much in love, but their love was illicit. That's all I can say. I won't come here again."

Her eyes darkened with fear. "Don't say that. You must come. Don't you understand? You are a medium. The spirits are calling you here."

"I can't be an eavesdropper," I said.

Her eyes blazed with a passionate intensity. "You foolish girl, don't you understand? There is a lost spirit out there who is calling to you. What you have heard, you have been meant to hear."

"But I didn't ask to be a medium. Why doesn't this spirit call on you?"

Sudden tears welled up in her eyes and she said, "If I knew the answer to that, I would know the answer to a secret that has been hidden for many years. You are the key that can unlock that secret."

"I had another vision yesterday. A terrifying one. No, no," I pleaded. "I can't go on with this."

Instantly alert now, her sharp eyes bored into mine. "You had another vision? What was it?"

She listened intently while I told her and when I had finished, I said, "Now you see why I can't go on. There's something evil here. I want no part of it."

"But you *are* a part of it," she said in a voice that chilled me to the bone. "You have been chosen. There is much I haven't told you because you are not one of us. I didn't want to frighten you then, but you are too deeply involved now to back out."

"Ask the spirit to use you as his medium then," I said angrily. "Go into the house right now and ask."

Very slowly, she shook her head. "There is no house, miss. It burned to the ground many years ago."

Her words stunned me for the moment, but then I turned and pointed to the house. "Why do you lie to me? I'm looking at it right now."

"Only you can see it, miss," she said softly.

I didn't want to believe this was happening, and with rising panic, I strove to prove my point. "You were in it yourself. We sat on the wooden bench together and talked."

She shook her head. "We sat on the parched ground."

"Parched ground? That ground is abloom with

heather—the tallest, most beautiful heather eyes have ever seen and the fragrance of it is like some heavenly perfume."

"Bring someone else here with you. Ask them what they see, but tell them nothing." Her eyes softened then and she put her arm around me. "Dear girl, don't fight what is meant to be. None of us asks for what we are. Accept it as a gift. In God's own time, all will be made clear. Truth will rise to the surface and wrongs will be avenged."

"Answer me this," I said, still unable to come to terms with the extent of my visions. "Do you know who the shepherd is?"

"He was my brother, Pasha."

"Was?"

"He burned to death in these woods many years ago."

My head was reeling, and she said, "You are very pale, miss. Our caravan is close by. Come with me and I will give you a potion. It's made from a plant found in the woods. Our people have used it for generations. It will quiet your nerves and ward off a headache."

Like a sleepwalker, I let her lead me through the forest. I simply could not accept the fact that the little house in the woods existed only in my mind, and yet I knew in my heart that it was so. Hadn't I entertained the thought that it was an enchanted cottage? Hadn't I found the heather almost too beautiful to be real?

The blue caravan was parked in another clearing. As we approached it, Rashev and his wife and baby stepped outside. The toddler ran up to his grandmother and pulled on her skirt.

Sonia looked down on her grandson with undisguised affection. "Go with your mother, Rao. I am busy."

The child's mother called him back and then the three of them walked off into the forest.

When they were out of sight, Sonia turned to me. "That boy will be a great man. It is written in his palm." Then her expression grew cynical and she added, "My son has been a disappointment to me. He is not a leader and his woman is nothing, but the child will be different."

I was still trying to come to terms with what she had told me about the house and I found I had a hard time paying attention to her family problems. I regretted coming, but I had no idea how to find my way out of the forest now. I would have to stay until Rashev came back and consented to take me home.

As always, she read my mind. "You have nothing to fear from us, miss. My son won't be gone long and when he returns, you'll be feeling better, I promise you. Now please, sit down under that tree and rest while I mix the potion."

Too sick to argue, I did as I was told and when she handed me a steaming cup of a thick, dark liquid, I drank it down.

Taking the empty cup from my hand, Sonia smiled with satisfaction. "You'll see, miss. This will work faster than Dr. McAllister's medicine. It's the same thing, but we know how to brew the roots and . . ."

I never heard the rest of her sentence and when I awoke, I saw that Rashev was back. He stood outside the caravan watching his mother, who was seated on the ground with a deck of cards fanned out in front of her.

"The king of spades has turned up three times," she said.

"What does that mean?"

"It means he has chosen her."

"And why should he do that? She is not one of us."

"Fool. If I knew, I would tell you."

"Sometimes I think it is you who are the fool. Keira wants to leave and so do I, Mother. There is nothing for us here."

Sonia's voice was full of anguish. "No, Rashev, not yet. Would you deny me my revenge? I must find out who murdered Pasha."

"We leave in two months and that's final."

Sonia smiled. "Agreed. The two of spades has come up twice. That's a sign."

"Then wake the English woman up. I'm ready to leave."

The following day, Colin drove me over to Thornton Manor. Vanessa was in one of her outrageous moods and I could see from the beginning we would get nothing accomplished.

"What did you think of the secret room?" she asked as soon as we were alone in the classroom.

"I have no right to think about it at all, and neither have you," I said. "And if you were punished for going there, it was no more than you deserved, Vanessa."

She gave me a sly smile. "I wasn't punished. My father knows nothing about it. Surely you don't think my grandmother would tell him. Why, the very mention of Lady Violette's name gives her the vapors."

"Childbirth deaths are a terrible shock, Vanessa. Everybody in a family looks forward to new life."

"Pooh, just because her old baby died. It was a boy, you know." A reflective look crossed her face and she paused, tapping her pencil on her desk. "He would be in his twenties now," she mused. "I would surely hate him, so I'm glad he died. Now he's just a little bunch of bones. Do bones ever disintegrate, miss?"

Her insensitivity revolted me. "That's disgusting, Vanessa. Have you no compassion?"

"Why should I? If he was here, I wouldn't be."

I couldn't argue with her logic and I was too concerned with my own problems to pursue the subject.

"Let's concentrate on history," I said.

"Yes, let's. History repeats itself. Isn't that right, miss?"

"Yes, it is. That's why it's important to be aware of the past."

She broke into a triumphant smile. "Be aware then, miss. My father's had three wives and all of them have died. Wouldn't you say a fourth wife would be taking a risk?"

Her lips were smiling, but her eyes were not. Was she warning me or threatening me?

"I don't think that's a subject we should be discussing, Vanessa."

"Oh, you're always so proper, aren't you, miss. Everybody knows my father wants a male heir, so he's bound to marry again. He'll probably go to London to find a suitable wife this time, though," she speculated, giving me a disparaging look. "That's where he met my mother."

"I see, and where did he meet Lady Diana?" I asked.

"Right here in Thornton Wood. Her father had a small estate on the outskirts of town and when he died, my father helped Diana manage the property." She smiled knowingly. "When he married her, it all became his anyway."

So Diana had grown up near Thornton Wood, I thought, and in that case, she and Philip McAllister could have been childhood sweethearts.

"Do you know how she died?"

I gave her a startled look and said, "No. I presume she took sick."

She started to laugh. "Oh, that's funny. She took sick all right, from eating poisoned herbs."

I felt a chill run down my spine. "Vanessa, you shouldn't say such things."

"Why not? It's the truth. She had this little package of weeds hidden in a drawer. I caught her eating them and I laughed. She got very angry and said they were to help her get pregnant and when she had a son, I'd be sorry because he would be Thornton Manor's heir."

"It was probably a perfectly harmless tonic," I said.

"Oh no, miss. After awhile, it made her daft and she threw herself off a cliff."

I was relieved when Mrs. Cathcart poked her head in the door and announced it was time for lunch. My head was buzzing and I did not want to hear anymore of Vanessa's bizarre theories.

If Diana had consulted Philip about getting pregnant it was not inconceivable that he would have given her a tonic, but I couldn't believe he would have deliberately poisoned her no matter what their past relationship had been.

Lady Thornton did not present herself for luncheon and Miss Hamilton informed Sir Evan that her ladyship was "indisposed."

He gave her an annoyed look. "Perhaps you would prefer having your lunch sent upstairs then, Miss Hamilton."

I wish Sir Evan would give me such a choice, I thought. These interminable luncheons with the family were a burden I would gladly relinquish.

Lady Thornton made me feel uncomfortable and Vanessa was always unpredictable. I was constantly on edge lest she say something outrageous and cause her father to lose his temper.

The disagreeable Miss Hamilton, on the other hand, was completely predictable and I knew she would find some excuse to remain in Sir Evan's presence.

"Thank you, Sir Evan, but I'll stay downstairs. I've given Lady Thornton a sedative, so I'm confident she'll be asleep for several hours."

Thank God for small favors, I mused. At least today I would not have to endure Lady Thornton's glassy stares and morbid fixation with my birthmark.

After lunch, I freshened up and then reported to Sir Evan's study. He was already there and looking over the mail, which Farnsworth had just brought in on a silver tray.

Picking up a rather bulky envelope, he handed it to me and said, "This is for you, Olivia. It's from a law firm in London."

I stared blankly at the printed name in the left hand corner: Edward L. Tattersall, solicitor.

Chapter Sixteen

I tore open the envelope and read:

Dear Miss St. Claire:
  It is my duty to inform you of the death of Lady Wynfield, wife of the late earl of Wynfield.
  In her will, Lady Wynfield has bequeathed to you the sum of 300 pounds as a token of her affection and gratitude for services rendered by your mother while in Lady Wynfield's employ as governess at Wynfield Towers.
  Upon receipt of the enclosed waiver, a check for said amount will be drawn up and forwarded to you. With sincere wishes for your good health, I remain,

Edward L. Tattersall.

  P.S. At the late Lady Wynfield's request, I also

enclose a letter which she penned to you shortly
before her death.

I was surprised and puzzled.

"Lady Wynfield died," I said.

Sir Evan looked up from reading his own mail. "I'm
sorry. You knew her quite well, didn't you?"

"Only as a child. My mother was her daughter's governess and we lived at Wynfield Towers until I was
eleven. She has very kindly mentioned me in her will.
I'm to receive three hundred pounds."

"So, you are an heiress," he teased. "What shall you
do with your fortune."

"Put it in the bank for my old age."

I did not mean to be ungrateful, but three hundred
pounds was nothing to Lady Wynfield, and although
it may have salved her conscience, it hardly made up
to me for the pain she had caused my mother. I was
anxious to read her letter though, but I decided to wait
until I could do so in private.

Sir Evan seemed restless and he walked over to the
window and looked outside. "Do you ride, Olivia?" he
asked.

"I took riding lessons when I was at Wynfield Towers," I answered, "but I haven't ridden for years."

"It's not something you forget. I'll tell you what—
let's play hooky today and go riding."

"But I have no riding habit."

"That's not a problem. There's one here that should
fit you. It'll do for now, but we'll have Miss O'Shay
make you a new habit. After all, when guests come up
from London, they'll expect to ride, and as my hostess,
you'll be expected to join us."

I could hardly refuse, but I couldn't help wondering whose riding habit I would be wearing. One of his dead wives'? The thought made me feel ghoulish.

He left the room and returned a few moments later with a brown worsted habit and riding boots. "I'll meet you at the stable," he said. "Don't be long."

I locked the door lest Farnsworth intrude, and changed into my borrowed clothes. They looked brand new, but whomever they had belonged to had been a little thinner than I was, for the riding habit was tight, but the boots fit quite well.

Sir Evan was waiting for me at the stable. "You'll be riding Penelope, a very gentle mare. I bought her for my late wife, but Diana never rode. She was afraid," he added.

"Afraid of horses?"

"Afraid of everything," he mumbled more to himself than to me.

The groom helped me to mount and I said, "I don't know about this. I don't exactly feel like I was born in the saddle."

He laughed. "You'll do fine. We'll take it slow today and next time you'll feel more secure."

I had liked riding as a child and Caroline and I had spent a lot of time exploring Wynfield Tower's rolling hills on horseback.

Those had been carefree, happy days and I felt a little nostalgic remembering them. Lord Wynfield had treated me like a second daughter and although Lady Wynfield had been preoccupied with her own interests, she hadn't been unkind.

Her ladyship had thrived on a busy social life and

Wynfield Towers' ballroom was the scene of some wonderful memories for me.

Caroline and I would sneak out of bed and hide on the balcony whenever there was a ball so we could listen to the music and watch the handsomely dressed couples dancing below.

Lady Wynfield wouldn't see us, but Lord Wynfield would, and he used to wink his eye to let us know that it was all right, we had his permission to be there.

He was very kind to us children, and my rather strict mother always deferred to his more permissive views.

I was anxious to read Lady Wynfield's letter, for perhaps at long last a question that had plagued me for years could be put to rest.

"You seem deep in thought," Sir Evan said.

"Oh, I was just thinking about when I used to ride over Lord Wynfield's estate. It was very beautiful and had been in the family for years. I think it dated back to the fifteenth century."

"Thornton Manor dates back to the fourteenth century."

"And it's been in your family all that time?"

"Yes. It once encompassed the entire village of Thornton Wood, but some of our more careless ancestors let portions of it get away.

"My grandfather was the last perpetrator. He sold the land on the other side of the forest to Lord Fenwick's ancestor and Amberwood was built about a hundred years ago."

His eyes scanned the hillside. "He should never have parted with any of the estate. Land is the only thing that lasts."

I said, "You feel strongly about Thornton Manor, don't you?"

"It's all I have."

I thought it a strange thing to say. Had he forgotten that he had a daughter?

He seemed to read my mind. "I don't have an heir. Vanessa is a woman and what passes on to her will not belong to a Thornton."

"Vanessa's heirs will be your heirs," I said.

"It's not the same thing."

I hadn't paid much attention to where the horses were leading us, but now I saw that we were approaching the forest.

It looked dark and forbidding, and remembering my vision of a man writhing on the ground with his body in flames, I shuddered.

Sir Evan said, "What's wrong, Olivia?"

"I was just thinking about that Gypsy who burned to death in the woods."

An angry expression crossed his face. "Vanessa has been punished for mentioning that. She upset her grandmother so much that day, Miss Hamilton had to give Lady Thornton a sedative. That girl takes a fiendish delight in the macabre," he added with a scowl.

"But who could have done such a thing?" I asked.

He gave me an impatient look. "I don't know. Boys, probably. A bunch of young scamps from the village used to frequent the woods. They could have done it. The Gypsies are hardly a popular lot, you know."

"But that's inhuman," I said.

Pulling his horse up close to mine, he reached across the animal and grabbed my arm. His eyes flashed with sudden anger and his voice hardened.

"Forget about it, Olivia. It happened over twenty years ago." Then he suddenly shifted moods, smiled, and patted my hand. "What colour riding habit would you like me to order from Miss O'Shay?"

Feeling like I was dealing with Vanessa, I accepted his mood swing with equanimity and answered, "I think green would be nice."

"Then green it shall be," he said gaily.

We took the horses back to the stable and Sir Evan promised me I should have a new riding habit come Sunday.

"Then we shall go for a longer ride," he said.

We went back to work, but I found it hard to concentrate. The day had produced some very disturbing revelations and I needed to come to terms with them and to find out the contents of Lady Wynfield's letter. I didn't think I could cope with a Thornton family tea, so I asked Sir Evan if I could be excused early.

I conveniently arrived at Amberwood too late for tea and too early for dinner, so I took advantage of the opportunity to escape to my room and read Lady Wynfield's letter.

My dear Olivia,

I am writing to apologize for the way I treated you and your poor mother after Lord Wynfield died.

When his lordship's will provided so generously for your mother, I thought it was because you were his child. I wanted nothing to do with either of you. You see, it was Lord Wynfield who brought the two of you to Wynfield Towers. He said he had hired Jenny St. Claire in London, but that was not the whole truth.

Several months ago, when I was setting my own affairs in order, I confided my suspicions to Mr. Tattersall and he very adamantly denied the accusation in Lord Wynfield's name.

Mr. Tattersall told me that one blustery, bitter cold night when he and Lord Wynfield were returning from a business trip, they came upon a woman and her infant lying in the roadway.

Mr. Tattersall said that the woman had collapsed with the child in her arms and that they had gathered them into their carriage and taken them to a nearby inn.

A doctor was called, who confirmed that the woman was suffering from exposure, but the child whom she had cradled next to her body had miraculously escaped harm.

Later, when the woman had regained consciousness, she had appeared terrified and refused to reveal anything about herself except for her name, Jenny St. Claire. Lord Wynfield and Mr. Tattersall believed the name to be a fictitious one, but they did not press the matter, for it was obvious that the poor woman was running away from some terrible danger.

She begged the men to take her to London with them so she could find work, and Lord Wynfield, who was the soul of generosity, could not refuse.

She told them she was by profession a governess and her intelligence and genteel manner attested to that fact. Moreover, she confided that she would not be seeking such a post again because she could provide no references.

It was then that Lord Wynfield offered to bring your mother to Wynfield Towers as Caroline's governess with no questions asked.

Never once was I sorry until jealousy made me turn my back, not only on you and your mother, but on the memory of my beloved husband. I'll never forgive myself for doubting him, and I'm sorry about your mother, too. She was the soul of integrity and I don't know how I could have thought two such honourable people could have deceived me. . . .

I could read no more. I was as guilty as she, for hadn't the same ugly suspicion crossed my own mind?

But now that I knew Lord Wynfield was not my father, the mystery of my birth deepened. What was my mother running away from? And, if I was not Olivia St. Claire, who was I?

True to his word, Sir Evan kept me busy all that week. I did manage to get Colin to deliver a note to Philip, explaining that I would be unable to see him on Sunday because I was needed at Thornton Manor.

When I arrived early that afternoon, Sir Evan presented me with a handsome green worsted riding habit and he insisted that I try it on so Miss O'Shay could make any necessary alterations.

It was a perfect fit though, and he said, "You look much too pretty to do any work, Olivia. Keep the riding habit on and we'll go for a ride." When we were mounted and riding out of the stable he told me he had something he wanted to show me.

Feeling a little more comfortable on horseback this time, I followed his lead across a meadow until we came to a narrow road that I immediately recognized because I had traveled it with Philip just the week before.

We rode a short distance and once again arrived at the Donovan cottage. At least I thought it was the Donovan cottage. For last week's delapidated old shack had been transformed by a new thatched roof and a fresh coat of whitewash.

"Are you surprised?" Sir Evan asked.

"Amazed." I could hardly believe my eyes. The transformation was so miraculous.

"Care to go inside?"

I hesitated. "I don't want to intrude on them."

He dismounted and said, "Nonsense. How can I intrude? The house belongs to me and they are my tenants. Come, I want to show you I'm not the ogre you think I am."

So saying, he dismounted and reaching up, lifted me down and then tied the horses to the hitching post.

Striding up to the cottage, he knocked once and a little girl opened the door. I recognized her as the child who had herded her brothers and sisters outside when Philip and I had arrived the Sunday before.

She curtsied and moved back to let us enter. The Donovan family, neatly dressed in their Sunday clothes, were all gathered together in the front room.

"Welcome to me humble cottage, Sir Evan," Frank Donovan said, and his wife looked at me and smiled awkwardly.

"Good to see you again, miss," she murmured.

"How is the baby?" I asked.

"Just fine, miss. Dr. McAllister's medicine took all the sickness away."

"Sir Evan has given us a cow, so now the children have milk," her husband quickly added with a nervous glance in Sir Evan's direction.

The room did not have the bare, unkempt appearance of a week ago and I noticed that some additional furniture, used, but in good condition, had been acquired.

I was glad to see all the improvements, but I felt embarrassed for the Donovans. It seemed so patronizing to barge into their home and put them on display.

Fortunately, Sir Evan was as anxious to leave as I was and we only stayed for a few minutes.

"Now, do you feel better about the Donovan family?" he asked when we were outside and he was unhitching the horses.

"Much better. It was kind of you to help them," I told him.

I didn't mention that it had been an imposition to call on them. He was an aristocrat and wouldn't have understood, but I couldn't forget that he had seen a need and given it his instant attention. Philip had misjudged Sir Evan and I would make it my business to tell him so.

We continued our ride and it was a pleasant afternoon. Later Sir Evan drove me home and Lord Fenwick insisted that his son-in-law stay for dinner.

Sir Evan seemed to have a special affection for Amberwood. A sentiment that could be easily attributed to its warmth and conviviality. But I couldn't help wondering if in part it was also because Amberwood reminded him of his beloved Violette.

The House in Thornton Wood

*   *   *

Several days later, I returned to the woods. I wanted to see the house again. Sonia had told me the truth, I didn't doubt that, but I hadn't seen the shepherd whom she claimed was her brother, Pasha, for a long time and I couldn't help wondering if this was because I now knew he was a ghost.

Would the little house, too, be gone? Would I see, instead of the purple heather, a parched, ashen ground where no living thing grew?

I hoped not. I hadn't asked to be Pasha's medium, but for whatever reason, he had chosen me. He had brought me to Thornton Wood and to the little house in the woods so I could hear some tragedy from the past being played out. I understood none of it, but I would see this thing through until the bitter end.

I was relieved to find that the house stood as before, surrounded by its little garden of heather. Smelling its sweetness, I ran through the swaying purple blooms to open the door and for a moment, I just stood there, disoriented.

The inside of the house was different. Gone were the cobwebs and rickety furniture. White curtains framed the windows and a round wooden table and two chairs sat in front of the hearth.

A delicate vase, looking out of place in the rustic little house, had been filled with heather and placed on the mantle, and a cot, covered over with a quilt, graced the far corner of the room.

How could you do this? I told you I would come back for you.

The man's voice was wrenched with anguish.

You were gone such a long time! the woman said.

What difference does time make? I would have waited for you forever.

Oh my darling, you don't understand. This has nothing to do with us. I don't love him, but it was my duty to marry.

We were married, he shouted. *Didn't we say our vows right here in this room?*

Her voice was soft and pleading. *I promised to love you forever and I do, believe me I do. Nothing will change. We can still meet here. He'll never know. Look, I've fixed the house up for us. It'll be our very own secret place.*

You planned it this way. You never intended to give up your other life for me.

You don't understand. In my world, marriages are made to protect property. It's our way of life. Oh my darling, please don't turn away. We can't change the system. Believe me, I do love you and I shall die if you leave. I can't live without you. Please, tell me you'll stay.

An eerie silence filled the room then and I thought it was over, but he spoke again and his words hung suspended in the air like harbingers of doom.

Oh God, I wish I had the strength to leave, but you have bewitched me and I would see you dead before I would give you up.

I did not want to believe what my ears had heard and I ran outside. The pieces were beginning to fit together. The woman had said her lover was gone for a long time.

Philip had left Thornton Wood and gone away to medical school. Had he come back and found Diana married to Sir Evan Thornton?

Vanessa had seen Diana take a herbal medication

and the disembodied voice had spoken of his mistress's death. Sonia's warning rang in my ears.

The Prince of Darkness is waiting for you in Thornton Wood.

Like the crack of a whip, the man's gruff voice broke through my thoughts. "What are you doing up here?"

He stood in the clearing only a few feet away, but the sun blurred my eyes and I didn't recogonize him until he had covered the short distance between us.

Then, grabbing me by the shoulders, Philip said, "What's wrong, Olivia? Why are you so upset?"

"Leave me alone," I cried, trying to break away. "It was you, wasn't it? You used to come here to meet Diana."

He stared down at me with hooded eyes. "What has that to do with us?"

"Answer me, Philip. Did you used to come here to meet Diana Thornton?"

"I met her in the woods, yes. Evan Thornton wouldn't let me come to the house."

Incredulous, I stared back at him. "You expected him to let you come to the house?"

"She was sick, Olivia. He wouldn't let me treat her. I think he was trying to kill her."

Oh dear God, what next? I thought. The accused is now the accuser and whom am I to believe?

Chapter Seventeen

"I want you to stay away from Thornton," he said.

"I work for Sir Evan Thornton."

"Work for him? You went horseback riding with him Sunday. That wasn't work, though you told me I couldn't see you because you would be *working* at Thornton Manor."

"Sir Evan took me to the Donovan cottage Sunday. He wanted to show me what he had done for the family. He's fixed up their house, given them a cow. He's not the ogre you think he is," I defended my employer.

"Oh, yes he is, Olivia. That and more. Thornton's trying to impress you and you're falling for his fine talk and fancy ways. You think he's a gentleman, and maybe you think it would be nice to be the next Lady Thornton," he snapped. Then he grabbed me roughly by the shoulders. "I'm not a fine talker and I don't have fancy ways, but I know what kind of a husband Thornton was, and I'd rather see you dead than married to him."

I gasped. He said the same thing to Diana, I thought. "Let me go," I cried, squirming out of his arms. "I have to get home."

I started to run, but with very little effort he caught up to me. "I'm sorry. I shouldn't have said that, but I know what I'm talking about, Olivia. Thornton is dangerous. Please don't let yourself become involved with him."

"I don't need your advice, thank you. Your own reputation is far from spotless, Philip."

He threw up his hands. "I know all about my reputation. I'm a thirty-two-year-old bachelor, Olivia. I haven't been a saint, but that's all over now. I'm ready to settle down and I'd like it to be with you."

He looked so vulnerable that I felt myself falling under his spell again and when he took me in his arms, I gave myself up to the rapture of his kiss.

I let him part my lips and ravage my mouth with his tongue. I let his hands caress me and when I felt his fingers fumbling at the buttons of my shirtwaist, the wild and wanton side of me surfaced. Suddenly, I had no conscience, no shame, only a burning desire to give myself completely to this man.

Ever so gently, he laid me down on the soft grass. I let him finish unbuttoning my blouse and push my camisole down to my waist.

"You're so beautiful, Olivia," he whispered.

A gentle breeze floated over my bare breasts, hardening my nipples and I gasped when he lowered his head to claim them.

Lost in the delicious agony of first passion, I pressed him to me and ran my fingers over his strong back. I would have let him take me right there on the forest floor, but he raised his head and whispered, "I don't have a castle to offer you, Olivia, but if you marry me, I'll make you my queen."

His words confirmed my worst suspicions and I pushed him away. "You lied to me, Philip. You did have an affair with Diana," I accused him, hurt replacing my desire.

He stared back at me with angry eyes. "You certainly pick a fine time to start an argument. Is that what Thornton told you?"

I was about to say that I had heard it with my own ears, that he had told Diana he would make her his queen, but I stopped myself. He wouldn't understand about visions and words frozen in time.

"Thornton is a liar," he said. "I never touched his wife. Diana had melancholia, brought on, no doubt, by him. I was only trying to help her."

I think if he had admitted the affair, I could have accepted the fact and gone on to believe he had nothing to do with Diana's death, but he stared me down and his lips curled with sarcasm when he said, "I would expect you to believe Thornton over me. After all, he's an aristocrat!"

He left me lying there and I don't think I have ever felt so confused or so miserable.

I was moving back to Thornton Manor. Since the damaged wing had been repaired and renovations were now complete, there was no reason for me to remain at Amberwood, and Sir Evan needed me close at hand so we could make the final arrangements for Lord Fenwick's reception.

I didn't want to leave. Amberwood was beauty and graciousness personified. But more than that, from the very first, I had been drawn to the house. Like a lost child, I felt I had finally found my way home.

I should miss Nanny and Lord Fenwick and I certainly wasn't looking forward to spending time in the company of Lady Thornton and Miss Hamilton, but I had known all along that my stay at Amberwood would be a temporary one.

"Oh dear," Nanny said when I told her. "I was hoping we could keep this arrangement. I've loved having you, Olivia, the way I loved having dear Genevieve. Oh, why couldn't those workmen have dawdled over their renovations?" she added peevishly.

I laughed. "I shan't be far away and I promise to visit."

Her china-blue eyes grew misty and she said, "Forgive me, I'm a foolish old woman, but I lost Genevieve and Lady Violette, and I don't want to lose you, too."

I was touched. "I shall visit every Sunday afternoon until you tire of me."

Brightening, she said, "You're a dear gel, Olivia, just like Genevieve. I wish you could have known her. You would have liked her."

I told Lord Fenwick the news over dinner. "I want to thank you for your hospitality." I smiled at my gracious host. "The renovations have been completed and Sir Evan has requested that I return to Thornton Manor."

"I know," he said. "I was sorry to hear it. We've enjoyed having you, my dear. Nanny and I shall both miss you."

Later that evening he took me aside. "Thornton Manor is not a happy home, Olivia, but if anyone can bring the sunshine back to that gloomy old house, it will be you. Sir Evan tells me you've already worked wonders with Vanessa. My own daughter, Violette, was a headstrong girl," he admitted, "but Vanessa is a troubled one and I want you to know that if for any reason things don't work out at Thornton Manor, you can always come back to Amberwood. This is a large estate and I could use the services of a secretary."

His kindness brought tears to my eyes. "Thank you, your lordship. I would love to stay at Amberwood, but I have an obligation to Sir Evan and I really do want to help Vanessa."

I got the impression there was something more he wanted to say for he paused, but after giving whatever it was consideration, he shook his head and, giving my hand a reassuring pat, said, "God go with you, my dear."

The following morning, Colin loaded my traveling bags into the carriage and I kissed Nanny good-bye.

"I want you to have this," she said, placing a small cross and chain in my hand. "It belonged to Genevieve," she explained with a sigh. "The poor girl was grief-stricken, and in her haste to leave, she left it behind."

It was not an expensive piece, but knowing how much the legendary Genevieve had meant to Nanny, I was touched. "Thank you," I said. "It's beautiful and I shall treasure it always."

I felt sad as the carriage pulled away and Amberwood disappeared from my view. I had spent eleven years at Wynfield Towers and another ten at the little house in Sussex, yet for some inexplicable reason, I thought of Amberwood as home.

There was yet another reason why I was reluctant to leave. Philip was not welcome at Thornton Manor and as long as I remained at Amberwood, I could still nurture the faint hope that he might come to see me and somehow manage to prove that he had nothing to do with Diana's death.

It was mid-afternoon when I arrived at Thornton Manor. Sir Evan was out, attending to estate business, Mrs. Cathcart informed me, and Vanessa had gone riding.

"In one of her moods, she was," the housekeeper said. "I saw her racing that poor pony across the meadow like the devil himself was after her."

I had hoped that Vanessa would be on hand to welcome me, but her tantrum and Mrs. Cathcart's chilly reception only served to remind me that nothing had changed at Thornton Manor, and despite Lord Fenwick's aspirations, I saw little hope of bringing any sunshine to these gloomy halls.

"Shall Colin take my bags up to my old room?" I asked, for he stood at the open door, my portmanteau and traveling bag in his hands.

Mrs. Cathcart's frosty reply took me by surprise. "You won't be using your old room, miss. Sir Evan has assigned you a room in the main wing of the house."

We followed her up the grand staircase to a large room overlooking the gardens. It obviously had been renovated and newly decorated, but it had none of the charm and warmth of my bedroom at Amberwood. I understood Mrs. Cathcart's attitude now. She had considered me a peer and now I was being elevated to a status that she did not think my position warranted. In truth, I would have to agree with her and I recalled Philip's words.

Maybe you think it would be nice to be the next Lady Thornton.

Good Lord, I thought. Is that what Mrs. Cathcart thinks? And Lady Thornton and Miss Hamilton? Do they all see me as a calculating woman who has connived my way into my employer's favor?

"I'll send someone to help you unpack," she said.

"That won't be necessary, Mrs. Cathcart. I've always unpacked for myself."

Having placed my bags in the room, Colin had disappeared and Mrs. Cathcart said, "I'll send Maggie. Otherwise Colin will only be distracting her from her other duties."

I was standing at the window contemplating the latest developments at Thornton Manor when Maggie knocked on the door. I didn't need her help, but Maggie's chattiness and warmth would be a welcome change from the icy reception I had just received.

"So good to have you back, miss," she said, and I breathed a sigh of relief. At least one person at Thornton Manor was glad to see me.

"We're all looking forward to the ball, miss. 'Course cook got her nose out of joint when she heard Sir Evan had hired a London chef to prepare the banquet." Maggie giggled. "Puffed herself up like a pouter pidgeon, she did." Opening my portmanteau, she mechanically began to place handkerchiefs and underwear in the bureau drawers. "They're saying Sir

Evan means to use Lord Fenwick's reception to announce his coming marriage."

My mouth must have hung open, for Maggie looked enormously pleased by my reaction and she nodded her head knowingly. "It's true, miss. Gladys, one of the upstairs maids, overheard him tell Lady Thornton. 'Course Lady Thornton took to her bed over it, but then Lady Thornton takes to her bed over most everything."

"Who—who is he planning to marry?" I asked haltingly.

"Gladys didn't hear the young lady's name, but it's probably Miss Polly Anderson, miss. Sir Evan almost married her once, but then he married Miss Diana Chase instead. The Chase property adjoined Thornton Manor, and of course Sir Evan wanted to acquire the land."

Polly Anderson, I thought. Yes. I recalled the name. I had addressed an invitation to a Miss Polly and her father, Colonel John Anderson.

I blushed to think that even for a moment I had considered the possibility that Sir Evan could consider his daughter's governess as a prospective bride. Philip, with his warped imagination, had planted the thought in my mind, but I had let it take root and grow, I admitted. And hadn't I done the same thing to Lord Wynfield and my own sainted mother?

It appears I have a habit of jumping to conclusions, I mused. Dear God, have I also jumped to conclusions about Philip? Lost in my own thoughts, I hadn't been listening to Maggie until I was startled out of my reverie by the word, *Gypsy*.

"What did you say?" I asked her sharply.

"I said, a Gypsy come to the back door asking for you, miss."

"What did she say?"

"I don't know, miss. Cook run her off. What do you suppose a Gypsy woman wanted with you?"

"I don't know," I answered truthfully.

The news disturbed me. Why hadn't Sonia communicated with me mentally, as before?

"I don't want nothin to do with no Gypsies, miss. They're touched by the devil. They cast spells and put curses on people. My mum told me when she was a girl, somebody set one of them on fire in the woods."

"That was a horrible thing to do," I said.

Maggie shuddered. "I know, miss, but that's the only way to kill a witch or a sorcerer."

I resented her rationalizing such a diabolical act. "They're human beings, Maggie. When they're cut, they bleed. And when they're set on fire, they die a horrible, agonizing death."

Sensing my disapproval, Maggie quickly changed the subject. "Some of these gowns are mussed, miss. I'll just take them downstairs and press them."

I didn't want to use the servants for my own personal needs. "That won't be necessary, Maggie. You have enough to do. I can press them myself," I answered, but she was eager to smooth my ruffled feathers.

"Don't give it another thought, miss. I have to press all Miss Hamilton's gowns. Guess I can do as much for you."

Before I could protest again, she had gathered up the offending gowns. "You'll be satisfied. I'm good with an iron," she said and smiled wickedly. " 'Course, sometimes Miss Hamilton's gowns get a little bit scorched, but that won't happen to none of yours, miss."

Left alone in the room, I smiled to myself. Evidently, I wasn't the only one who found Miss Hamilton a pain in the neck. My thoughts grew serious then. Why had Sonia come to Thornton Manor? Always before we had communicated with each other mentally. Why not now?

I would have to see her, I thought and what better time than right now. Sir Evan was out, Vanessa, too, for that matter. She was probably only sulking over some imagined slight, but I could use her absence as an excuse to get out of the house. If Mrs. Cathcart or anyone else questioned me about leaving, I could always say I was looking for Vanessa.

Changing quickly into my riding habit, I slipped quietly out of the house. No excuse was necessary, as I met no one on my way to the stable. I had the groom saddle Penelope and I rode off, not exactly sure where I was going, but hoping that sixth sense that had guided my footsteps before would not desert me now.

I gave Penelope her head and she took off at a fast pace, not in the direction of the forest, as I had assumed, but away from it. When I realized we were going toward the village, I pulled on the reins, but the mare would not stop.

Threatening to unseat me, the possessed animal raced over fields, digging up tufts of earth as her hooves pounded the soft ground. I hung on for dear life, knowing that if she threw me, I would surely break my neck.

The mare did not slow her pace until we were on the edge of town and then, as though free of her demons, she plodded along at a snail's pace down one narrow street after the other.

I was unfamiliar with the village of Thornton Wood, having only been to Philip's office and the fairground, but every town has its slums and these streets reminded me of the area I had stumbled upon in York when I'd been accosted by a bunch of drunken revelers spilling out of a pub.

Looking around at the houses, I noticed a woman peering out at me through a window. I urged Penelope on, but the mare came to a dead stop and the woman in the window opened the door and came running toward me.

Up close, her wrinkled chalk white face, rouged cheeks, and dyed red hair gave her a grotesque appearance. "Hello, dearie. Name's Pearl," she said. I dug my heels into Penelope's flanks, but the horse still would not budge.

"Come inside," she urged. "Sonia's gone into one of her trances, but she's been waiting for you, Miss St. Claire."

A creepy feeling washed over me and I gave the woman and the house a dubious glance. "Where is Rashev and the caravan?"

"One of the shopkeepers accused Rashev's woman of stealing, so they got out of town, but Sonia's staying with me. My clients," Pearl added with a patronizing smile, "find it amusing to have their fortunes told."

Common sense and my own strict upbringing told me not to go inside, but something even stronger made me dismount, tie Penelope to the hitching post, and follow the woman.

The small front room was gaudily furnished and the

red-globed lamp that hung in the window confirmed my suspicions as to the kind of house I was in. The woman led me through the parlour and back to the kitchen where Sonia lay on a cot.

Pearl spoke softly, "Here's Miss St. Claire, but take the potion first. I mixed it up like you told me."

Sonia acknowledged my presence with eyes that were full of pain. Empathizing with her, I said, "Don't try to talk. I'll wait until you feel better."

She drank the potion that Pearl gave her and a few minutes later, Sonia sat up and said, "I've been so worried about you."

Pearl discreetly left the room then, and I said, "Why did you come to Thornton Manor? You've always met me in the woods."

"Because I was afraid to go there. Rashev had to leave town. It's not safe for Gypsies to be found in Thornton Wood now. Keira, fool that she is, has turned the villagers against us again."

"But you're still here," I said.

She nodded. "I'm safe here and I must see this thing through. I've waited more than twenty years to avenge my brother's death. I'll not be cheated of it now that the truth is about to be revealed."

"I don't see what any of this has to do with your brother," I said.

"It has everything to do with him. God works in mysterious ways and the spirit world is not ours to fathom. The truth will be revealed through your eyes and ears."

"My eyes have seen nothing, except for a phantom whom you claim to be your brother's spirit, and I haven't seen him since I was lost in the maze," I added. "I hear voices, but I do not see the people who speak."

"All in good time," she said. "It requires enormous energy for those from the spirit world to materialize, but words once spoken remain in the atmosphere forever. Even the ungifted hear them from time to time. They attribute the sounds to the wind or some other natural force," she added with a shrug.

"As for Pasha, you are here. You are doing his bidding. He has no further need to appear to you," she explained.

"I'm tired, Sonia," I said. "What I hear at the house in the woods is very distressing. I think it concerns Lady Diana Thornton."

I didn't mention Philip. To put my suspicions into words would somehow confirm them, and I wasn't ready yet to do that.

She looked puzzled. "Let's reserve judgment until we're sure. All will be made clear, but I must warn you again. Be careful and trust no one. I saw another fire. This time flames consumed a large copper vat."

"What does it mean?" I questioned. "I've seen that copper vat, too."

"I don't know, but you must go back to the woods. You must learn more. Only then can you protect yourself against the Prince of Darkness."

Pearl came back into the kitchen then. She had removed her shawl, exposing plump bare arms and an enormous bosom barely covered by the low-cut purple gown she wore.

"Will you be up to telling fortunes tonight?" she asked, and Sonia nodded her head.

Just then a young girl came down the back stairs that led to the kitchen. Surprised by our presence, she halted abruptly and hung back in the shadow of the landing, but I had caught a glimpse of her. A small blond girl with a rosy complexion, she wore a night-gown and was barefoot.

Why, the child is no older than Vanessa, I thought.

Pearl turned angrily on the girl. "Get upstairs, Nellie. Dr. McAllister'll be here any minute. And don't be hiding under the bed, I don't want to have to drag you out."

Speechless, I felt my breath catch in my throat. The cad, I thought. Is there no end to his depravity?

Chapter Eighteen

Overcome with panic, I stood up.

"I must leave," I told Sonia.

"Promise me you'll go back to the woods," she pleaded, and grabbing me by the hand, she gazed deeply into my eyes.

"Yes, yes, I'll go," I said impatiently.

She held my hand in a tight grip. "Promise on your mother's grave."

"I promise on my mother's grave," I cried.

Anything to get out of here, I thought, for I would rather die than meet Philip face-to-face in this house.

"So long, dearie," Pearl said, giving me an impudent smile. "Come back when you have more time. Me and my girls'll teach you some tricks."

Her coarse laughter followed me out the door. I stood a moment, glancing frantically up and down the street, but I saw no sign of Philip, or anyone else for that matter.

A thick, pea-soup fog had gathered while I had been inside the house and it added to the wretched atmosphere that clung to this sordid part of town.

I mounted the mare and urged her on. I wanted to get out of Thornton Wood as fast as possible and without running into Philip McAllister.

Tears streamed down my cheeks, for I had fallen in love with him and now I knew it was Philip the Gypsy had warned me against.

Sadly, I faced the truth. He had been Diana Thornton's lover and may have taken her life, and now he was about to corrupt a child. The man was a pervert and a monster and I thought of the two missing girls in the village. What had he done to them?

Oh, why had he asked me to marry him? I wondered. Or had he only wanted to give me a false sense of security so I would be easier to seduce?

The fog was growing thicker and I asked the mare to increase her pace, but once outside the village, I hesitated. Cutting across open fields the way we had come would save time, but it would be dangerous in this weather.

Common sense told me to take the road, but it was growing late. I would soon be missed and where could I say I had been all this time?

Dropping the reins, I once again let the unseen hand that had guided the mare the first time take over.

Penelope headed for the open fields and I prayed that the mysterious spirit that had followed me since the day my mother died would guide us safely back to Thornton Manor.

Fog has a menace all its own and riding through the swirling mists, I felt I had stepped off the earth and was plunging through space.

I controlled my terror by remembering Sonia's words: *You are the key that can unlock a secret that has been hidden for many years.*

I am needed, I thought. Therefore I shall be protected, at least for now.

Over hills that rose like humps on a camel's back we raced. I could not see three feet in front of me, but Penelope never faltered and I felt like the horse's hooves had risen above the ground.

Suddenly an approaching light pierced the fog and a gruff voice shouted, "Who goes there?"

"I am Olivia St. Claire, governess at Thornton Manor," I answered.

The man approached and holding the lantern up to my face, said, "Thank God!" Then he shouted in a booming voice, "She's found. Tell Sir Evan the young lady's safe." He turned back to me then. "We've had a search party looking for you, miss. Easy it is to get lost in the fog."

I was grateful to the man for supplying me with an excuse. Conceivably, a rider could spend hours wandering around in circles on a day like this.

"You're safe and sound now, miss. I'll ride ahead and you follow my light," he said in a reassuring voice.

I wondered what he would have thought if I had told him I had been to the village and back again in less time than it took a two-horse coach to make it one way.

Sir Evan met me at the stable. His riding clothes were mud-splattered and there was a cut over his eye.

"Thank God you're safe," he said, rushing up and lifting me out of the saddle.

"Your eye," I said. "What happened?"

He wiped the blood away with his hand. "It's nothing. I took a fall out there, but you, Olivia. How did you ever find your way home in this fog?"

"I don't know," I answered honestly. "Penelope just seemed to know the way."

"Come into the house," he said, grasping my arm and tucking it inside his. "You must get out of those damp clothes and rest. We'll discuss this later."

I was grateful for his concern and I felt guilty that he had taken a fall because of me.

"You're the one who's hurt," I said. "I'm so sorry to have caused all this trouble."

"It's all Vanessa's fault," he said irritably. "The groom told me you went to look for her."

Good Lord, I thought. I had almost forgotten about the child.

"Is Vanessa all right?" I asked.

"Of course. She was home long before the fog gathered but she's going to be punished for this."

I had used Vanessa as an excuse and I couldn't let the child be punished on my account.

"Please, Sir Evan. Don't punish her. The fog was not her fault and I don't want my first day back to be an unpleasant one for Vanessa."

"Very well," he said. "But she's a lucky girl to have you for her champion."

We were walking toward the house and the fog was still thick, so I couldn't see his face when he said, "I still don't see how that horse ever found her way back. She's not taken out enough to know her way around

241

the grounds; the grooms exercise her in the paddock.

Did he suspect I had been with someone? Philip, perhaps?

Maggie informed me that Mrs. Cathcart had sent her up to help me dress for dinner.

"Sir Evan's orders," she added. "Guess that didn't set so well with Mrs. Cathcart, the old pea-hen."

I was relaxing in a tub of hot water brought up by two scullery maids from the kitchen. Too depressed to carry on a conversation, I ignored Maggie's words. My mind was focused on only one thing, Philip's treachery.

I should have known better than to fall in love with him, I told myself.

Philip was everything my mother had warned me against in a man. He was sensual, earthy, and he discussed things no gentleman would ever bring up in the presence of a lady. And yet, I mused, all those things had been part and parcel of the appeal he had held for me.

"I hung your pressed gowns in the wardrobe, miss. Which one should I lay out?"

"None of those, Maggie," I answered. "Thornton Manor isn't as formal as Amberwood. There's a lilac silk with a lace collar in the back of the wardrobe. I made it myself on the sewing machine when I was at Amberwood. That one will do for tonight."

I had found the material in the sewing room when I was stitching up my knickerbockers and Nanny had said I could make a dress out of it.

"Gawd almighty, miss. You can't wear that," she said.

The dress was plain, but the material was of good quality and I had been taught to sew by my mother.

"Why not?" I asked, a little miffed.

"Oh, miss. You can't wear lilac," she cried. "Sir Evan don't allow nobody at Thornton Manor to wear that color. It was his first wife's favorite, you know, and Sir Evan can't bear to look at it. Why, Mrs. Cathcart don't even allow lilacs to be brought into the house. That was her favorite flower," she added.

The poor man, still grieving after all these years. My thoughts turned to Philip then. The cad, he couldn't begin to comprehend a love like that.

"How about this one?" Maggie said, holding up a dainty pink gown that Miss O'Shay had made for me.

"Fine," I answered.

I didn't care what I wore. I hated the thought of dining with the Thorntons, but I couldn't insult Sir Evan. He'd been so kind and he'd requested that I join the family for meals.

Maggie wanted to dress my hair, but I declined.

"It's my job," she said and I was afraid I had hurt her feelings.

"You'll have to make allowances for me, Maggie. I'm not used to being waited on. After all, I'm an employee here the same as you," I told her.

"Oh no, miss, not the same as me. You're a refined, educated lady and I can't read or write."

"Would you like to learn?" I asked.

"Oh yes, miss."

"Then I shall teach you. It'll be my way of repaying you for all the nice things you do for me."

She blushed. "Pressing clothes and fixin' hair ain't nothin', but I'll take you up on your offer, miss."

Maggie wound tiny pink rosebuds into my hair and I was reminded of the day I had gone to the fair with Philip and he had bought a pink rose and placed it in my hair.

I had worn this same gown that day, I recalled, and the thought made me want to change it, but Maggie had gone to too much trouble placing the roses in my hair.

I thought about that day, though, as I went downstairs. Philip had been so attentive and we had had such a wonderful time.

I think I had started falling in love with him then and I could still taste the sweetness of his good-bye kiss. No man had ever kissed me before, but now a memory that should have been beautiful was tainted.

So deep had I been in reminiscence that I hadn't even seen Vanessa standing at the foot of the stairs. Her voice startled me and I almost tripped.

"Oh miss, I'm so sorry you got lost because of me."

I held tightly to the bannister and said, "It wasn't your fault, Vanessa."

"Yes, it was. I was mad and now I can't even remember why. I don't know what gets into me sometimes. One of my nursemaids used to say I had the devil in me."

"That's nonsense," I said.

"No, it's not. Some people are possessed by the devil."

"Well, you're not," I said.

She gave me a strange look. "I hope you're right. I don't want to be. Maybe you'll drive my devil out," she said. "Like what's-her-name did."

"What are you talking about?"

"You know, John-Vi-Ev."

She pronounced the French name in English syllables.

"You mean Genevieve, Lady Violette's governess?"

"That's right. Everybody says *dear, sweet* Lady Violette was a hellion, but her governess turned her into a perfect little lady. Maybe you'll turn me into a perfect little lady and then my father will love me, too," she said wistfully.

I linked her arm in mine. "Your father loves you dearly, Vanessa, but he doesn't always approve of some of the things you do."

Ever the chameleon, she changed colours right before my eyes.

"Well, I don't always approve of some of things he does either, so there. And don't try to change me, because I don't want to be just another *shrinking violet,*" she declared, emphasizing the last two words and laughing hysterically at her own joke.

Unlinking arms, she walked ahead of me into the dining room.

Will I ever understand her? I thought, doubting if either my mother or the legendary Genevieve could have handled Vanessa.

Perhaps it would be best if I went back to London. Let Vanessa's new stepmother contend with her, I told myself. I wasn't really helping the girl and I wanted to get as far away from Philip as possible.

Swear on your mother's grave, Sonia had said, and I had promised.

I also had promised to help Sir Evan with Lord Fenwick's reception, I reminded myself.

I'd go to the house in the woods one more time, and

whether or not Sonia was satisfied, I'd leave as soon as the reception was over, I decided.

Sir Evan rushed up to me as I entered the dining room.

"You look lovely, my dear, and none the worse for your adventure," he said gallantly.

The cut above his brow gave him a dashing, masculine look and mitigated the effect of his almost too perfect aristocratic features.

The others were already seated at the table and Farnsworth pulled out chairs for Vanessa and myself. I meant to sit on the end this time, directly across from Miss Hamilton, but once again Sir Evan intervened.

"Sit here, Olivia," he said, indicating the chair to his right and directly across from Lady Thornton.

"Good evening," I said before taking my place.

Lady Thornton's perpetually rigid mouth barely opened as she murmured, "Good evening, Miss St. Claire."

"We heard you were lost in the fog. That must have been a frightening experience," Miss Hamilton said.

Sir Evan looked at me and smiled. "As a matter of fact, it was a most unusual experience. The horse brought her home and the one she was riding has only been out of the paddock a few times. My own horse, who should know these grounds like he knows his stall, managed to step in a rut and throw me."

"Perhaps someone or something was guiding the horse Miss St. Claire was riding," Lady Thornton said, and again, her eyes riveted themselves to my birthmark.

"You mean like a guardian angel?" Sir Evan asked.

"Or something else supernatural," his mother answered.

Sir Evan gave me a warm smile. "Well, whatever it was, we're certainly grateful. The replies to our invitations are starting to come in—fifty already this morning," he announced, making a smooth transition to a more pleasant subject.

Vanessa wasn't ready to drop the old one, though, and she said, "Maybe Miss St. Claire put a hex on the horse."

"Don't talk nonsense," her father said abruptly.

"Cook says people with special signs can hex animals and put spells on people," Vanessa replied with a laugh.

"That will do, Vanessa," Lady Thornton said, her voice shaking with some repressed emotion.

I couldn't tell if it was anger or fear or a combination of both.

"Leave the table," her father ordered. "Why do you have to spoil every pleasant occasion?"

Her face a storm cloud, Vanessa stood up and said, "I was only poking fun at cook's superstitions. Miss St. Claire doesn't need magic. Some man always comes along and helps her out." The last was spoken with a sarcastic look in her father's direction.

"Like when I lost her in Amberwood's maze," she continued. "Dr. McAllister brought her home and I heard her tell him a shepherd showed her the way out."

Vanessa ran out of the room then. Sir Evan looked perplexed and angry, but both Lady Thornton and Miss Hamilton looked absolutely terrified.

* * *

Most of my time for the next several weeks was taken up with plans for the reception. Vanessa and I were not able to meet very often and I was certain she resented it, a fact that added to my guilt when Sir Evan was called away one afternoon and I sneaked out of the house to go to the woods. I should have spent the time with Vanessa, but I had promised Sonia over two weeks ago that I would take a trip to the little house in the woods.

I hadn't told Sonia it would be my last visit, but now that I was sure these conversations were between Philip and Diana Thornton, I didn't want to hear them.

Let Sonia's brother use her as his medium, I thought. She was a more appropriate channel than I was anyhow.

Maybe the house will have disappeared and I'll be off the hook, I mused as I climbed the hill and followed the now-familiar jagged path to the clearing.

The house was still there, though, and I braced myself for what I was about to hear. But never in the farthermost reaches of my imagination could I have prepared myself for the shock I was about to receive.

From the outside, the cottage looked exactly the same. But inside, it felt different. A chilliness I had never noticed before seemed to permeate the air. It was a strange kind of cold, and almost at once I associated it with the feeling I had experienced in Sonia's tent the day of the fair—the day she had used the crystal ball, and we had both felt a presence join us.

Come away with me, the man said.

I jerked my head around, almost expecting to see him standing over by the cot.

We'll go to America. We'll have no past, just the present and whatever future we dare to make.

Oh, my darling. Aren't you happy with me?

I'm happy when I'm with you, but what about all the other times when you're with him? I go crazy thinking about you then. I imagine you in bed with him. Does he do this? he asked and there was a long pause.

My foolish heart broke all over again and jealousy became a physical ache that twisted in my chest like a knife.

The woman spoke in a voice husky with passion. *Nobody has ever loved me the way you do.*

Say you'll come to America with me, he pleaded. *We'll be happy. I'll make something of myself, you'll see. There are plenty of opportunities there. Any man can get rich and I'll work my fingers to the bone for you.*

All the passion suddenly left him and in a voice so low I had to strain my ears to hear him, he said, *Say you'll come because I can't go on like this. I'm leaving with you or without you, my love.*

Oh my darling, forgive me. I'll come with you, but don't ever leave me. I can't live without you, Pasha.

Nor I without you, Violette.

I gasped. Pasha and Violette, not Philip and Diana!

The room seemed suddenly charged with electricity and my breath caught in my throat as the faint outlines of two figures slowly took shape and materialized before my eyes.

He was dark and handsome with curly black hair that reached to the nape of his neck and I recognized him immediately as the cab driver and the cowl-draped shepherd. Only this time, he was naked and his muscular young body held his lover in a passionate embrace.

They parted and the fair-skinned young woman looked straight at me with unseeing eyes. Violette Thornton was even more beautiful than her portrait. She, too, was naked and her pearly white skin looked even paler next to the body of her Gypsy lover.

Long silver-blond hair hung to her waist and framed a face of exquisite, ethereal beauty.

You meant it. You won't change your mind, he said.

She reached up and kissed him.

No, Pasha. I can face anything with you, but I can't face losing you.

You won't ever be sorry, he said, picking up his clothes from the floor and putting them on.

Her clothes lay in a pile at the foot of the cot and she, too, began to dress.

Go quickly. You first, she said, kissing him again.

He ran to the door and blew her a kiss. *Til Thursday,* he intoned.

When he had gone, she finished dressing. I had hardly recovered from the shock of finding out who these people really were when someone knocked at the door and Violette hurried to answer it.

How did you know where I was? she asked, and the other person, whom I could not see, murmured an answer.

Violette held the door open and said, "Come in, Genevieve."

The young governess stepped inside and pushing her hood back, exposed her face.

She was not as beautiful as her pupil, but nevertheless Genevieve's warm brown eyes and generous mouth mirrored the beauty of her soul.

Though time had taken away her youth and the dewy freshness of her complexion, and the years had dusted her dark hair with silver, I would have recognized my mother anywhere.

Genevieve Piaf and Jenny St. Claire were one and the same person.

Chapter Nineteen

I wanted to rush forward and embrace this young woman who had become my mother, but although I could see her, I knew that she could not see me.

These were only brief vignettes from the past, and I could not break the barrier that separated their time from my own.

Gathering Violette's hands in hers, Genevieve frowned and said, *What are you thinking of? What you are doing is dangerous. If Sir Evan should find out—*

Oh, Genevieve don't scold. I love Pasha and I'm going to America with him.

Ever practical, my youthful mother answered, *Think, Violette. How will you live?*

Pasha will succeed. I know he will.

He's a shepherd. He has no money and neither do you.

Pasha was destined to become his people's leader. He was chosen as a child to be king, but he gave it all up for me. That's why he's a shepherd. There's no place for a Gypsy over here, but in America things will be different.

Oh Violette, you're building castles in the air.

And what if I am? If we are poor, I won't even care. Just so long as Pasha and I are together.

She searched Genevieve's face for some sign of compassion and then lowering her eyes, Violette said, *When you fall in love, Genevieve, then you'll understand.*

And what of honour? You married Sir Evan Thornton.

The question coming from the lips of the pretty, dark-haired girl was so typical of the mother I had known that tears welled up in my eyes.

Yes, I thought. Mama would think of honour, for it was ingrained in her nature and she had ingrained it in mine. She could no more condone what Violette was about to do then I could condone Philip's callous manipulation of a child, prostitute or not.

And so nothing had changed. Philip McAllister was still a man without honour and that I could never accept.

The two young women in front of me stared for a long time into each other's eyes and then Violette spoke.

Dear Genevieve, you've been my mentor, my teacher, and my friend. Don't desert me now.

I could never desert you, Violette.

Then hear me out. There's something else you should know.

A faint rustle outside the window alerted me to the

253

fact that someone was out there listening.

I wanted to cry out, to warn them, but I knew it was useless. I could not reach back and alter the events of the past.

Suddenly, all motion stopped and like mechanical dolls, the two figures froze in place. Violette's unblinking eyes still held within them a plea for understanding and Genevieve's slightly parted lips and anxious expression showed her concern.

The figures wavered for a moment and then slowly began to fade. Once again the warmth of a summer's day flooded the room and I stood there, unable, myself, to move. I mentally willed my mother to come back, to speak to me, but the young girl she once had been was gone and the frail, hollow-cheeked woman I had loved lay buried on a windswept hillside in Sussex.

Choking back a sob, I ran outside. At the edge of the clearing, I turned and looked back. The house and the heather were gone and in their place lay a parched and barren field.

Slowly I walked down the jagged path and when I reached the bottom of the hill, I sat down under the big tree where I'd first heard Pasha and Violette as children. More confused now than ever, I leaned back and rested my head against the trunk.

Nanny had said my mother disappeared after Violette's death. Where had she gone? And who was my father?

She had not known him while Lady Violette was alive. That much was clear, for I recalled Violette's words.

The House in Thornton Wood

When you fall in love, Genevieve, then you'll understand.

Lady Violette had lived for love, but my mother had lived by a strict moral code. She had been married to my father, of that I was certain, but who was he? And why had my mother been found alone and frightened on a country road with me in her arms?

All will be made clear. Sonia had said.

But how could that be accomplished now? The house in Thornton Wood had completely disappeared, almost as if the final chapter had been written, but it couldn't have been. Too many unanswered questions remained, not the least of which was why I was chosen to be the medium in the first place.

I got back to Thornton Manor just in time for Vanessa's lesson and hurried upstairs to change my clothes.

No one was in the corridor, so I was startled when Miss Hamilton stepped out of the shadows. She stood in front of me, barring my path and said, "You're up and out early, Miss St. Claire."

"I'm an early riser," I said.

Her small snakelike eyes took in my cycling clothes. "Isn't your attire a little unconventional for a governess?"

"I don't wear it in the classroom," I said, "and, if you'll excuse me, I was just about to change."

She blocked my way. "I'm acquainted with Mrs. Truesdale, you know."

"Yes, I believe you mentioned that you had gone to school with her."

"I wrote her a letter and asked her why she had sent you to Thornton Manor. She told me a messenger had advised her that Sir Evan required the services of a governess."

"That's right," I said.

A malicious smirk played at the corners of her mouth. "Sir Evan did not send that messenger, but you did, didn't you?"

"Certainly not."

"You didn't see a shepherd, either," she insisted. "You were trying to frighten Lady Thornton, weren't you?" The tip of her tongue darted out of her mouth and she flicked it nervously over her lips.

Once again, I was reminded of a serpent, and pushing past her, I said, "I'm sorry, I have to get ready for class."

"I don't know how you've gotten your information," she called after me, "but I know what you're up to and it won't work. You can frighten Lady Thornton, but you can't frighten me."

After our encounter in the hall, Miss Hamilton and I only spoke out of necessity. Evidently, she thought I had some ulterior motive for coming to Thornton Manor, but I was beyond caring what she thought. As soon as Lord Fenwick's reception was over, I was leaving Thornton Wood forever.

The reception and ball promised to be a gala event. Twelve Londoners and fifty more guests from Thornton Wood, York, and other surrounding towns had accepted Sir Evan's invitation to honour one of England's most respected subjects.

Those from London would arrive Friday afternoon and stay at Thornton Manor until Sunday. Other guests would be housed overnight at Amberwood after the ball and Sir Evan had even reopened his late wife's home on the outskirts of Thornton Wood in case it should be needed.

A London chef had been engaged and he and his staff were due to arrive several days ahead of time to arrange the kitchen to their liking; news of which caused Thornton Manor's cook to have a cat fit, according to Maggie.

Sir Evan was deeply grateful to me for my assistance and he treated me with such kindness that I hadn't the heart to tell him I had decided to leave.

He, as a matter of fact, spoke like my tenure would continue on a permanent basis.

"Next year we shall spend the winter in London," he said as we worked together assigning guests to the different houses. "I've been thinking about purchasing a townhouse there. Vanessa will be coming out in four years and it would be advantageous to set up residence beforehand. Would you like that, Olivia? We can attend the opera and the ballet. It would expose Vanessa to some culture. That would be a good idea, don't you think?"

I wondered what his wife would think of his plan to include me in attending these cultural events, but since his engagement had not yet been announced, I could only say, "I should enjoy it very much, Sir Evan."

I was busy, but not a day went by that I didn't think of Philip. I knew I should forget him, but little incidents kept reminding me of him.

Every time I looked at the rose garden, I thought of the day Philip had pinned a rose in my hair. He had given me my first kiss and I relived that moment over and over in my mind.

I thought how much his patients respected him and how kind he'd been to the Donovan family. Even the things that used to annoy me about him—his outspoken manner and ungentlemanly disregard for the proprieties—didn't seem so bad, in retrospect.

I could overlook the rumors about Diana Thornton. After all, they were only rumors, but I had seen little rosy-cheeked Nellie with my own eyes and I had to ask myself, what kind of man would force himself on a child?

I thought about Sonia and I was sorry that I hadn't been able to help her. I wanted to tell her that the voices belonged to Pasha and Violette and that they were planning to run away together.

I wanted to let Sonia know that the little house in the woods had disappeared and whatever power I had been given to look into the past had disappeared with it.

I wanted to say good-bye and tell her I was leaving Thornton Wood, but Sonia would no longer meet me in the forest, and I could not bring myself to go back to Pearl's.

I supposed I should always wonder about my mother's secret and why she had carried it to her grave. But, knowing Mama, I could only conclude that her silence was meant to protect me.

I treasured the little cross and chain, first because it had belonged to my mother and second because it had been given to me by a woman who had been very dear to us both.

Whenever I got the chance, I visited Nanny and always I turned the conversation around to Genevieve. I loved to hear Nanny tell about my mother when she was young and I longed to tell her who I really was, but of course I couldn't.

Nanny told me that Genevieve had confided that before coming to England, she had entered the novitiate of Notre Dame de Nemours, a French order of nuns. However, before she could take her vows, the government, which was violently anti-clerical, had closed down all the convents and dispersed their members.

I was not surprised to hear this, for my mother had been a deeply religious woman. It also helped me to understand her contemplative spirit and the somewhat puritanical views she held on relations between men and women.

Poor Mama, I thought, she wanted so much to see me marry an upright gentleman of high moral standards and I have fallen in love with a scoundrel.

Consequently, I would remain a spinster for I could never marry without love and unfortunately I had fallen in love with a man I could never marry.

In the weeks that followed, Vanessa's studies and my work with Sir Evan kept me busy and confined to Thornton Manor. I had very little contact with Lady Thornton, who spent most of her time in her room, and on the rare occasions when she did put in an appearance, acted like she was under sedation.

The ever-solicitous Miss Hamilton was always by her ladyship's side, so much so, in fact, that they might have been joined at the hip like a pair of mismatched Siamese twins.

The situation failed to bother me, though, for my relationship with Vanessa had improved to a remarkable degree. The rapport that I had always hoped to attain with this misunderstood, mercurial child suddenly seemed within my reach and I thought of Genevieve and Violette.

Time passed quickly and in a matter of days, guests would be arriving for the reception. Very soon now, I would be leaving Thornton Wood and Philip McAllister forever, I mused.

"You look pensive," Sir Evan observed.

We had been working together in his study and I had not realized he had been watching me.

"You're not nervous about your part in the reception, are you?" he asked.

I supposed I should have been, but my other problems had taken precedence.

"I just want to do well and justify your faith in me," I replied.

"Then you have absolutely nothing to worry about. You'll outshine every woman there and I shall be very proud of you."

I thought it a strange thing to say, considering the fact that his future bride would be attending the reception.

He studied me a moment and then said, "Lord Fenwick tells me you visit Nanny Grey."

"Yes. I'm very fond of Nanny."

"Still seeing McAllister?" he asked.

The question took me by surprise. Did he think I went to Amberwood to see Philip?

"No. I won't be seeing Dr. McAllister anymore," I answered.

He looked relieved. "A wise decision and I hope what I am about to say won't upset you, but Lord Fenwick has asked me to invite McAllister. I can't very well

refuse his request, since it *is* his lordship's reception,"
he said with a scowl.

I tried to act casual. "Shall I address an invitation to
Dr. McAllister, then?"

"That won't be necessary," he replied. "I sent one of
the servants to his office with a verbal invitation this
morning." Then he smirked and added with disgust,
"A gentleman would consider such an invitation in-
sulting, but McAllister showed his ignorance by accepting."

So I would see Philip McAllister once again, I
thought. The prospect was unnerving, but feeling Sir
Evan's eyes upon me, I did my best to hide my anxiety.

That night, alone in my room, I thought about the ball
and a feeling of exhilaration and triumph overrode my
apprehension. Philip would see me looking my best
and not as a governess, but in a position of honor as
Sir Evan's hostess.

I would be beautiful and desirable and completely
beyond the reach of a womanizing country doctor. I
played out a scene in my mind. Should he ask me to
dance, I would not refuse, for it would be a breach of
etiquette to do so.

The orchestra would play a waltz and Philip would
take me in his arms for the very last time.

I'm going back to London, I would say.

He would be shocked and perhaps ask me why.

I would tell him I preferred the hustle and bustle of
city life, and, smiling gaily, I would add, *There's quite
a demand there for social secretaries and one gets to
meet so many important people that way.*

Regret for all the things that might have been would

fall like a shadow across his face and he would know that I had never really taken him seriously.

A pinging sound caught my attention and I sat up and listened. Someone has thrown a stone at the window, I thought, and raising it, I peered down into the garden.

A hooded figure stepped out of the shadows, and I drew back. It looked up and waved an arm, beckoning me down.

Consumed by an uncontrollable urge, I left the window open and throwing a shawl over my nightgown, I stepped out of the room.

The gaslights in the corridor had been extinguished and I had to feel my way down its length. When I reached the staircase, though, I was relieved to see that the lamp on the newell post still burned.

It cast shadows on the walls, and I almost turned and ran back upstairs again. Suppose the figure in the garden was not Pasha's spirit, but someone else wearing a cloak and hood?

No, it must be Pasha, I thought, for why else would I have felt such a strong impulse to follow the summons?

Hurrying through the hall to the dark conservatory, I felt for the French doors that would lead me outside to the gardens.

My heart was beating wildly. What did the spirit want of me now?

Slipping outside, I felt the cool night air on my face. A full moon shone down on the flagstone walkways and my eyes, more accustomed to the darkness now, darted around as I tried to get my bearings.

My bedroom overlooked a stone bench, and spotting it, I left the path and picked my way over the damp grass in my thin night slippers. Turning around, I gazed up at my open window. This was the spot, but where was the spirit?

I heard a faint, rustling noise and suddenly a human hand reached out of the shadows and clutched mine.

"Don't scream," a familiar voice said, and my startled eyes stared into a face partially concealed by a hood.

It fell back and I cried out, "Sonia! I thought you were Pasha's spirit."

She grasped my hands eagerly. "Why? Has he been in communication with you?"

"No, I think the connection is broken," I answered.

Knowing this would distress her, I drew her over to the bench and said, "Sit down and I'll tell you everything that has happened."

When I had finished, she wiped tears from her eyes. "I always suspected it was Lady Violette. She was beautiful and spoiled and she destroyed my Pasha. He was destined to be a king, and because of her, he turned himself into a lowly shepherd." She gazed sadly down at her feet.

"She loved him, Sonia." I said, trying to explain his behaviour.

"Then why didn't they leave and go to America?"

"I don't know."

Her eyes widened. "Maybe Lady Violette changed her mind. Maybe she broke Pasha's heart and he did this to himself."

"I don't know, but I can't help you anymore. I'm leaving Thornton Wood and going back to London."

"No, you can't. It isn't finished yet. I have to know what happened."

"But don't you understand? I can no longer see the house. It disappeared after the last vision."

"Then the house is no longer useful," she said, and finished with her stock phrase, "All will be made clear."

"Perhaps," I said, humoring her.

Pulling the hood over her head again, she looked up at the sky and said, "Dawn will be breaking soon. I must get back. I didn't come before because we were quarantined."

"Quarantined?"

"Dr. McAllister quarantined the house," she answered. "No one could leave and no one could enter. Pearl was furious. She said it would ruin her business."

"But why was the house quarantined?"

"You remember Nellie, the girl who came downstairs when you were there?"

"Yes, I certainly do."

"She's dead," Sonia said in a matter-of-fact tone.

I gasped. "But Nellie was only a child."

She nodded. "That was the problem. Nellie came down with a red rash the day you were there. Pearl had sent for the doctor and when he examined her, he said she had typhoid. Dr. McAllister put a quarantine sign on the door and isolated all of us. Poor Nellie got worse and a couple of days later, she died."

Stunned, I stared back at her. I had completely misjudged Philip. He had gone to Pearl's house in the capacity of physician, not client.

Chapter Twenty

Slipping back inside the house, I closed the French doors and leaned against them.

Sonia's story had completely exonerated Philip and I felt ashamed that I had been so ready to condemn him. I had been wrong about Diana Thornton, too, and now I was certain that Philip had been telling me the truth all along.

He had been her physician, not her lover, and my suspicious mind had accused him of all kinds of despicable crimes, even murder.

My face burned remembering the way I had twisted poor Pasha's words and convinced myself they were Philip's. Suspicion, I thought, works its insidious way into the very soul of those afflicted with it.

Consumed with remorse, but at the same time gloriously happy, I cried tears of joy. Philip was innocent.

The man I loved was good and kind. And I, like a fool, had lost him, I suddenly realized.

But I can get him back, I told myself. Philip's angry with me now, and he has every right to be, but he's coming to the reception and surely in that romantic setting, love will triumph.

Once again I imagined us on the dance floor in Thornton Manor's ballroom.

Only this time I saw myself looking into his eyes and saying, *I'm sorry I misjudged you, Philip. Can you forgive me?*

He'd be gruff at first, but then he'd smile and tell me he was glad I'd finally come to my senses.

We'd slip away from the crowd and he'd ask me to marry him again and this time I'd say yes.

Encouraged by my fantasy, my spirits lifted and I walked confidently out of the dark conservatory and into the hall.

Feeling like my feet had wings, I fairly floated up the dimly lit staircase. Once again, shadows danced on the wall, but the eerie old house held no Oterror for me now. I was too happy to know fear.

Once in my room, I snuggled down in the deep feather bed and dreamed rosy dreams about the future. I felt sorry for Sonia, but I preferred to be finished with the past, my own as well as those whose tangled lives I had unwittingly been made privy to.

The choice, however, was not mine to make, as I would soon come to learn.

The London chef, who turned out to be French, and his staff arrived the following day. Monsieur Claude spoke very little English. However, I suspected him of using this handicap to his own advantage.

He set about reorganizing everything in the kitchen and when cook protested, he gave her a Gallic shrug and pretended he did not understand.

I don't know what I should have done without Mrs. Cathcart, who handled the situation with her customary aplomb. Somehow she managed to soothe cook's ruffled feathers and with her firm, professional manner she kept Monsieur Claude in line, as well.

When the London guests arrived, Sir Evan insisted that I be at his side and I was introduced as, "Miss St. Claire, my daughter's governess."

I smiled and greeted each guest in what I hoped was an acceptable manner. I was curious, though, about only one guest and when I met her, I was surprised.

I had pictured Polly Anderson as being blond, elegantly tall, and, of course, beautiful. She would be poised, maybe even haughty, I thought, a sort of ice princess who would complement Sir Evan's own aristocratic good looks. So I was completely taken aback when I was introduced to her. Miss Anderson was blond, and that turned out to be the only thing the young lady had in common with my mental image.

Almost childishly small, she had a sweet face that was deceptively youthful. However, on closer inspection I could see that she was in her late twenties.

Her age automatically labeled her a spinster and she wore the label with a self-conscious, almost apologetic air. Her widowed father, a tall, robust man of military bearing, stood behind her and I was reminded of a sparrow cringing in the shadow of an eagle.

"So nice to meet you, Miss St. Claire," she said.

Her hand in mine was cold and I had the outlandish notion that she was on the verge of curtsying to me.

How would she ever cope with Vanessa, I thought; or with Sir Evan, for his mood swings were as unpredictable as his daughter's. And then there was the eccentric Lady Thornton and her shadow, the obnoxious Miss Hamilton . . .

Colonel Anderson stepped forward then and smiling broadly said, "How young and pretty you are, my dear. Vanessa is a lucky little girl. Poor Polly's governess was rather a dragon." He laughed and turned to his daughter. "A formidable woman was Miss Krause, aye Polly?"

"I was terrified of her," she answered weakly.

As I am terrified *for* you, Miss Polly Anderson, I mused, looking down on this frail, insecure woman who was slated to be Sir Evan Thornton's fourth wife.

Somewhere in the back of my mind, Vanessa's singsong voice came back to me.

My father's had three wives and all of them have died. Wouldn't you say a fourth wife would be taking a risk?

After the London guests had been shown to their rooms, I put the servants to work setting up chairs in the small gallery next to the dining room. Sir Evan had engaged a violinist from York for this evening's after-dinner entertainment.

Tomorrow night the reception and ball would be held and guests from Thornton Wood and surrounding towns would arrive. The evening was scheduled to end with a magnificent display of fireworks, and on Sunday afternoon the overnight guests would depart.

I was looking forward to the festivities, but I was looking forward more to seeing Philip and straightening out the mess I had so foolishly made of our relationship.

I checked with Mrs. Cathcart and was relieved to hear that all was going well in the kitchen. Then, glancing in the dining room, I saw that the butler was overseeing a group of young maids who were busily engaged in setting the long banquet table for this evening's dinner.

Hostessing a social event of this magnitude was an awesome responsibility for someone of my inexperience, but everything was moving like clockwork under Farnsworth and Mrs. Cathcart's able direction.

A false sense of security made me smile to myself. All was in order. I was young. I was in love and my intuition told me that tomorrow night would probably be the most exciting night of my life.

For the ball, I would be wearing an elegant white satin gown trimmed with red roses, but this evening I had thought to wear the simpler red velvet gown that had been copied from the one my mother had made.

I was only an acting hostess and I didn't want to appear pretentious and foolish before Sir Evan's guests, but an hour before it was time to dress, a servant delivered a package to my room. Inside was a black lace shawl and pinned to it was a note from Sir Evan.

Please wear this tonight with your yellow satin gown. The shawl will complement the gown and you will complement them both. Evan Thornton

The handmade lace shawl was exquisite and certainly expensive. Both the gift and the fact that he even recalled the gown Miss O'Shay had made so many months ago disturbed me, but I told myself Sir Evan was a complex, erratic man who was given to bursts of extreme generosity.

Then, too, I supposed this was his way of showing gratitude for my help with the reception. I wished he hadn't, though. The shawl was beautiful, but the gown was a little too flamboyant for my taste and I felt over-dressed and a little self-conscious as I hurried down-stairs.

Entering the drawing room, I was relieved to see that I was the first to arrive.

"You take your duties very seriously, don't you, my dear?"

Startled, I looked around as Sir Evan rose up from a large wing chair in a corner of the room.

"You surprised me. I didn't think anyone was here."

"I'm sorry. I just wanted to compliment you on your punctuality. You make a perfect hostess, Olivia," he said, coming closer and standing beside me. "My late wife was never on time, a serious breach of etiquette for a hostess. Wouldn't you say?"

"I don't know," I stammered. "Perhaps she was very busy and time got away from her."

He smiled. "Diplomatic, too, and beautiful, I might add. Do you like the shawl?"

"It's very handsome. Too handsome really, Sir Evan, You shouldn't have . . ."

He waved his hand. "Nonsense. Nothing is too hand-some for you, Olivia. But tell me, are you enjoying yourself?"

"Oh, yes."

"You've made quite a favorable impression on our

London guests. Colonel Anderson and Miss Polly find you charming."

Blushing, I answered, "That's very nice of them. Miss Polly Anderson is a very sweet person."

"Yes, and her father is very influential in diplomatic circles, but that is no longer of importance to me. An accomplished and charming wife can be an asset by herself."

He paused for a moment and then added, "I'm a man of some means and importance. In time I shall probably come into a considerable fortune and I want an heir to carry on the Thornton name. That, coupled with sincere affection, is not a bad basis for marriage. Don't you agree?"

I didn't know why he was telling me all this, but I nodded agreeably.

"Then you understand my sentiments."

"Yes, of course."

"And how do you feel about it, Olivia?"

Surely, he was not asking me for advice, I thought, but perhaps because of Vanessa . . .

"Vanessa may be a little difficult at first," I said. "I will talk to her though and do my best to make her understand."

"You will win her over, but don't say anything about this for now," he added, as guests began entering the room.

I gave him a reassuring nod.

Little Miss Polly and Sir Evan were mismatched in my opinion, but it certainly wasn't my place to say so.

Vanessa had been given permission to dine with the family and their guests this evening, but she would not be allowed to attend the reception and ball tomorrow night.

She looked deceptively sweet in an ankle-length pink taffeta dress with draped overskirt over four tiers of ruffles. Simulating a bustle, the overskirt was caught up in the back and tied with a bow.

Her hair, always a problem, had been tamed for the time being, but I didn't doubt it would soon spring back to life and frizz up like spun sugar on a stick.

Lady Thornton and Miss Hamilton had entered the drawing room with Vanessa and I was relieved to see that Vanessa was staying close by her grandmother's side. My little sharp-tongued pupil did not act up when she was in Lady Thornton's company, I had noticed, and I attributed this to the fact that Lady Thornton's love for her granddaughter appeared to be unconditional.

Most of the guests were people of Lord Fenwick's age, and if they thought it unusual that Sir Evan's mother had relinquished her role of hostess in her son's home to a governess, they were too polite to show surprise.

Aperitifs were served in the drawing room, and guests engaged in conversation for about twenty minutes before Farnsworth appeared and, with a nod of his head, informed Sir Evan that dinner was ready to be served.

Sir Evan took Miss Polly into dinner, as was to be expected, but I thought it odd that he had practically ignored the poor girl in the drawing room.

Escorted by Colonel Anderson, I, the hostess, was the last to enter the dining room. I found the colonel an affable, if slightly overbearing man, but he was a good conversationalist and the elderly gentleman on my left, though pleasant, was deaf and had little to say.

The food, prepared by Monsieur Claude and his staff, was excellent. However, I was not accustomed to French cuisine and I was a little dismayed later to learn I had eaten frog legs.

We ladies retired to the drawing room after dessert, but the gentlemen joined us for coffee. Sir Evan gave no evidence beyond the usual courtesies that Miss Polly Anderson held a particular interest for him and I found their relationship a strange one.

Lady Thornton retired soon after dinner and Vanessa caught my hand and said in an undertone, "This is boring. Can I be excused?"

"Your father wanted you to meet his guests, Vanessa."

She tossed her head. "So, I've met them. They're old and boring and Miss Polly Anderson is a simpleton."

"Hush," I whispered, drawing her away from the others. "The musicale will be beginning soon. Don't you want to stay for that?"

"I hate that dumb kind of music. Father won't let me stay for the ball tomorrow. That's what I'd really like to see."

Recalling my own early years, I said, "Sneak out of bed, then, and watch from the balcony. No one will know you're there. That's what I used to do when I lived at Wynfield Towers."

"You did something naughty, miss? I can hardly believe it," she said in that sing-song voice that boded trouble.

Instead of taking offense, I jollied her along. "I just confessed, didn't I? I'll make a bargain with you, Vanessa. Stay for the musicale and be nice to all your father's guests, and I won't tell anybody you're up there tomorrow night."

"Not even my father?"

I shook my head. "Nobody. It'll be our secret."

"What a charming gown," she said to Miss Polly, who was standing nearby with a dazed expression on her face. Her father was busy shouting into the ear of Sir Anthony Blakesley, my deaf dinner companion.

Grateful to have been rescued, Miss Polly bobbed a curtsy to old Sir Anthony and immediately joined Vanessa and me.

"Thank you," she said, giving Vanessa a tremulous smile. "It's India silk. Papa brought the material back with him from Bombay. I think this bright indigo blue much too harsh a colour for me. It is not at all becoming." She turned to gaze at me with a generous smile. "It would be more beautiful on someone like Miss St. Claire."

Vanessa showed little interest in the gown, but her face lit up at the mention of Bombay. "I would love to go to India. It's such a fascinating place and they have some very barbaric customs." Her eyes glowed with macabre delight. "I read that when a man dies, his widow is placed beside him on the funeral pyre and burned to death."

Sonia's chant automatically popped into my head. *Tongues of fire, light the pyre. The tide will turn and the devil will burn.*

I half expected Miss Polly to faint, but she answered in her soft, little girl voice, "Suttee is no longer practiced. The British banned it a long time ago."

A little deflated, Vanessa dropped the subject, but

out of the corner of my eye, I caught a glimpse of a young man standing in the doorway. Has there been a late arrival? I wondered.

"Excuse me," I said, slipping away to check the hall. There was no one there and I thought perhaps I had mistaken one of the young footmen for a guest.

When I returned to the drawing room, the musicale was about to begin and we moved into the small gallery and took our seats.

Thank God for the entertainment, I thought. If nothing else, it would effectively silence Vanessa.

The performance by Alfred Bosco, a very talented young musician, was wonderful and I soon lost myself in the music.

One melody was particularly beautiful, but the selection ended abruptly and the soloist explained that it had been taken from an unfinished movement discovered and published after the composer's death.

"The melody haunts me," he explained, "for I shall never know the ending."

I understood his feelings. For the rest of my life I would wonder how Violette and Pasha's story had ended, and why my mother had never told me about her past.

Guests were leaving their places and saying goodnight, and as I stood up, I again caught a glimpse of a young man standing in the hall. He stopped and I stared across the room at him.

This time there could be no mistake. He was wearing evening clothes and his dark, handsome face was not obscured by a hood. This was Pasha, an unbelievably beautiful young man with a regal air.

And why not? I thought. Hadn't he been born to be king?

I knew no fear. It seemed somehow right and comforting that he should have returned.

"Excuse me," I said, brushing past several of the guests in my hurry to reach him.

Already he was fading, but his dark eyes met mine in a silent plea. For what? I wondered.

"What's wrong, Olivia? You look like you've just seen a ghost."

Sir Evan was staring at me with steely eyes. A cold draft swept across my shoulders and I shuddered.

Someone had just walked over my grave.

Chapter Twenty-one

A full moon bathed Thornton Manor in a silvery glow, transforming the ugly grey dragon into a more benign image. Carriages converged on it from all directions as guests began to arrive for the Reception and Grand Ball in honor of Lord Charles Spencer Fenwick.

I stood in the garden and looked up at the house. I would be leaving it soon and after tonight I would know where I would be going.

Either I would be taking up residence in Thornton Wood as the wife of a sometimes exasperating, but thoroughly lovable country doctor, or I would be going back to London.

The clatter of carriage wheels on the gravel driveway summoned me back inside the house. I was Sir Evan's hostess and I must welcome our guests.

The uneasy feeling that had made me seek these few

moments of solitude persisted, though. I wanted to hide in the garden and let this long-awaited night pass me by.

Coward, I chided myself. If Philip rejects you, you have no one to blame but yourself. But it wasn't only the thought of facing Philip that bothered me. It was seeing Pasha last night.

Not that I was afraid of him, for I had come to know this Gypsy outcast first as an engaging and vulnerable boy and then as a man caught in the throes of a great and all-consuming love. Moreover, I had been an unwilling witness to his cruel and ignoble death.

No, I did not fear Pasha; I pitied him. However, what bothered me was his return. The past had not been buried. There was more to come and the very thought filled me with a terrible foreboding.

"I knew you would not disappoint me by being late," Sir Evan said, as I entered the drawing room. Kissing my gloved hand, he stood back and studied me from head to toe. "How magnificent you look, my dear. Turn around, let me feast my eyes upon you."

Feeling foolish, I did as he asked. I was wearing the white satin ball gown trimmed with roses in what Sir Evan had referred to as "regal red."

"You look like a princess who is about to become queen," he said. His smile and the way his eyes glittered in the candlelight reminded me of Vanessa and for some inexplicable reason, a chill ran down my spine.

Lord Fenwick entered the drawing room then and the three of us repaired to the ballroom to await the arrival of our guests.

"My dear, you look positively charming," Lord Fenwick said. "All is well with you, I trust." His kind eyes looked deeply into mine as if he hoped to read his answer within their depths.

Sir Evan interrupted. "She is a delight to behold, isn't she, my lord."

"Aye a delight in every way," Lord Fenwick answered. "Nanny and I sorely miss Olivia."

Sir Evan opened the double doors and we entered the ballroom, which had been transformed into an indoor garden by the decorators. The walls were adorned with trellises of white latticework entwined with ivy and fresh flowers and the scent of roses and gardenias perfumed the air. And through the far doors I could see into the large gallery where supper was to be served. The glimpse I caught of a long table lavishly set with gold-plated dinner service and Venetian crystal promised even more splendor.

As guests arrived, Farnsworth escorted them to the ballroom and as I chatted with everyone my attention was drawn away from the entrance, but every now and then I would glance up, hoping to see the arrival of a tall, familiar figure.

I had almost given up hope when I saw him, and the image I had carried in my mind did not compare with the flesh-and-blood man.

Philip looked ruggedly handsome in white tie and tails, but I smiled when I noticed he was the only man in the room who was not wearing gloves.

The Prince of Wales was said to have set a precedent by forgetting his gloves once, but I was sure Philip neither knew nor cared about that. Rather, I could almost hear him say, *What do I need gloves for? My hands aren't cold.*

Dear Philip, my beloved rebel. Kind hearts are more than coronets and though you would dispute it, you are as much a gentleman as any man here, I thought.

I lost track of him when he descended the marble steps and began mingling with the crowd. But he's here, I told myself and even though we shall not actually meet until after supper, there will be plenty of time at the ball.

Supper was served at nine. Guests were seated at two twenty-five-foot-long banquet tables and since I would be sitting at the end of the head table, I had placed Philip near the front of the second one.

In my fantasy, we had not met until the ball and it seemed important that we follow the same pattern.

The elaborate meal served by liveried footmen drawn from all three houses consumed two hours of precious time. I was anxious for it to end and the ball to begin, but had I known the startling revelations and resultant terror this night would hold, I would not have been so impatient.

At last it was over. Gentlemen remained in the gallery to smoke and the ladies were invited to the small gallery while servants readied the ballroom for dancing.

Lady Thornton excused herself and, accompanied by Miss Hamilton, she retired for the evening. I gathered she did not wish to be present when her son announced his engagement to Miss Polly.

I couldn't understand why Lady Thornton should object. The young lady was certainly well-connected and docile enough to suit the most demanding mother-in-law.

The ball began at eleven and Lord Fenwick claimed

my first dance. He wore a disturbed expression and as we glided across the floor, he said, "Evan has just confided the news to me, Olivia. This is a hasty decision, and I don't think the announcement should be made tonight."

I looked up at his very serious face with surprise. "You disapprove, your lordship?" I asked.

"I do, and not for reasons you may think. My concern is for you, my dear."

Did he think I feared losing my position at Thornton Manor?

"Don't worry about me. I shall be just fine," I said gaily.

I couldn't confide in him yet, but if all went well with Philip, this dear man would be the first to know, I decided.

Changing the subject abruptly, he said, "I went to Ireland after my daughter's marriage and a year later, when Violette died, I was still there. I've always regretted that. For as the years passed . . ."

He never finished the sentence for the dance ended and before he could lead me off the floor, Sir Evan appeared beside me to claim the next waltz.

He was an accomplished dancer, but my head reeled as he turned faster and faster in an almost frenzied ever-widening circle until the other dancers drifted to the sidelines and we had the whole floor to ourselves.

Whereupon, he abruptly stopped and raised his hand to the orchestra for silence.

I caught my breath and planted my feet firmly on the floor as the dizzying sea of faces swam before me.

"Honored guest, ladies and gentlemen," Sir Evan

said. "I would like to announce my forthcoming marriage to Miss Olivia Rachel St. Claire."

A hush fell over the assembly and then well-wishers converged on us offering congratulations. Through hazy, disbelieving eyes, I swept the room looking for Philip. I saw Lord Fenwick's concern, Miss Hamilton's hate, and finally Philip's tall figure in the back of the room.

His expression was one of utter disgust and I stood helpless, surrounded by people I scarcely knew as Philip turned on his heel and walked out of my life forever.

I couldn't bear it, and brushing past the knot of people surrounding us, I murmured, "Excuse me," and fled the room.

Picking up my long train, I slung it over my arm and ran down the corridor to the front of the house. Farnsworth stood at the door, a puzzled expression on his pasty old face.

"Where is Dr. McAllister?" I demanded.

"He just left, miss."

I ran outside just in time to see his ancient buggy racing out of the driveway at breakneck speed.

With tearful eyes, I re-entered the house and suddenly stared into Sir Evan's blazing eyes. "What the hell do you think you're doing?" he demanded.

"Sir Evan, you have misunderstood," I said and then catching a glimpse of Farnsworth still at his post, added, "We must talk."

"My sentiments exactly," he said, grabbing me by the arm and propelling me toward his study.

Once inside, he shut the door and turned to face

me. "What was the meaning of that disgraceful performance in the ballroom, miss?"

"You misunderstood, or perhaps it was I who misunderstood," I stammered. "I thought you were going
to announce your engagement to Miss Polly Anderson."

"I don't need Miss Polly Anderson anymore," he said
coldly. "I preferred doing you the honor of becoming
my wife."

"But I'm in love with someone else," I cried.

His expression, more demonic than Vanessa's could
ever have been, made me cringe. "You dare to tell me
that you would choose McAllister, that ignorant peasant, over the lord and master of Thornton Wood!"

"I'm sorry, Sir Evan. I didn't mean to hurt you."

"Hurt me, miss? You are a governess, a poor girl with
no connections. I offer you a kingdom and you dare
to scoff at it?" His glittering eyes turned crafty and he
added, "When Lord Fenwick dies, I shall control all of
Thornton Wood. My family dynasty will come back to
me then. Think, Olivia. I shall rule like a feudal lord,
the way my grandfather and all the Thorntons before
him ruled.

"They affixed taxes, assigned tenant quotas, and
those who did not meet them were punished. They
held absolute sway over life and death in Thornton
Wood, and so shall I," he shouted, raising his fist and
crashing it down on his desk.

Suddenly all frenzy left him; his mood changed, and
altering his expression, he spoke in a perfectly rational
voice. "We'll discuss this again, Olivia, but for now do
me the courtesy of returning to our guests. I told everyone that the excitement had made you ill. Kindly re-

frain from contradicting me. We'll leave matters as they are for the time being."

The ball that I had so eagerly awaited was over now and guests were seated in lawn chairs waiting for the fireworks to begin. Colourful Japanese lanterns hung from the trees and they cast an eerie glow over the well-manicured lawn behind the manor house.

Everyone had accepted the fact that the excitement of becoming engaged to Sir Evan Thornton had proved too much for me. I supposed among themselves they gossiped about the poor girl with no connections who had schemed and manipulated herself into her employer's favor, but on the surface they appeared cordial and kind.

Miss Polly Anderson, who had every reason to wish me ill, was effusive in her good wishes and I believed her to be sincere. Perhaps she was relieved to be out of the running for Bride Number Four, but nevertheless, I found her to be a thoroughly nice person.

Sir Evan was busy consulting with the man he had hired to conduct the fireworks display and as I stood looking out over the lawn, I stiffened.

A Gypsy playing a violin strolled among the guests. The haunting melody was familiar and I suddenly identified it as the unfinished composition we had heard the night before. He passed under one of the lanterns and I gasped. Pasha, looking more handsome than I had ever seen him, wore a red bandana over his head and a gold earring in his ear. As he approached me, he abruptly lifted the bow, cutting off the last note. It drifted out into the night as his eyes met mine. Then raising his hand he beckoned for me to follow him into the house.

You cannot choose because you have been chosen, Sonia had said, and so I slipped quietly away from the crowd and walked back to the house.

It was deserted as servants eager to see the fireworks lined the porch and stood on the lawn behind the guests. I knew they could not see him, but they were too busy chatting among themselves to even notice me as I passed them.

I followed him down the hall toward the kitchen. He was several feet ahead of me and when he reached the door leading to the hidden staircase, he turned and disappeared.

Slipping back the two heavy bolts that locked the door, I opened it. The enclosed staircase was bathed in a strange vaporous light. I knew where the stairway led and hesitantly, I started to climb its treacherous treads.

Encumbered by my gown's long train, I practically crawled up the steep, narrow steps. Several times I slipped and after what seemed like an eternity, I reached the top.

The door to the fourth floor was open, and the whole corridor was bathed in that same ghostly light, yet there was no sign of the spirit. My feet seemed to move of their own volition, although I already knew where they were taking me. Passing the other rooms with their sheet-covered furnishings, I thought that they looked even more eerie in this ethereal, sepia-toned light.

I entered Lady Violette's violet room and the door slowly closed behind me. Like a spectator waiting for a performance to begin, I stood immobile, eyes and ears alert to any sound or movement. The empty room looked exactly the same as I had last seen it, but suddenly the absolute silence was broken by the sound of a woman crying. The wrenching sobs continued for several moments and my eyes were drawn to the sumptuous canopy bed that dominated the room.

Ever so slowly, something large and bright began to materialize beside it. Inch by inch it took shape and form until I gasped when I recognized the large copper vat I had seen in my dreams.

Another movement made me tear my eyes away from the vat and look toward the bed where the nebulous shape of a woman's figure struggled to appear. It wavered for a second and then became clear and distinct.

Her long silver-blond hair was snarled and disheveled and her beautiful face was contorted with pain. "Help me," she sobbed, and another young woman with dark hair suddenly became visible at the foot of the bed.

She said nothing, but the malicious smile she wore on her face chilled me to the bone.

Even young, Miss Hamilton had been ugly, and her beady little black eyes mirrored the ugliness of her soul.

A willowy and much younger Lady Thornton appeared then, and going up to the bed, she silently placed a cloth on Lady Violette's head. She looked frightened and her eyes looked through me to the door.

"Here he comes," she said, shrinking back and making way for a very blond, very youthful Sir Evan.

His handsome young face was twisted in the same furious scowl I had seen him wear when he had confronted me this evening in his study.

Leaning close to his wife's face, he pointed and said, "See that copper vat, my dear? I had Miss Hamilton fill it to the brim with water. Do you know why?"

Her eyes wild with terror, the woman in the bed shook her head.

"Then I shall have to tell you, my unfaithful wife. If the son you bear is blond, I shall rejoice that a Thornton heir has been delivered." He paused a moment and glanced across the room. I saw his eyes glitter with macabre excitement. "But if the child is dark," he continued, turning back toward the bed, "I shall drown it in that vat like an unwanted kitten."

"No, Evan. For God's sake have mercy," she screamed.

He smiled then, a fiendish smile. "So you already know whose child it is, don't you? And you dare to beg for mercy? Well, I'll show your bastard no mercy, madam. No more mercy than I showed his father."

"What do you mean?" she said, reaching up and grabbing hold of his coat. "Pasha left. You told me so yourself."

Seizing her wrists, he wrenched himself free of her hands, and, tossing her back on the bed, he shouted, "Your Gypsy lover is dead. I ran him down and put a torch to him."

She stared back at him with horror and he continued in a calmer voice. "He had bewitched you, for surely you would never have chosen him over me. He died like a warlock should die. In flames."

Not a sound came from the woman in the bed and

Lady Thornton rushed up to her son. "Evan, for God's sake leave her be. She has fainted."

Ignoring his mother, he turned to Miss Hamilton. "I'll be outside. Call me the instant the child is born."

I shuddered as he marched past me and left the room.

Lady Violette had come to and once again she was crying and writhing in the bed. "Don't let him do this," she cried and then, "Help me, help me. . . ."

Miss Hamilton and Lady Thornton pulled back the covers and began to assist in the birth. I could not see what was happening, but after several moments had passed, I heard Miss Hamilton's triumphant voice. "It's a black-haired Gypsy boy! Sir Evan, Sir Evan come quickly," she shouted.

I watched in horror as the door burst open and Sir Evan appeared, his face like a fiend from hell and before his mother could stop him, he had snatched the blood-covered infant up and thrust him in the vat.

Violette's screams echoed in my ears and Lady Thornton lay on the floor in a dead faint. I felt ill as his hand continued to hold the helpless newborn under the water.

"It's dead," he said, removing his hand and wiping the water from his coat sleeve.

I think I must have passed out for a few moments myself, for when next I looked, Sir Evan and Miss Hamilton were gone and Lady Thornton and another woman were bending over the bed with their backs to me.

"Hear me, Violette. There is another child and you must push if you want it to live," Lady Thornton said.

Violette opened her eyes and stared at her mother-in-law. "Where is Evan?" she asked in a weak voice.

"Gone. Miss Hamilton followed to make sure he doesn't harm himself. I don't condone what he did, but he's distraught, as he has a right to be."

Sensing someone on the other side of her, Violette turned her head. "Genevieve," she cried.

"Push Violette," Lady Thornton said. "You must hurry before they come back."

"I can't. It's no use. It'll only die anyway. He won't let it live."

"He won't ever know," Lady Thornton said. "Genevieve is going to take the baby away and no one will ever know that there were two."

I felt weak, but I dared not faint, not now.

"Push, Violette," Lady Thornton urged and then another dearly familiar voice spoke.

"It's a little girl," my mother said.

No, not my mother, I thought, as tears streamed down my face.

"Violette's gone," Lady Thornton said.

"No," Genevieve cried in an anguished voice.

"It's better this way," Lady Thornton answered and then looking down at the child, she began to tremble. "Oh dear God, he was a warlock and we are cursed," she mumbled.

"What are you talking about?" Genevieve said.

Lady Thornton wrapped the infant in a blanket and thrust it into Genevieve's arms. "Here, take her away, as far away as you can get. Leave tonight. Change your name and don't ever come back because he'll kill her."

"But what about Pasha?"

Lady Thornton hesitated, but she kept her son's secret. "Pasha's gone," she answered. "He left with the other Gypsies. Raise the child as your own and never tell anyone what happened here this night." Pushing Genevieve and the baby toward the door, she said, "Go now, before it's too late!"

All sound, all movement suddenly ceased and as before the figures in the melodrama froze into place. Fear and a terrible uncertainty clouded the youthful face of the only mother I had ever known.

The motionless body of the woman who had given me birth lay sprawled in the bed and Lady Thornton's paralyzed face was permanently etched with horror as her rigid eyes stared down at the tiny hand that protruded from the blanket. It bore a fiery birthmark that resembled tongues of fire!

The vision ended, but a voice from the present spoke to me from the doorway.

"So, you think to be the fourth Lady Thornton!"

Chapter Twenty-two

Miss Hamilton carried a lamp. I wondered why and then it suddenly dawned on me that she could not see the light which the spirit had provided, and that without it, the whole fourth floor was in complete darkness.

"You scheming little nobody," she said, advancing into the room. "I've known all along what you were up to. I tried to get rid of you the very first night you came here."

"So it was you who set the fire outside my room," I said.

"That's right. I set the fire in the stable, too, and I shot at you in the woods. I was trying to frighten you away, but you insisted on staying and turning your tarnished charms on Sir Evan."

"I certainly did not."

"You don't fool me, Miss St. Claire. Even your name sounds like something somebody made up."

I almost laughed, thinking how my poor Genevieve had done just that, probably borrowing the name from The St. Claire Arms, the first inn she would have come upon on her escape from Thornton Wood.

"What were you anyway, a London actress down on your luck?" she scoffed.

"You'd be surprised if I told you my background," I said.

"Oh, no I wouldn't. I was on to you from the beginning, and when I saw you kissing Philip McAllister in the woods, I knew you meant to marry Sir Evan and carry on an affair with your lover on the side." She laughed then. "That was something his first wife did and learned to regret." Her eyes glittered maliciously.

"What is your interest in Sir Evan?" I asked.

"I happen to love Evan Thornton. I'd do anything for him, anything. Do you understand?"

"Yes, I do," I answered. And I did understand, only too well.

"When his first wife died, I thought he'd turn to me," she said, looking off into space like she had forgotten I was even there. "So handsome he was, even after his hair turned white."

"That was after his wife and child died, wasn't it?" I asked, trying to draw her out.

"That's right," she said, still talking more to herself than to me. "Violette drove him to do what he did. It turned his hair white, but afterwards he couldn't remember anything that had happened," she paused, "either that night or the other night."

I assumed she was referring to the baby's murder and Pasha's.

"Then he had to go and marry Esther," she said. "But she could only give him that brat of a girl. I got rid of Esther," she said matter-of-factly. "I know all about the plants that grow in the woods."

"You poisoned Vanessa's mother?" I asked, horrified anew at the depth of the treachery I was uncovering.

"Of course, but very slowly. Everybody thought she was just getting weaker and weaker."

"And what about Diana?"

"It didn't work as well with her. Drugs have different reactions in different people. It drove her mad, but that was fine. I didn't have to kill her. She did it herself."

I knew she meant to kill me, too, and I was becoming frightened. Everyone was outside watching the fireworks. I could hear the rockets exploding even as we spoke.

"I have no intention of marrying Sir Evan. The announcement was a mistake," I said. "So, if you'll excuse me, I should be getting back downstairs."

She barred my way, and reaching into her pocket, she pulled out a small revolver. "Loving a man who rejects your love can drive a woman crazy," she said. "But I'm not so crazy that I will let you leave this room alive."

A third voice spoke. "Come with me, Araminta."

Lady Thornton stood behind Miss Hamilton, whose first name I had not heard until now. Placing her hand very gently on Miss Hamilton's shoulder, she added, "I need you in my room."

Miss Hamilton whirled around and faced her patient. "You don't need me. You're trying to help her get away. Why? You don't want him to marry her any-more than I do."

Lady Thornton's eyes met mine. "That's true, but I have other reasons."

Knowing now that Lady Thornton had recognized who I was and that she had only tried to protect her son's secret, I felt nothing but pity for her. I would not even be alive today were it not for her.

"Lady Thornton," I addressed her. "Please believe me. I never intended to marry your son. I love Philip McAllister. I told Sir Evan that tonight. The announcement was a mistake." And then, because I knew that I would never leave this room alive, I heard myself add, "Thank you for saving my life and for giving me a wonderful mother."

"She told you." A flicker of concern passed over her face.

She would have been terrified if I had explained how I knew, so I let her think Genevieve had confided in me.

"Evan's not responsible," she hastened to explain. "His father went mad and the family curse has been passed on to Vanessa."

Miss Hamilton suddenly grew impatient listening to a conversation she could not fathom.

"I don't know what the two of you are talking about," she said. Then grabbing Lady Thornton's arm, she shoved her into the room. The older woman stumbled and landed at my feet.

"You were afraid she was a witch and now you're on her side. Then die with her like a witch," she screamed, hurling the oil lamp across the room.

The rug burst into flames and Miss Hamilton ran to

the door, but it had slammed shut and she couldn't get it open.

I tried to beat the fire out, but Miss Hamilton ran across the room and pulled me away. "You're going to burn, witch," she shouted.

She held on to me with a maniac's super-human strength while Lady Thornton lay on the floor with a dazed expression on her face.

"Lady Thornton," I yelled. "Open the door and get help."

Instead, she ran over to us and tried to pull Miss Hamilton away from me, but she was no match for the other woman's superior power.

Flames reached the bed hangings and then the flimsy curtains caught fire and fell in a burning mass on the floor. Outside the exposed window, rockets shot up in the air and sprayed the darkened sky with a shower of bright multicolored lights.

When she saw the fire could not be put out, Miss Hamilton shoved me aside and made a dash for safety. The room was filling up with smoke and I could barely make out Miss Hamilton's figure as she struggled in vain to open the door.

Her maniacal laughter added to the terror of the raging inferno and like one possessed, she darted from one end of the room to the other resembling a rat caught in a trap.

I helped Lady Thornton to her feet and recalling Philip's instructions from the first fire, I thrust my shawl over her head.

"Keep your face covered," I whispered. "And don't speak. You'll inhale smoke."

Then, ripping the train from my gown, I held it up

to my own face. Holding Lady Thornton's arm, I propelled her forward, through the thick, suffocating smoke toward what I hoped was the direction of the hallway.

When I bumped into wood, I felt around, praying I had reached the door and not a solid wall. My hands felt for the doorknob and when I grasped it, I screamed with pain. The metal was as hot as molten lava.

The first thing I saw when I opened my eyes was a beautiful filigree border of vines and flowers. It looked like the handsome stucco work that had decorated the walls of my bedroom at Amberwood.

I must be dreaming, I thought, or perhaps I am dead, for I certainly could not be at Amberwood.

As my eyes became more focused, I dared to look around me. The pale green walls, the bed hangings, and the matching floral drapes in green and rose were the same.

I heard a door open softly and a small, white-haired little woman tiptoed into the room.

"Oh, Nanny," I cried. "Am I dead, or am I home?"

Her sweet smile brought tears to my eyes. "Oh, dear girl, you're home at Amberwood." Then turning around, she spoke to someone else. "She's awake, doctor."

Doctor, I thought, loving the sound of the word, but of course it could not be Philip, or could it possibly be?

His massive figure dwarfed Nanny and his vibrant personality filled the room. I looked into his eyes and the concern I saw there warmed my heart.

"Oh, Philip," I cried in a rasping voice unlike my

own. "It was all a mistake. It's you I love."

"Hush, don't talk so much. You inhaled a lot of smoke," he cautioned.

I could barely speak above a whisper, but I managed to ask the most important question, "Do you forgive me?"

"I love you, you stubborn woman. Now will you be quiet, or shall I have to bandage your mouth as well as your hands?"

I held my hands up to my eyes. Swathed in white bandages, they looked gigantic.

"Don't talk. Just listen," he instructed. "Your hands were badly burned and I've dressed them. I'll tell you as much as I know, but as your doctor, I forbid you to talk. Agreed?"

I nodded my head and he kissed me very gently on the forehead. "When you're better, I'll do better than that," he promised with a smile. Then he sat on the edge of the bed.

"Thornton Manor was badly damaged in the fire," he told me. "That's why you and Lady Thornton were brought here to Amberwood. She was not burned and neither were you, except for your hands. But you both inhaled too much smoke. Actually, she saved your life by dragging you out of that room after your fingers were burned."

He read the question in my eyes and answered it.

"Miss Hamilton died in the fire. No one could have saved her and you're not to think about it. I don't know what the three of you were doing up there, but that's beside the point. I have always respected Lady Thornton and it was she who told me you had no intention of marrying her son.

"She said you told her you were in love with me. Did you? Just shake your head yes or no," he said, holding up his hand.

I nodded.

"Then why the hell didn't you tell me? Don't answer that," he said. "You can tell me later and yes, I apologize for my bad language," he added quickly. Leaning down, he very gently kissed me on the lips. "I'm not much of a gentleman yet, but if you promise to marry me, I'll try to change."

I nodded my head vigorously and he shouted, "Nanny, what do you think? Olivia has promised to marry me!" Then looking like a sheepish, boisterous lad, he lowered his voice and said, "I'll leave the room now and let you rest."

But he didn't leave immediately. With passion and love burning in his eyes he captured my mouth with his own, in a kiss that I felt clear through my body. A kiss that left me in no doubt that we truly belonged together.

I tried to sleep, but my heart was too full of mixed emotions: happiness because Philip and I were together at last; sadness because of all the pain the past had revealed; and confusion because I needed to sort all of it out in my own mind.

I was Violette and Pasha's daughter, and Mama, whom I now knew to be Genevieve, had been my foster mother. As a girl, she had sought tranquility in the convent, but she had wound up in Thornton Wood where all her principles had been tested.

She had stood by my birth mother through adultery and she had raised a bastard child with all the love she would have bestowed on her own flesh and blood.

The House in Thornton Wood

I loved her with all my heart and I would never forget her, but I also had come to terms with the rash child-woman who had given me birth and the father who could not rest until I had been told the truth about my heritage.

My thoughts then turned to Lord Fenwick and Amberwood. Hadn't I always felt a granddaughter's affection for this gentle man who was in reality my grandfather?

And hadn't I felt that Amberwood was my home since first I laid eyes upon it? This was why my father had brought me to Thornton Wood. Not for revenge. It was Sonia who craved revenge. Pasha only craved love.

As for Sir Evan, I could never forgive him for murdering my father and my innocent baby brother, but the past was dead. I never wanted to see him again, but to openly accuse him now would only hurt his mother and ruin Vanessa's chances of ever escaping the Thornton curse.

I thought of her mercurial moods and her rages, and I feared for her. No, I told myself as I drifted off to sleep, I would do nothing to jeopardize Vanessa's brave, but fragile hold on reality.

I didn't get to talk to Lady Thornton until several days later.

She was alone in the garden, admiring Amberwood's late-blooming roses when I joined her.

"I want to thank you, Lady Thornton," I said. "Philip told me you saved my life."

"Not completely," she answered. "If that young man hadn't gotten the door open, we would both be dead."

"What young man?"

"I don't know who he was. It was hard to see in the smoke. Perhaps he was one of the servants."

"Perhaps," I answered.

"He should be rewarded."

I smiled a secret smile. "I'm sure he will be, Lady Thornton," and motioning her to sit down, I said, "I want you to know that I didn't come to Thornton Manor for revenge. I love Vanessa and I would do nothing to hurt her. So, as far as I am concerned, the past is dead."

Her eyes filled with tears. "Thank you, my dear. I appreciate your generosity, but then you were raised by a very warm and generous woman." She bowed her head in a gesture of humility and added, "If I thought ill of you, Olivia, it was because I was terrified when I saw the mark on your hand and realized who you were. I was the only person in Thornton Wood who knew you even existed, and I was positive you had come back to wreak havoc on us all."

She paused and sighed deeply. I understood the tremendous emotional strain she was under and my heart went out to this victimized and misunderstood woman.

Composing herself, she bravely continued. "You see, after Evan murdered your brother, he ran off and didn't return until the following day. He didn't even know Violette had died yet, but horror and guilt had turned his hair completely white at the age of twenty-one.

"Afterwards," she explained, "he acted like he didn't remember any of it, and to this day, I'm not sure whether it came back to him or not, but as you say, there is Vanessa to consider.

"Evan's father lost his mind, and his father before him, so insanity is in Vanessa's blood." Turning to me then, with eyes full of pathos, she said, "You're grateful to me now, but please, for my granddaughter's sake, I beg you never let the truth come out."

"You have my word, Lady Thornton," I promised.

Sir Evan's mother then assured me I would not have to face Sir Evan regarding our so-called "broken engagement." She would advise him that my decision was irrevocable and that I was to wed Philip McAllister. At the time, neither she nor I could foresee that poetic justice would render such a precaution completely unnecessary.

Philip and I were married in Amberwood's beautiful drawing room. I wore a simple pale blue dress that I had made myself. Neither fancy nor particularly stylish, it would serve a country doctor's wife well for many a year.

I carried a bouquet of roses from the garden, and tucked inside among the pinks and whites was a perfect violet one, *the Lady Violet rose.*

I would press it and keep it so that in years to come, when the truth would hurt no one, I could show it to my grandchildren and tell them the story of their great-grandmother who had been a beautiful lady with a rose named after her.

My secret grandfather, who thought of me as a nice young woman whom he was quite fond of, gave the bride away. And dear Nanny, who laughed when I called her a bridesmaid, stood beside me.

Looking up at my tall, dark, and handsome groom, my heart swelled with pride. Philip was the prince of my girlhood dreams, the only man I would ever love.

My thoughts turned then to the silver-haired Prince of Darkness. Already he was lost in the tide of the Gypsy's chant, but I would not think of that now.

This was my wedding day and I was blissfully happy.

When the short ceremony was over, Philip kissed me and I knew I would never miss the balls, the fancy clothes, or even my beloved Amberwood. My place was with my husband and nowhere else would I rather be.

We cut the wedding cake that Mrs. Bodine had so lovingly made and Lord Fenwick opened a bottle of his best champagne.

"A toast," he said, raising his glass. "To the bride and groom—two wonderful young people that I like to think of as my grandchildren."

When we left, I kissed him good-bye and with a teasing smile that hid a tear, I said, "Thank you for that beautiful toast, Grandfather."

Epilogue

As I look back on the events that happened that year in Thornton Wood, I wonder how we all survived. Of course, all of us did not, which leads me to the matter of poetic justice.

Was it fate, a Gypsy curse, or merely coincidence that turned perpetrators into victims and rendered harsh, if overdue sentences?

Miss Hamilton's obsession with fire proved her own undoing. She was a willing accomplice to murder and I cannot help but feel that she got exactly what she deserved, but I do not believe my father's gentle spirit caused her downfall; and Sonia, who was far more vengeful, did not even know about Miss Hamilton.

As for Sir Evan—What happened took place while Lady Thornton and I were recuperating at Amberwood, but it was a long time before I could bring myself to think about Sir Evan's death and the peculiar circumstances that surrounded it.

Because of those circumstances, the constable was called in and after declaring Sir Evan's demise to be accidental, he requested that Philip sign the death certificate.

Philip was given a copy of the constable's report and in it, the witness, Sir Evan's groom, recounted the events leading up to the accident:

Sir Evan Thornton and meself were riding through the woods when Sir Evan noticed the remains of a campfire still burning in a clearing. I didn't see it meself, but Sir Evan did.

About twenty feet away stood a blue caravan. Sir Evan dismounted and he marches right up to that caravan and tells them Gypsies they're about to set the whole bloody woods on fire.

The Gypsy man said their fire was out and Sir Evan got angry. He told the Gypsy to come see for himself. They both walk over to the clearing and the Gypsy laughs and says he don't see no fire.

Just then a little Gypsy lad runs out. He's about two years old and this little nipper holds his hands out like he's feeling for the fire. Then he looks up at Sir Evan and laughs. The bloody Gypsies get in the van then and they race out of the woods like the devil hisself is after them.

Sir Evan starts to stamp out the fire and that's when it happened. So help me, I never seen nothing like it. Flames ten feet tall shot out of the

ground and before I could get down off me horse,
Sir Evan was done for.

Was it an accident? I shall never know, but the child
was Sonia's grandson and she had predicted he would
have great powers.

I never saw Sonia or her grandson again, but after
Sir Evan died, my birthmark began to fade. It finally
vanished altogether and Philip attributed it to the salve
he had used to heal my burns. But, recalling the chant,
I had to wonder. Once their purpose had been served
had the tongues of fire disappeared along with the
past?

Vanessa and Lady Thornton still live at Thornton
Manor. Lady Thornton is very old now, but she was
Vanessa's mainstay after Sir Evan's death. Though he
never gave his only daughter the affection she craved,
Vanessa idolized her father and my silence has pre-
served her illusions.

We kept in touch and I saw Vanessa frequently
while she was growing up, not so much in later years.

She never married. I think she was aware of her own
defects and preferred to let the Thornton curse die
with her rather than pass it on.

More just than her father ever was, she has earned
the respect of her tenants. Vanessa manages both her
property and her fortune shrewdly and those who
think to take advantage because she is a woman soon
change their minds.

My life as a country doctor's wife has been happy
and deeply fulfilling. Philip's practice has not made us
rich, but it has rewarded us in other ways. I've watched
children who might have died without my husband's

skill grow to adulthood and my heart swells with pride at the respect and affection Philip's patients show him.

The mystery of Thornton Wood's two missing girls was also solved. One was found hiding out in the Scottish hills with her lover, the highwayman who had been plaguing Northumberland's travelers.

The other girl turned out to have been poor little Nellie. The child had run away from a brutal father only to wind up working at Pearl's and losing her life to typhoid.

My dear Nanny died shortly after my marriage, but the Earl of Fenwick, whose Christian name was Spencer, lived to see his great-grandson, Philip Spencer McAllister almost grown.

I never told Lord Fenwick he was my grandfather, but his affection for both Philip and myself was no less diminished by that fact. He loved our son, Spence, in a very special way and when Lord Fenwick died, he left Amberwood in trust for his namesake.

Spence came into his inheritance at the age of twenty-one and a year later he married and brought a lovely bride to Amberwood.

They love the house as I did and someday perhaps when my two-month-old granddaughter has grown up a little, I'll tell her a story about the beautiful, violet-eyed lady whose portrait still hangs in Amberwood's hall.

I'll tell her about a curse and a Gypsy chant, and if her grandfather is listening, he will probably shake his head and think that my imagination is running away with me.

But I'll just smile and tell her another fairy tale about

a gentle spirit and how he brought an insecure young woman to Thornton Wood where she met two princes, one good and one evil. She married the good prince and lived happily ever after.

ACROSS A STARLIT SEA

REBECCA BRANDEWYNE

They were betrothed before she was born. She has no say in her future, no voice with which to protest the agreement made by her father that irrevocably binds her to Jarrett Chandler, a man whose hot blood and swift temper can make him as savage as their native Cornish moors . . . a man determined to claim what he's been promised. Unwilling to be a helpless pawn, Laura fights him in every way she knows. But even she has to admit that the tingling which courses through her body as Jarrett takes her in his iron embrace is not fueled solely by fear. Yet to succumb to the tortuous longings means she may have to forfeit the security of innocence and delve into desires that threaten to drown her in a sea of passion.

_____52440-6 $5.99 US/$7.99 CAN

Whispers of Goodbye

Karen White

I need you. I am so afraid. . . . As soon as she reads the words, Catherine sets off for Louisiana to help her sister. Upon entering the moss-draped woods surrounding the house, Cat finds herself immersed in a mystery as murky as the mighty Mississippi River. For Elizabeth has disappeared, and Cat suspects her sister's husband knows more than he is saying. His dark eyes tell her he has great sadness; his arms speak of much of warmth; and his lips have a language all their own. But not even a whisper of her sister. Drawn into a web of family secrets and ancient superstitions, Cat hardly knows what to fear most: the deadly cottonmouth snakes, the deceptively peaceful swamps, or the dashingly powerful man who can steal her breath and sear her heart.

The Shadowing
Joan Overfield

Evil is the first word that comes to mind when Anne Garthwicke arrives at Castle MacCairn. Duty bound to help her father appraise the holdings, she has no choice but to stay. And her trepidation deepens after meeting the laird. Proud and powerful, he embodies all the wildness of the Scottish highlands and incites dreams of carnal passion such as Anne has never experienced. Achingly tender one moment and roughly forceful the next, Ruairdh MacCairn has a beast within straining to break loose. And according to legend, it is only a matter of time before the monster will escape. Anne already knows her heart is lost, but she can only hope that when the moment of fate arrives, her body won't be sacrificed as well.

___52458-9 $5.99 US/$7.99 CAN

THE
PERFECT
WIFE

Victoria Alexander

The Earl of Wyldewood has decided that an ideal spouse should be pleasant to look at and have little effect on his well-ordered life. After meeting Sabrina Winfield, he thinks he has found the woman to fit the bill. But appearances can be deceiving, for beneath Sabrina's delicate beauty lies the most infuriatingly stubborn, wildly adventurous woman he's ever known. And his plans for a proper marriage are about to go dreadfully awry, for now all the earl can think about is silencing her biting repartee with kisses, diverting her schemes with seduction, and forever surrendering his heart and soul to her capable hands.